AUTHORS PRAISE ELLE JAMES AND *TO KISS A FROG!*

"Fun and fanciful, when it comes to romance Elle James rocks!"
  —*USA Today* Bestselling Author Pamela Morsi

"Elle James delivers voodoo magic and great fun with a biochemist heroine and a hero who oozes sex appeal even in his amphibian persona. A definite one-sitting read!"
  —*USA Today* Bestselling Author Merline Lovelace

"Take a hot and steamy ride into the Louisiana bayous in *To Kiss a Frog*, a delightful, sexy romp. Elle James has done a marvelous job of twisting a clichéd fairy tale—and having the heroine be the savior of the 'frog.' Look out for heroes fallen under Voodoo curses!"
  —Award-winning author Lori Avocato

"*To Kiss a Frog* is a fast-paced delight with a charming heroine and a captivating hero. A must read."
  —Award-winning author Judi McCoy

HER NAKED PRINCE?

Was that a bare leg she could see through the glass case standing between them? Elaine's gaze slid downward.

The man glanced down, too, his eyes widening. A faint red stained his cheeks. He folded his arms across his bare chest and quickly leaned against the counter. "Can I help you?"

It took her several seconds to locate her tongue before she could reply. Was he completely naked? "I need you," she stammered.

The man smiled and a wicked eyebrow rose up under the stray lock of hair that had fallen back over his forehead. He didn't comment, nor did he move, staying firmly in place, the counter covering him from the waist down. "You want me?"

Heat crept up her neck and into her face, when Elaine realized what she'd said and what she'd tried to see. "I mean I'm here about the bed."

His smile broadened.

TO KISS A FROG

ELLE JAMES

LOVE SPELL

NEW YORK CITY

LOVE SPELL®

March 2005

Published by

Dorchester Publishing Co., Inc.
200 Madison Avenue
New York, NY 10016

ISBN 0-505-52620-4

The name "Love Spell" and its logo are trademarks of Dorchester Publishing Co., Inc.

Printed in the United States of America.

Visit us on the web at www.dorchesterpub.com.

ACKNOWLEDGMENTS

To my editor, Kate Seaver, who found me! Thank you, thank you, thank you! To my writing friends of Mt. Helicon Muses who made me laugh and kept me sane through the long writing process. To my sister, Delilah Devlin, who convinced me to write and whose talents never cease to amaze me. And most of all to my dear family whose love, patience, and understanding allowed me the time and creative energy to make this book come alive. I salute you!

CHAPTER ONE

Bound to a cypress tree, Craig Thibodeaux struggled to free his hands, the coarse rope rubbing his wrists raw with the effort. A fat bayou mosquito buzzed past his ear to feast on his unprotected skin. The bulging insect had plenty of blood in its belly, much more and the flying menace would be grounded.

What I wouldn't give for a can of bug repellent.

Craig shook his head violently in hopes of discouraging the little scavenger from landing.

The dark-skinned Cajuns who'd kidnapped him stood guard on either side of him, their legs planted wide and arms crossed over bare muscular chests. They looked like rejected cast from a low-budget barbarian movie, and they didn't appear affected by the bloodsucking mosquitoes in the least.

"Hey, Mo, don't you think you guys are taking this a little too far?" Craig aimed a sharp blast of breath at a bug

1

crawling along his shoulder. "I swear I won that card game fair and square."

The man on his right didn't turn his way or flick an eyelid.

Craig looked to his left. "Come on Larry, we've been friends since you and I got caught snitching apples from Old Lady Reneau's orchard. Let me go."

Larry didn't twitch a muscle. He stared straight ahead, as if Craig hadn't uttered a word.

"If it will make you feel any better, I'll give you back your money," Craig offered, although he'd really won that game.

He'd known Maurice Saulnier and Lawrence Ezell since he was a snot-nosed kid spending his summer vacations with his Uncle Joe in Bayou Miste of southern Louisiana. He had considered them friends. Until now.

Granted, Craig had been back for less than a week after an eight-year sojourn into the legal jungles of the New Orleans court system. But his absence shouldn't be a reason for them to act the way they were. An odd sensation tickled his senses, as if foreshadowing something unpleasant waiting to happen. Sweat dripped off his brow, the heat and humidity of the swamp oppressive.

"Look guys, whatever you're planning, you won't get away with." Craig strained against the bonds holding him tight to the rough bark of the cypress tree.

"Ah, *chèri*, but we will." A low musical voice reached out of the darkness, preceding the appearance of a woman. She wore a flowing bright red caftan with a sash tied around her ample girth and a matching handkerchief covering her hair. Although large, she floated into the firelight, her bone necklace rattling in time to a steady drumbeat building in the shadows. Her skin was a light brown, almost mocha, weathered by the elements and age. But her dark brown eyes shined brightly, the flames of the nearby fire dancing in their depths.

Despite the weighty warmth of the swamp, a chill crept down Craig's spine. "Who's playing the drums? And who's the lady in the muumuu?"

The silent wonder next to him deigned to speak in a reverent whisper, "It's all part of Madame LeBieu's magic."

Craig frowned and mentally scratched his head. Madame LeBieu . . . Madame LeBieu . . . oh, yes. The infamous Bayou Miste Voodoo Priestess. He studied her with more interest and a touch of unease. Was he to be a sacrifice in some wacky voodoo ceremony?

"Are you in charge of these two thugs?" Craig feigned a cockiness he didn't feel.

"It be I who called upon dem." She dipped her head in a regal nod.

"Then call them off and untie me." Craig shot an angry look at the men on either side of him. "You've obviously got the wrong guy."

"Were you not de man what be goin' out with de sweet Lisa LeBieu earlier dis very evening?"

"Yes," Craig said, caution stretching his answer, as dread pooled in his stomach. He didn't go into the fact that Lisa wasn't so sweet. "Why?"

"I am Madame LeBieu and Lisa be my granddaughter. She say you dally with her heart and cast it aside." The woman's rich, melodious voice held a thread of steel.

Craig frowned in confusion. "You mean this isn't about the card game? This is about Lisa?"

"No, dis be 'bout you mistreatment of de women."

"I don't get it. I didn't touch her. She came on to me, and I took her home."

"Abuse not always takes de physical form. You

shunned her love and damage her chakras. For dis, you pay."

Craig cocked an eyebrow in disbelief. "You mean I was conked on the head and dragged from my bed all because I refused to sleep with your granddaughter?" He snorted. "This is a new one on me."

"Craig Thibodeaux, I know your kind." Madame LeBieu shook a thick brown finger in his face. "You break hearts wherever you go, dating one woman after another and no love to show for it. You've wielded your loveless way for de last time." Madame LeBieu flicked her fingers, and the flames behind her leaped higher. Then, reaching inside the voluminous sleeves of the caftan, she whipped out an atomizer and sprayed a light floral scent all around him. The aroma mixed and mingled with the dark musty smells of the swamp's stagnant pools and decaying leaves.

"So you're going to douse me in perfume to unman me?" Craig's bark of laughter clashed with the rising beat of the drums. The humor of the situation was short-lived when the mosquitoes decided they liked him even more with the added scent. Craig shook all over to discourage the beggars from landing.

"Ezili Freda Daome, goddess of love and all that is beautiful, listen to our prayers, accept our offerings, and enter into our arms, legs and hearts." Madame LeBieu's head dropped back, and she spread her arms wide. The drumbeat increased in intensity, reverberating off the canopy of trees shrouded in low-hanging Spanish moss.

The pounding emphasized the throbbing ache in the back of Craig's head from where Madame LeBieu's henchmen had beaned him in his room at the bait shop prior to dragging him here. The combined smells of perfume and swamp, along with the jungle beat and chanting nutcase, made his stomach churn. The darkness of the night surrounded him, pushing fear into his soul.

Craig had a sudden premonition that whatever was about to happen, he was not going to like and had the potential to change his life entirely. Half of him wished the woman would just get on with it, whatever it was; the other half quaked in apprehension.

The voodoo priestess's arms and head dropped, and the drums crashed to a halt. Silence descended. Not a single cricket, frog, or bird interrupted the eerie stillness.

Craig broke the trance, fighting his growing fear with false bravado. "And I'm supposed to believe all this mumbo jumbo?" He snorted. "Give me a break. Next thing, you'll be waving a fairy wand and saying bibbity-bobbity-boo."

Madame LeBieu leveled a cold, hard stare at him.

Another shiver snaked down Craig's spine. With the sweat dripping off his brow and chills racing down his back, he thought he might be ill. Maybe even hallucinating.

A small girl appeared at Madame LeBieu's side, handing her an ornate cup. She waited silently for the woman to drink. Craig noticed that his two former friends bowed their heads as the voodoo lady sipped from the cup then handed it back to the girl. The child clutched the cup as if it were her dearest possession and bowed at the waist, backing into the shadows.

With a flourishing sweep of her wrist, Madame LeBieu pulled a pastel pink, blue and white scarf from the sleeve of her caftan, and waved it in Craig's face.

"Mistress of Love, hear my plea.
Help dis shameless man to see."

5

"You know I have family in high places, don't you?" Craig said. Not that they were there to help him now.

Madame LeBieu continued as though he hadn't spoken.

"Though he's strong, his actions bold,
his heart is loveless, empty cold.
By day a frog, by night a man,
'til de next full moon, dis curse will span."

Craig stopped shaking his head, mosquitoes be damned. What was the old lady saying? "Hey, what's this about frogs?"

"A woman will answer Ezili's call,
one who'll love him, warts and all."

"Who, the frog or me?" He chuckled nervously at the woman's words, downplaying his rising uneasiness. His next sarcastic statement was cut off when Mo's heavily muscled forearm crashed into his stomach. "Oomph!"

"Silence!" Mo's command warned of further retribution should Craig dare to interrupt again.

Which worked out great, since Craig was busy sucking wind to restore air to his lungs. All he could do was glare at his former friend. If only looks could kill, he'd have Mo six feet under in a New Orleans minute.

Madame LeBieu continued:

"He'll watch by day and woo by night,
to gain her love, he'll have to fight,
to break de curse, be whole again,
transformed into a caring man."

6

"You didn't have to knock the wind out of *my* sails." Craig wheezed and jerked his head in Madame LeBieu's direction. "*She's* the one making all the noise, talking nonsense about frogs and warts."

Mo's face could have been etched in stone.

The old witch held her finger in Craig's face, forcing him to stare at it. Then she drew the finger to her nose and his gaze followed until he noticed her eyes. A strange glow, having nothing to do with fire, burned in their brown-black centers. Madame LeBieu's voice dropped to a low, threatening rumble.

"Should he deny dis gift from you,
a frog he'll remain in de blackest bayou."

With a flourishing spray of perfume and one last wave of the frothy scarf, Madame LeBieu backed away from Craig, disappearing into the darkness from whence she'd come.

Craig's stomach churned and a tingling sensation spread throughout his body. He attributed his discomfort to the nauseating smells and the ropes cutting off his circulation. "Hey, you're not going to leave me here trussed up like a pig on a spit, are you?" Craig called out to the departing priestess.

A faint response carried to him from deep in the shadows. "Don't tempt me, boy."

As soon as Madame LeBieu was gone, the men who'd stood motionless at his side throughout the voodoo ceremony moved. They untied his bonds, grabbed him beneath the arms and hauled him back to the small canoelike pirogue they'd brought him in.

Forced to step into the craft, Craig fell to the hard wooden seat in the middle. When the other two men

7

climbed in, the boat rocked violently, slinging him from side to side. One man sat in front, the other at the rear. Both lifted paddles and struck out across the bayou, away from the rickety pier.

"So what's it to be now?" Craig rubbed his midsection. "Are you two going to take me out into the middle of the swamp and feed me to the alligators?" He knew these swamps as well as anyone, and the threat was real, although he didn't think Mo and Larry would do it. Would they?

"No harm will come to you what hasn't already been levied by Madame LeBieu," Mo said. Dropping his macho facade, he gave Craig a pitying look. "Man, I feel sorry for you."

"Why? Because a crazy lady chanted a little mumbo jumbo and sprayed perfume in my face?" He could handle chanting crazy people. He'd represented a few of the harmless ones in the courtroom. "Don't worry about me. If I were you, I'd worry more about the monster lawsuit I could file against the two of you for false imprisonment."

"Going to jail would be easy compared to what you be in for." Larry's normally cheerful face wore a woeful expression.

The pale light of the half-moon shimmered between the boughs of overhanging trees. Craig could see they were headed back to his uncle's marina. Perhaps they weren't going to kill him after all. Madame LeBieu was probably just trying to scare him into leaving her granddaughter alone. No problem there. With relatives like that, he didn't need the hassle.

Besides, he'd been bored with Lisa within the first five minutes of their date. Most of the women who agreed to go out with him were only interested in what his money could buy them. Lisa had been no different.

The big Cajuns pulled up to the dock at the Thibodeaux

Marina. As soon as Craig got out, they turned the boat back into the swamp, disappearing into the darkness like a fading dream.

Tired and achy, Craig trudged to his little room behind the shop, wondering if the night had been just that. A dream. He grimaced. Dream, hell! What had happened was the stuff nightmares were made of. The abrasions on his wrists confirmed it wasn't a dream, but it was over now. He would heed the warning and stay away from Madame LeBieu's granddaughter from now on.

He let himself in through the back door and stared around the place while flexing his sore muscles. The room was a mess from the earlier scuffle, short-lived though it was. Craig righted the nightstand and fished the alarm clock out from underneath the bed.

Without straightening the covers he flopped onto the mattress in the tiny bedroom. It was a far cry from his suite back home, but he'd spent so many summers here as a boy, the cramped quarters didn't bother him. He was bone tired from a full day's work, a late-night date gone sour, and his encounter with Madame LeBieu. What did it matter whether the sheets were of the finest linen or the cheapest cotton? A bed was a bed.

"Just another day at the office." Craig yawned and stared at the ceiling. It would be dawn soon and his uncle expected him up bright and early to help prepare bait and fill gas tanks in the boats they rented to visiting fishermen.

Craig closed his eyes and drifted into a troubled sleep where drums beat, witches wove spells, and frogs littered the ground. A chant echoed throughout the dream, "By day a frog, by night a man, 'til the next full moon, dis curse will span."

What a crock!

* * *

Professor and research scientist Elaine Smith moaned for the tenth time. How the staff must be laughing. Brainiac Elaine Smith, member of Mensa, valedictorian of her high school, undergraduate and masters programs, with an IQ completely off the scale, and she hadn't had a clue. Until she'd opened the door to the stairwell in the science building to find her fiancé Brian with his hands up the shirt of a bosomy blond department secretary while sucking out her tonsils.

The woman saw her first, broke contact and tapped Brian's shoulder. "Uh, this is a little awkward." She twittered her fingers at Elaine. "Hi, Dr. Smith."

"Elaine, I can explain," Brian said, his hands springing free of the double-D breasts.

Without a word, Elaine marched back to the lab. She'd only been away for a moment. If the drink machine on the second floor had worked, she wouldn't have opened that door. Thank God she'd made this discovery before she'd been even more idiotic and married the creep.

She crossed the shiny white floor to her desk and ran her hand over her favorite microscope, letting the coolness seep into her flushed skin. With careful precision, she poured a drop from the glass jar marked *Bayou Miste* onto a slide. With another clean slide, she smeared the sample across the glass, and slid it beneath the scope.

The routine process of studying microorganisms calmed her like no other tonic. Her heartbeat slowed and she lost herself in the beauty of microbiology. She didn't have to think about the world outside the science department. Many times in her life, she'd escaped behind lab doors to avoid the ugly side of society.

"Elaine the brain! Elaine the brain!" Echoes of children's taunts from long ago plagued her attempts at serenity.

Elaine snorted. Wouldn't they laugh now? Elaine the brain, too stupid to live.

A tear dropped onto the lens of the microscope, blurring her viewfinder, and the lab door burst open. Elaine scrubbed her hand across her eyes before she looked up. She'd be damned if she'd let the jerk see her cry.

"Elaine, let me explain." Brian strode in, a sufficiently contrite expression on his face.

He'd probably practiced the expression in the mirror to make it look so real. Elaine wasn't buying it. She forced her voice to be flat and disinterested. "Brian, I'm busy."

"We have to talk."

"No . . . we don't." She turned her back to him, her chest tightened and her stomach clenched.

"Look, I'm sorry." Brian's voice didn't sound convincing. "It's just . . . well . . . ah, hell. I needed more."

Elaine's mouth dropped open, and she spun to face him. "More what? More women? More conquests? More sex in the hallways?"

He dug his hands in his pockets and scuffed his black leather shoe on the white tile. When he looked up, a corner of his mouth lifted and his gray eyes appeared sad. "I needed to know I was more important than a specimen, that I was wanted for more than just a convenient companion."

"So you made out with a secretary in the stairwell?"

"She at least pays attention to me." He shook his head. "I should have broken our engagement first, but every time I tried, you'd bury yourself in this lab." He ran a hand through his hair and stepped closer. "It would never have worked between us. I couldn't compete with your first love."

"What are you talking about?"

"Your obsession with science." He inhaled deeply and

11

looked at the ceiling, before his gaze came back to her. "Face it, Elaine, you love science more than you ever loved me."

"No, I don't!" Her denial was swift, followed closely by the thought, *Do I?*

He crossed his arms over his chest and stood with his feet spread slightly. "Then say it."

"Say what?"

"Say, I love you." Brian stood still waiting for her response.

Elaine summoned righteous indignation, puffed out her chest and prepared to say the words he'd asked for. She opened her mouth, but the words stuck in her throat like a nasty-tasting wad of guilt. Instead of saying anything, she exhaled.

Had she ever really loved Brian? She stared across at his rounded face and curly blond hair. He had the geeky-boy-next-door look, and he'd made her smile on occasion. She'd enjoyed the feeling of having someone to call her own, and to fill the lonely gap in her everyday existence.

But did she love him? After all the years of living in relative isolation from any meaningful relationships, was she capable of feeling love?

Her chest felt as empty as her roiling stomach. He was right. She couldn't say she loved him when she knew those words were a lie. And as much as she didn't like conflict, she disliked lying more. How long had she been deluding herself into thinking they were the perfect couple?

"It's no use, Elaine. Our marriage would be a huge mistake. The only way you'd look at me is if I were a specimen under your microscope. It's not enough. I need more. I need someone who isn't afraid to get out and experience the world beyond this lab."

Brian turned and walked out, leaving a quiet room full of scientific equipment and one confused woman.

Afraid to get out? Elaine glanced around the stark clean walls of the laboratory, the one place she could escape to when she wanted to feel safe.

Dear God, why can't I be like normal people? Brian was right. She felt more comfortable behind the lab door than in the world outside.

When she stared down at the litter of items on the table, blinking to clear the tears from her eyes, she spied the jar labeled *Bayou Miste*. The container had come to her in the mail, an anonymous sample of Louisiana swamp water. She stood, momentarily transfixed by the sight of the plain mason jar, a strange thrumming sound echoing in her subconscious, almost like drums beating. Probably some punk with his woofers too loud in the parking lot.

With an odd sense of fate, she leaned over the microscope, dried her tear from the lens with a tissue, and studied the slide. Her skin tingled and her heartbeat amplified. Here was her opportunity to get away from the lab. If she couldn't solve the microcosm of her love life, she could help solve the pollution problems of an ecosystem.

CHAPTER TWO

Light glinted off the mirror on the eastern wall of the tiny bedroom, nudging Craig out of a deep sleep. He cracked an eyelid and stared at the persistent glare. Sunlight on the mirror? The sun never shown directly into this room in the morning, only in the late afternoon. Glancing at the clock on the nightstand, he jerked awake—groggy, but awake.

Eight-thirty? As in eight-thirty in the evening? He squinted at the clock. Yes, the little red light indicating P.M. glowed and the sun only shone into his room on its way to the western horizon. Damn. His uncle knew he'd had a meeting with Jason Littington at one o'clock this afternoon. Why didn't he wake him earlier?

Craig stretched and flexed his muscles, surprised how agile he felt after being tied to a tree. He felt woozy, not like a concussion, but more like a hangover from too much alcohol and not enough water to replenish his brain cells. But, all in all, no harm had been done in last night's fracas.

14

Fuzzyheaded, but definitely hungry, he rolled out of bed—and fell a long way down to the floor. Too late, he realized he should have put his feet down first. As he fell, his body tensed, and his muscles braced for impact.

Craig landed on all fours, the wind temporarily knocked out of him. When his breathing returned to normal, he looked around.

Huh? He hadn't been drunk when he went to sleep the previous night. But here he was, crouched on the floor looking up. The bed he'd just vacated and the wooden nightstand towered over him. He shook his head to clear the haze. Something wasn't right. Perhaps it was because he was squatting.

Squatting? Why am I squatting?

He attempted to straighten, his muscles bunching in an unfamiliar way. When he tried to stand, he only leaped to another squatting position, and he was no taller than before. The nightstand and bed still loomed next to him.

Noises from the front of the store alerted him to his uncle's presence, and he crawled for the door, forcing his arms and legs to propel him. He'd never noticed how dusty and bumpy the wooden planks were. The going was slow and tedious, but eventually he made it to the doorway leading from the back room into the bait shop.

Craig opened his mouth to cry, "Uncle Joe!" but his voice croaked.

"I don't know where that boy gets off, leaving me here to answer to Littington," the old man muttered.

Craig forced air past his vocal chords, only to emit another croak. *I'm here, Uncle Joe,* he thought, willing his uncle to turn his way. *I was here all day. Why didn't you wake me up?*

Joe Thibodeaux had his back to him, rooting around behind the counter, shifting small boxes of weights and hooks, searching for something.

"Damn!" Uncle Joe pulled back his hand. A hook protruded from his thumb, blood oozing around the gold metal. "This place needs a good cleaning. Couldn't find a snake if it stuck its head out and bit my hind end."

He gingerly eased the hook from the digit and dabbed the blood against his T-shirt. Then, he turned and circled the counter, practically stepping on Craig. "What the heck?" Uncle Joe used the tip of his sneaker to push Craig out of his way. "You don't belong in here. Go on. Get on out of here. I ain't got time to mess with you." His uncle strode for the door leading out to the dock.

A fly buzzed past Craig's head and he froze, his gaze tracking the insect's flight. An urge so powerful, a primal instinct older than time, erupted in his brain. He struggled to control it, fought to stop it, but he couldn't help himself. How could he deny what his body insisted on doing? He watched in horror as his tongue snaked out to snatch the fly from the air, and he swallowed it whole.

His eyes bulged. *Was that my tongue? I saw my tongue out in front of my face?* Making the next logical connection, Craig gagged. Bluck! He'd swallowed a fly! He stuck his tongue out and pawed at it with his hand to remove the bug guts and germs. It was then he noticed his skin.

The room spun and Craig sat down on the floor. He blinked his eyes several times, and then held out his arm again. It wasn't tanned and sprinkled with manly black hairs, like it had the night before. His skin was smooth, shiny and—and—green!

Numb with shock, he crawled to the glass display cabinet with the expensive fishing reels. He bunched the muscles in his legs and jumped high enough to peer at his reflection in the glass. A mottled green water frog looked back at him.

No way!

He jumped again. The frog came into view again.

This couldn't be happening. He was still asleep and this was just a continuation of the whole voodoo thing—one long crazy nightmare. People just didn't change into frogs overnight—no matter what that voodoo witch would have him believe. He was asleep, right? He bunched his legs to take another look. Propelling himself off the ground, he realized a little too late that he'd miscalculated and whacked his head into the glass.

Damn!

Not only did he see the frog again but, based on the pain in his head, he wasn't asleep either.

His legs trembled and he leaned against the cabinet, feeling his miniscule frog heart pounding against his slick white chest. A chest like the one on the frog he'd dissected in high school. Not a chest a man could pound his fist against.

Heck. Now what was he supposed to do? Somehow, he had to find that voodoo witch and get her to undo what she'd done.

Shadows lengthened in the bait shop. The sun was setting and Uncle Joe hadn't turned on the inside lights.

Craig's skin tightened, stretching and pulling. He trembled with the force of every cell in his body splitting and changing in a miraculous metamorphosis. A roaring sound filled his ears and he watched as everything around him shrank.

Focus, Elaine. She had a mission to accomplish, come hell or high water. By the looks of the long causeways she'd crossed getting here, high water it was. If she concentrated on her mission, she wouldn't keep thinking of Brian's betrayal or the millions of gallons of water surrounding her.

With a shiver coursing down her spine, she sent a fervent prayer to the heavens that she wouldn't have to get in it. She hoped everything she had to do, she could do from a boat or dry land. Egad, a boat. Another shiver shook her body.

Elaine had inherited her mother's cursed fear of water. No one incident could be blamed for her irrational panic in regard to getting in over her head, much to her chagrin. There was no logic in this crippling fear. Ever since she was a child, she'd been deathly afraid of entering water deeper than her bathtub, much preferring to shower.

Then why the hell didn't she send a graduate student to the bayous instead of coming herself? She sighed. She'd face a thousand miles of swamp filled with water just to get away from the university and the disaster of her love life.

Elaine had spent the entire trip from Tulane to Bayou Miste fuming and berating her blind stupidity. Why hadn't she seen through Brian's lies? Throughout their four-month courtship and ultimate engagement, he'd been kind, attentive and accommodating of her need for space to do her work. What more could she want?

Passion, love, and most of all fidelity? Was that too much to ask? They'd been engaged, for heaven's sake.

She slammed her palm against the steering wheel. If she hadn't seen it with her own eyes, she'd never have believed Brian was having an affair. Right under her nose!

No matter. She was much better off without him.

When Elaine pulled into the little town of Bayou Miste, Louisiana, on the edge of the Atchafalaya Basin, she had completed her self-coaching session. She was a worthy and intelligent scientist whose work was important to the protection of a fragile ecosystem. She would locate the source of pollution killing the creatures that lived in the swamps. Once her research was complete, she would document her findings and take whatever action was necessary to close down the source and force them to clean up the mess they'd made.

But, as much as she tried to use logic and reason, Brian's rejection still stung. Was something wrong with her? Would she ever feel more passionate about a man than science?

The trip had taken longer than Elaine had anticipated. She hoped the marina was still open. She wanted to move into her rental cottage and set up her lab as soon as possible.

Bayou Miste could barely be called a town. Main Street ended in the parking lot of Thibodeaux Marina, beyond which spread endless miles of swamp. Dilapidated houses lined both sides of the street for the equivalent of one city block. It was a good thing she'd made her arrangements before she came. Only one rental house existed in the entire town and it was all hers for the next three weeks.

An unsettling thought struck her and she glanced up, breathing a sigh of relief when she saw electrical lines. By the looks of the buildings, the town had to have been built more than seventy years ago, maybe a hundred. Peeling paint curled off the sides of a few houses. Weather and the swamp humidity had done their job to try to convert the structures into recycled compost.

The marina's bait shop was in the same condition, except where someone had applied a fresh coat of white paint to a square patch about seven feet tall and seven feet wide. The bright white contrasted sharply with the graying boards. The can and paint brush stood against the wall, waiting for the painter to pick up where he'd left off.

The dock stretched to the side and behind the bait shop located at the center of the marina. No one stirred in the lingering heat of the late evening. She understood why. She flipped her visor down and checked her appearance, attempting to smooth the frizz her hair had become in the moist air. It was no use. Her hair knew no boundaries with one hundred percent humidity. She gave up.

Much as she hated to admit it, Brian had a point. She hadn't been out of the laboratory in a while. Mixing with people and being sociable were not easy for her in the best of circumstances. Invariably, she clammed up and stood like a lump or, on occasion, she blurted out her opinions and alienated everyone within earshot. She preferred to read or walk alone. She didn't mind chatting with other scientists, sharing information on past experiments or theories.

Outside the university environment, though, she felt lost. What did normal people talk about? What could she find in common with them? Well, it wouldn't be an issue while she was in Bayou Miste. She would collect her specimens, conduct her studies and not be bothered by social obligations.

Elaine pushed her glasses up on her nose, gathered her purse and her courage and climbed out of her practical, four-door sedan. After a few deep breaths of thick swamp air, she almost gagged. The rank smell of fish and stagnant water almost had her retreating to the car again. She squared her shoulders and marched up to the door of the bait shop, pointedly ignoring the water beyond.

Mr. Thibodeaux had said she could find him here. Not only did he own the marina, dilapidated as it was, but he was also the landlord of the house she'd be living in during her stay. She prayed the house was in better shape.

She pulled at the rusty handle on the screen door, hoping the inside of the bait shop didn't smell as bad as the outside. When the door swung wide, she stepped into the dark interior and inhaled deeply. Again, she choked. A combination of earthy, fishy, musty odors assailed her nostrils.

Her eyes slowly adjusted to the darkness after the waning light from the setting sun. Soft thumping noises emanated from the far end of the store, but she couldn't see well enough in the dim interior to make out a person. Why hadn't anyone turned on the lights?

"Excuse me," she called softly.

More thumping and scuffling ensued. Elaine thought she heard a faint moan, but nobody appeared.

She cleared her throat and tried again. "Excuse me." Her voice echoed off the walls, and she cringed.

Still no response.

What was wrong with these people? She knew she'd spoken loud enough this time to wake half the town. Perhaps the person behind the counter wasn't a person. Maybe it was a dog or cat.

A frown settled between her brows. Whatever it was might be trapped or hurt and need her help. She strode across the room and had almost reached the other end of the building when a man rose from behind the counter, his back to her.

Elaine stopped so fast she almost tipped over. Her eyes widened and her mouth fell open.

Wow!

She'd never seen such a beautiful specimen of the human male in all her twenty-six years. His broad, bare shoulders were solid and tanned, each muscle neatly defined and precisely curved. His back tapered down to a trim waistline, disappearing below the top of the counter to what promised to be sexy buttocks of firm proportions.

With his back still to her, he cleared his throat. "Am I . . . ?" He held his hands up to the meager light from the windows and flexed his fingers. Then, holding his arms in front of him, he plucked a hair. "Ouch!" He laughed out loud and shouted, "Thank God!"

Elaine stood in a silent stupor as the muscles in his shoulders flexed and extended with each movement. Her mouth went dry and not a single coherent thought surfaced.

He turned and treated her to the full force of his ice-blue stare. Ebony hair hung long around his ears and curled down the nape of his neck in dark waves. A single lock fell across his forehead and he pushed it back with a broad hand.

Elaine's fingers itched to pull the curl back down on his forehead. Her stomach turned flip-flops at the expanse of hard-muscled chest only a few feet away.

Startled by her reaction to the half-naked man standing in front of her, her eyes widened and she licked her lips. At least she *thought* he was half naked. Was that a bare leg she could see through the glass case standing between them? Her gaze slid downward.

The man glanced down, his eyes widening. A faint red stained his cheeks. He folded his arms across his chest and quickly leaned against the counter. "Can I help you?"

It took her several seconds to locate her tongue before she could reply. "I need you," she stammered.

The man smiled and a wicked eyebrow rose up under the stray lock of hair that had fallen back over his forehead. He didn't comment, nor did he move. He stayed firmly in place, the counter covering him from the waist down. "You need me?"

Heat crept up her neck and into her face when Elaine realized what she'd said and what she'd tried to see. "I mean I'm here about the bed."

His smile broadened.

Elaine pressed her hands to her cheeks, her mortification complete. Where had her intellectual vocabulary and scientific mind gone? She felt like a giddy, hormonal teenager instead of a revered scientist with numerous research articles and a book under her belt. "Oh, good grief, let me start over."

"Perhaps you should." His words seeped into every pore of her skin like butter on a hot potato. He could have mocked her sudden inability to articulate. Instead, he graced her with an encouraging grin.

Elaine's mouth opened, but her brain refused to engage. She had the overwhelming urge to run her tongue over his lips, to feel his chest under her fingers.

He cleared his throat. "Are you, or are you not, going to start over?"

Elaine gulped, then stammered, "I'm Elaine Smith." Wiping the sweat from her palm, she stuck her hand out.

"Craig Thibodeaux." His rough hand enveloped hers. The simple gesture sent tingles shooting through her, reminding every cell in her body she was female, single and over twenty-one.

The myriad of sensations raced from her fingertips to her lower extremities, moistening places that had no business being wet in the company of a strange man . . . a sexy as hell strange man. Maybe shaking hands with him wasn't such a good idea after all.

When her senses returned, she jerked her hand back

and rubbed it against her khaki slacks to still the spread of electrical impulses triggering an entirely chemical response throughout her body. Her reaction was pure physics and chemistry, nothing more, nothing less, she told herself. Besides, hadn't she just broken off an engagement? Get a grip.

"Mr. Thibodeaux, I spoke with you on the phone about renting a cottage for three weeks." She chose her words carefully, rather than uttering embarrassing nonsense like she had earlier.

"You must have spoken to my uncle Joe. He owns the place."

"Oh, I see." She dragged her gaze from the vicinity of his chest and scanned the interior again. "Where can I find him?"

"I think he's out on the dock. Why don't you go see?" Craig didn't make a move from behind the counter. "I'd take you out there, but I have something I need to do first."

The thought of the dock paralyzed her. Docks generally stretched over water. "I can wait," she said quickly. "Go ahead and finish what you were doing."

Craig frowned and glanced away. "No really, I don't want to hold you up. Just go on outside. He's sure to be within shouting distance. I'll be out in just a minute."

"Okay." Elaine stared at the door he indicated with all the anticipation of one heading for a guillotine. "Are you sure you don't want me to wait?"

"Positive. Please, go on."

Geez. He was in a hurry to get rid of her.

Good. She didn't have time for men. Remember? Besides, she couldn't possibly have anything in common with a dock hand like Craig Thibodeaux. She was better

24

off sticking with her scientific studies. She could have much more interesting conversations talking to herself. At least with her own company, she knew where she stood. A little voice popped into her head. *Yeah, hiding behind a microscope.*

Elaine liked to think she was moving at a swift walk toward the door. If she was honest, it was more like a snail's pace. But she didn't stop; she kept right on going. Even though the dock was scary, the marina owner's nephew left her more unsettled than the murky swamp around her. She reminded herself that she'd come to study frogs, not the mating habits of the Cajun swamp people. The less she saw of Craig Thibodeaux, the better off she'd be.

CHAPTER THREE

Once outside the bait shop, Elaine stood with a hand pressed to her chest and inhaled deep, calming breaths of the sticky, warm air.

What had come over her? The sight of one bare-chested male shouldn't cause her to take leave of her senses. Even if he was one of the most beautiful specimens of hot, spicy Cajun males she'd ever seen. With those piercing blue eyes and more than his share of dark curly hair on his head . . . and on his chest . . .

Elaine fanned the rising heat spreading up her neck into her face. Beads of perspiration sprung out on her forehead and upper lip.

No man had ever had this effect on her, not even Brian. And, frankly, it scared her. Elaine Smith was a scientist, not a driven-by-her-hormones teenager prone to mooning over sexy guys. Pushing loose tendrils of hair back from her damp forehead, she scanned the dock, looking for Mr. Joe Thibodeaux, with luck a much older gentleman with less sex appeal than his nephew.

Darkness had cloaked the landscape and the water was even murkier and more menacing than in the daylight. A boardwalk ran fifty yards to either side of the bait shop with short piers jutting out at thirty-foot intervals to allow boats to pull alongside for refueling or overnight docking.

Lights dotted every other pier, providing a safe port for returning fishermen. At the end of the long boardwalk stood a grizzled old man in baggy tan shorts and a tattered T-shirt. He was deep in conversation with an equally aged man sitting in a fishing boat.

Anxious to get settled in the cottage, Elaine focused on her goal, not the water. Thank goodness she couldn't see through the boards to the water below.

You can do it, one step at a time. Don't look at the water to your right or left, just concentrate on the next board in front of you. Thus schooling herself, she marched the length of the dock, slowing as she approached the men. She hung back far enough not to interrupt their conversation, but close enough for them to see her, and for her to overhear their words.

"I don't know what done it, Joe," said the man in the boat. "But I tell you there musta been twenty or so fish floatin' belly up."

"Now, Bernie, you sure you didn't see any sign of city folks in their flashy boats?" Joe scratched his scraggly whiskers. He lowered his hand to pat the faded picture of a leaping fish displayed across his chest. "Sometimes they fish all day just for the sake of catching. Then they dump all those dead fish before they leave."

Bernie shook his head. "I thought about that, but not a one of 'em showed signs of having swallowed a hook. That's when I found this." He reached under the seat in

27

front of him and pulled out a small alligator not much bigger than a baseball bat. Its body was already beginning to bloat and a milky film had formed over its eyes.

Elaine's heart sped up and she stepped forward. "May I see that?"

Two startled heads turned in her direction.

Elaine took a deep breath, inhaling the scent of decaying fish. Despite the rotting stench, she could barely contain her excitement and held out her hand to Joe. "Hi, I'm Elaine Smith. Are you Mr. Joe Thibodeaux?"

"That's me." Joe took her hand. "You that doctor from Tulane who called about renting the house?"

"I'm the one," she responded with a smile.

Joe frowned. "I thought you'd be older."

"Sorry to disappoint you. Is that going to make a difference?"

"No. Your money spends the same."

Bernie tossed the dead alligator onto the wooden dock and climbed out of the boat. "What's a pretty lady want with a dead 'gator?"

"I'm a scientist. I came to study the effects of pollution on the creatures that live in the swamp." She pushed her glasses up on her nose and squatted next to the alligator on the wooden planks. "Where did you find it?"

"In the swamp about five miles from here," Joe said.

Bernie frowned and stepped between Joe and Elaine, shooting a hard look over his shoulder at Joe. "I got a tongue. I can speak for myself." He faced Elaine and pulled his fishing hat from his head, displaying oily white hat hair and a gap-toothed smile. "Like Joe said, *I* found that 'gator and some dead fish in a lagoon about five miles from here. Durn shame, too. Used to be my favorite fishin' hole. Joe knows the one."

Her eyes widened, and blood pounded through her

veins. Elaine put her hand on Bernie's arm. "Would you take me there?"

Bernie's face flushed red and he twisted the hat in his gnarled hands. "Now, I'd like nothin' more than to take you there, but my wife, Lola, would skin me alive if she found out I took a pretty young thang out in the swamp. Yessirree. She'd plum skin me alive and feed my flesh to the 'gators."

Elaine turned to Joe. "Don't you rent boats?"

Joe held his hands up. "Now, don't get some fool notion of going off on your own to find them dead fish. You'd get lost as soon as you left the dock. Besides, the swamp ain't no place for a lady."

"I'm no lady. I'm a scientist." Elaine winced at her choice of words.

"Scientist or no, I don't rent my boats out to people I don't think can bring 'em back."

"Then perhaps you could help me?" Her lips turned up at the corners. "I'll need to hire someone for the next few weeks to take me out to gather frogs and fish for my studies."

"Folks around these parts do their frog-giggin' at night when the frogs are most active. If you're wanting frogs, you'll have to go out at night to get 'em. I'm no night owl, but I know someone who is," Joe said, looking over Elaine's shoulder. "Here's your man. My nephew Craig can take you."

Fingers of sensation trickled down her spine. Without having to look, she knew he stood behind her.

"Craig can take who where?" His voice was as sultry as the humid air, oozing sex appeal with every syllable.

How does he do that? Did he have some way of emitting testosterone that, combined with her dormant hormones, caused spontaneous combustion in her lower abdomen?

Elaine refrained from fanning her face, braced herself for impact, and executed a slow turn. The half-naked man from the marina stood in faded blue jeans, bare feet and a cotton shirt, untucked and hanging open. This unkempt man had no right to look good enough to eat, one lick at a time, like a very tall ice cream cone on a hot day. She was determined not to react as idiotically as she had previously.

"No thank you. I'll eat another guide."

All three men tilted their heads and narrowed their eyes.

Elaine stared back and then clapped a hand to her mouth when she realized what she'd said. "I mean, I'll get another guide, or go alone."

Joe shook his head. "Dr. Smith, you don't seem to understand. Craig's your best bet as a night guide. And my rule is no guide . . . no boat."

"What are you more afraid of, the swamp or me?" Craig dared her with a half smile and a tilted eyebrow.

Elaine frowned. This was the second time a man had accused her of being afraid. She'd be damned if she'd take that lying down. Although, with him, lying down held a certain appeal.

Jumpin' genetics, what was she thinking? Heat surged up her neck and into her cheeks. Thank God he couldn't read minds. Straightening her shoulders, she stared directly into his eyes and replied, "Neither."

"So, when do you want to start?" Craig asked.

Boy, he moved fast. Elaine felt a little out of breath. Although she struggled, she congratulated herself on keeping her inner turmoil from showing on her face. "I hope to have my lab set up by tomorrow night. Can you handle that, Mr. Thibodeaux?"

"Lady, I can handle anything you've got." He ran his

gaze from the top of her curly brown hair to the tips of her sensible black pumps.

Elaine gulped, forcing her chin to a defiant angle when she'd rather run like a scared rabbit in the face of a hungry wolf. "Good," she said, her voice squeaking. She cleared her throat and assumed her best professor voice. "I'll see you tomorrow at dusk. Please be on time and—" she eyed his open shirt and raised an eyebrow in what she hoped was a disdainful look, "fully dressed?"

"At your command, Dr. Smith," Craig said with a sweeping bow and several rolls of his wrist.

Elaine turned to address the elder Thibodeaux, who'd remained quiet throughout the exchange. "May we go to the house now?"

"Yes, ma'am!" He popped a smart salute, immediately softening it with an impertinent wink. Joe turned to his nephew. "You take care of Bernie's boat while I help Miss Smith with the rental house."

"Sure, but when you get back, we need to talk," Craig said, his expression serious.

Elaine stared from the older man to the younger one. What was that all about? She didn't know, but she'd do well to keep a close eye on the younger Thibodeaux . . . and her hands and thoughts to herself.

An hour later, Craig had tied up Bernie's boat, topped off the gas tanks and cleaned the seats and floors of all trash. Although it had been eight years since he'd visited his uncle, the activities were still second nature from all the summers he'd spent helping at the marina.

When Uncle Joe still hadn't returned, Craig paced the length of the dock. At every lamp post, he stopped and held an arm up in the circle of light. He batted away moths and mosquitoes to get a glimpse of his skin to make sure he wasn't turning green. Occasionally, he ran a hand through his thick black hair to reaffirm it was still there.

"What bug have you got up your butt, son? You're as twitchy as a trapped ringtail."

Craig spun to face his uncle, all the pent-up emotions of the past twenty-four hours gushing out in four words. "I'm in big trouble."

"Your daddy comin' down here?" Uncle Joe asked. " 'Cause if he is, I'm leaving. I can't take two minutes of his high-and-mighty act."

Craig shook his head. "No, it's worse."

Uncle Joe scratched the gray stubble on his chin. "Can't think of anything worse than that stiff-necked brother of mine comin' for a visit. So, spit it out."

Craig pushed his hand through his hair again. "You're not going to believe this."

With a frown, Uncle Joe laid a hand on Craig's shoulder, concern reflecting in his pale blue eyes. "Try me."

Pausing to phrase his words carefully, Craig shook his head. How did he tell his uncle that he was related to an amphibian? "Have you heard of Madame LeBieu?"

Uncle Joe nodded. "Seen her once or twice out in the swamps. She's been known to practice voodoo on occasion. Had a buddy of mine who swore he'd never get hitched. Said he had too many women to love before he saddled himself with a ball and chain. But Madame LeBieu slipped him a love potion and he went and married dog-faced Debbie Smith." Uncle Joe smiled and shook his head. "Dangdest thang. Every one of their poor kids looks just like Debbie."

"Well, I had a personal invitation to visit with her last night."

Uncle Joe's eyes widened and his shaggy brows climbed up his forehead. "She asked for you in person?"

"No, she insisted on my coming. Mo and Larry delivered an invitation I couldn't refuse."

"Holy cypress knees." Uncle Joe clapped a hand to the top of his head. "Did you do something to tick her off?"

Craig paced a few steps away and turned back to his uncle. "Not that I can remember. I went out with her granddaughter, Lisa LeBieu, earlier that evening. When Lisa came on to me, I took her home."

"That's gotta be a first." Uncle Joe shook his head.

"That's just it." Craig smacked his fist into his palm. "Lisa was mad I didn't take her up on what she was offering, so she got her voodoo grandmother involved."

"Not good."

"No, it's not." An image of the old voodoo witch materialized in his head along with the thrumming of the drums, tapping a tattoo at his temples. He pinched the bridge of his nose to dispel the picture and breathed in deeply. "It's real bad. I think she put a spell on me. Last night when I went to bed I was a man. This afternoon when I woke up, I was a frog." Craig's lips tipped in an ironic smirk.

"Say again?" Uncle Joe's bushy white brows twisted together in a confused frown.

Craig looked his uncle in the eye. "That old witch put a spell on me. When I woke up earlier, I was a frog."

"You don't say." Uncle Joe slapped his hand against his leg and hooted with laughter.

"Maybe you didn't hear me." Craig frowned as his uncle chuckled. "When I woke up this afternoon, I was a frog. As soon as the sun set, I turned back into a man."

"Got to admit that's the lamest excuse I ever heard for

not showing up for your meeting with Littington this afternoon. Not sure I liked that man, but I like your story."

"I'm not kidding, Uncle Joe. I was as ugly a green water frog as you've ever seen in the swamp and about this tall." Craig held his thumb and forefinger two inches apart. "Hell, you almost stepped on me a while ago when you poked your finger on that fishhook.

"That was you?" Uncle Joe scratched his head. "Didn't look much like you. Thought it was a stray from the swamps that got into the shop. Good thing I didn't step on you. How would I explain to your parents I killed their only son when I crushed him under my boot?"

"Uncle Joe." Craig's patience wore thin. "Perhaps you don't understand. This spell makes me a frog by day and a man by night. The old bat said something about having until the next full moon to figure out how to break it. That's less than two weeks." He snorted. "Otherwise, you're stuck with a frog for a nephew, forever. Hell, this sounds like some sick fairy tale."

"Yeah, boy. You done messed with the wrong voodoo queen. She don't give up until she gets what she wants." Uncle Joe shook his head. "What'd she say she wanted?"

Craig inhaled deeply and blew out. Apparently, living in the bayou made even the most down-to-earth men, like his uncle, believe in magic. Thank God. "As far as I can figure, I'm supposed to find someone who'll fall in love with me by the next full moon or I'm stuck as a frog."

Uncle Joe crossed his arms over his chest and tipped his head to the side. "Better get crackin'."

"What do you mean, get cracking?" Craig stared at his uncle, dumbfounded. "You don't suggest I go along with this crazy swamp woman, do you?"

"Don't see as you got much of a choice."

"I've got a choice, all right." Craig climbed into the

skiff. "I'm going to find that woman and make her undo what she did to me!"

"Won't do you no good." Uncle Joe shook his head sadly. "My cousin begged and begged, but when Madame LeBieu sets her mind to something, not even a hurricane as powerful as Camille could budge her."

With his hand poised to yank the pull string on the motor, Craig paused. "What do you mean?"

"Only way you're gonna fix this mess is to follow her instructions."

Craig laughed without humor and rolled his eyes. "Like I'm going to find someone to love me in that short a time? Hell, I haven't found anyone in the past twenty-eight years, how will I find someone in less than two weeks?"

Uncle Joe tapped a finger to his temple. "You got a point, son. But you better try, unless you fancy flies and bugs for dinner every night."

Craig sat down on the hard metal seat of the little boat and buried his face in his hands. "Great, I'm screwed."

Uncle Joe scratched the whiskers on his chin and stared up at the stars. "What about the scientist lady? Can't you make her fall for you?"

Craig looked up and snorted. "She's not my type." Although, with eyes the color of Spanish moss and soft curls framing her face, Elaine had her appeal, in a subtle way. She'd come across as vulnerable instead of intimidating like he suspected she'd been aiming for.

"And you've been more successful with the women you usually go out with?"

Craig's lips tightened.

Uncle Joe folded his arms across his chest. "Exactly. Maybe Madame LeBieu has a point."

Disgusted, Craig threw his hands in the air. "Oh, don't tell me you're on her side!"

"No, but you gotta admit, your track record isn't so great."

"And since when have you started keeping score?"

"Since you first started noticing girls back when you were a smart-mouthed teenager comin' to visit me on your summer vacations. That's when. And don't tell me you're here strictly for work. I know you had a run-in with a woman back in New Orleans and don't try to tell me different. Your daddy and I still talk, even though I don't know what he's saying half the time with all that lawyer jargon."

"I didn't come here to get away from a woman," Craig grumbled. "I have legitimate business with Jason Littington."

"Yeah, and I ain't partial to beer. Since when do you lawyers perform housecalls? And when do you plan to head back to New Orleans?"

Craig climbed out of the boat and walked a few steps toward the bait shop before he answered. "I'm not sure. Considering my present circumstances, I'm not certain I'll ever go back. You've got to help me out of this mess."

"You're ignoring my question."

"Look, if it bothers you for me to be here, I'll leave."

"Dug a finger in a festering wound, did I?" Uncle Joe dropped his arms to his side. "You know you're welcome to stay as long as you like. I can always use the help with the marina."

"Thanks, Uncle Joe," Craig said. "But that still doesn't fix my problem."

"Maybe an apology to Madame LeBieu and her granddaughter would be the place to start."

Craig ground his teeth. "The thought of apologizing to that old witch goes against the grain. I acted like a gentleman with her granddaughter and she considers that cause enough to sentence me to being a frog? I don't get it. But if apologizing will get her to lift the spell, I'll do it. Anything to keep from changing back into a frog."

"That's more like it. Sometimes you got to get humble. And in the meantime, be nice to the lady scientist. She might be your salvation."

Craig stomped back to the bait shop for bug repellent. He'd have to hurry if he planned to talk with Madame LeBieu before sunup. And he'd thought his law practice was stressful. So much for coming to Bayou Miste to conduct a little business and snatch a bit of peace and quiet.

"My words stand." Madame LeBieu's melodious voice held a hint of steel. She stood with her arms crossed over her massive bosom and her lips pressed into a stubborn line. The skirt of her Hawaiian-patterned muumuu billowed in the breeze blowing in off the gulf. "You must find a woman to love you before de next full moon, or your skinny little butt be a green hoppin' one forever."

"You can't be serious." Craig flung a hand in the air and paced the ground in front of the rickety porch. "How am I supposed to get a woman to love me when I'm a frog?"

"You got all night long to work yer magic, my friend."

He stopped in front of Madame LeBlieu. "Most people sleep at night."

"Dat be your problem."

"And where am I supposed to find an eligible woman in the swamps?"

"Bayou Miste has plenty single women. What about de scientist lady I sent—what come here on a mission? You be sure and help her find what she be lookin' for. Her heart is true and she cares, unlike you!"

Craig stood at the foot of the warped wooden steps, holding a lantern high to size up his adversary. He'd argued in some of the most hostile courtrooms and won cases against the best attorneys, but Madame LeBieu was in a league all her own. "I don't have time to date swamp women. I've got to complete the deal with Littington and get back to New Orleans. I can't go as a frog. Be reasonable."

"Looks to me as if your priorities have changed. If you don't do as I say, you won't have to worry 'bout going to work no mo'."

"I could sue you." He cringed as he said the words.

Madame LeBieu snorted. "Go ahead. No judge will take you seriously if you can't even show up in court." She laughed and turned to reenter her ramshackle clapboard house. "Sue me, ha!" Her chuckles could be heard even as the screen door slammed behind her.

"I'm doomed," Craig moaned. He glanced at his watch. The sun would rise in less than an hour. He'd have to hurry to get back to the marina before the transformation.

The screen pushed open again and Madame LeBieu stood with one chubby finger raised. "One other ting. The magic don't work if she know about your problem."

On the ride back through the swamps, he considered his options. Some options. He could do as Madame LeBieu said or stay a frog the rest of his life.

From where he sat, the vote was unanimous. He had to find a woman and make her fall in love with him in less than two weeks. Simple, right?

CHAPTER FOUR

Whoever said it was quiet in the country obviously hadn't spent time in the swamps. The raucous sounds of crickets, cicadas and frogs were every bit as loud as the traffic outside Elaine's little house in the suburbs of New Orleans.

Due to the strange bed and all the unfamiliar sounds and smells, Elaine had spent a restless night tossing and turning. When she'd managed to sleep in short spurts, her dreams had run the gamut from scenes of Brian and the secretary to dark and sinister swamps filled with eerie croaking frogs. A steady thrumming laced each dream, as if drums beat to the rhythm of her heart.

When the predawn grayness heralded the sun's rising, Elaine slipped out of bed and padded into the tiny kitchen to make a pot of coffee. Since she wasn't sleeping, she might as well start the day.

She'd unpacked only the necessities the night before, one of which was the coffeemaker. While the machine heated water, she returned to the bedroom to change into khaki slacks and a ribbed T-shirt. She was tugging a brush through her tangled hair when she heard a knock at the front door.

With a quick glance in the mirror, she sighed. What was the use in this humidity? Her hair bushed around her face in wild, wavy abandon. In a few swift motions, she swept the tresses back into a wide-toothed clip and raced for the door.

She turned the deadbolt and swung the door wide.

"Mornin' neighbor." A diminutive woman with hair the color of warm honey sailed through the door, a cloth-covered basket dangling from her arm.

Elaine stepped back, unsure how to react to someone barging into her home, temporary though it was.

"I smelled coffee a-brewin' and figured you were finally awake. Mind if I join you? I brought breakfast." The woman didn't seem to care that Elaine hadn't responded to her first words. She plunked the basket on the table and bustled around the kitchen like she knew it well.

The aroma of hot muffins filled the room, reminding Elaine she hadn't eaten. "Excuse me, should I know you?"

"Oh, bless my soul." The woman pressed a hand to her chest and then held it out to Elaine. "I'm Mozelle Reneau. I live right next door to you. I just finished bakin' a batch of the best blueberry muffins you'll taste in the entire parish, if I say so myself, and I thought, 'Mozelle, it wouldn't be neighborly of you to keep them all to yourself now, would it?' So I marched myself right on over here to see if my new neighbor would be interested in sharin' a muffin and a chat with a stranger, although I hope we're not strangers for long."

Elaine's eyes widened and she inhaled deeply along with Ms. Reneau. How could any one person talk so long, and fast, without taking a breath?

"And you are?" Ms. Reneau waited with eyebrows raised as if poised to pounce.

"Elaine," she managed to sputter before extending her own hand and saying more calmly, "Elaine Smith."

"And where might you be from, Ms. Smith?"

"New Orleans. And, please, call me Elaine."

"Why thank you. I'd be pleased to call you Elaine and I insist you call me Mozelle. There! Now that we're properly introduced, we can become quite chummy over a hot, fresh muffin and . . ." she sniffed, eyed the coffeepot and smiled, ". . . coffee."

Mozelle moved around the tiny kitchen, taking down clean plates and coffee mugs from cabinets, more at home than Elaine. "We have an occasional visitor to these parts from New Orleans. Mostly, they come to fish. Once in a while, they like it so much here, they stay."

"Really?" Elaine asked politely, when Mozelle paused to breathe.

"Certainly. Why, our own Mr. Thibodeaux is a New Orleans transplant to these swamps. He and that nephew of his are quite the scoundrels. I like sugar in my coffee, no cream. What's your preference?"

Elaine sat at the small dinette table with the white-speckled Formica top. "The younger one."

"Pardon?"

Elaine's face burned and she mumbled, "Only sugar, please."

"Me too. I like mine hot and black with a couple of spoonfuls of the sweet stuff. As I was sayin', Joseph Thibodeaux is the black sheep, if ever there was one in the

Thibodeaux family. And by the looks of it, that young nephew of his could be followin' in his footsteps."

"Why do you say that?" Elaine shifted in her seat, slightly embarrassed to be encouraging the gossipy Ms. Reneau.

"Craig used to come visit his uncle durin' the summer. He and his friends were always pullin' pranks and into things they ought not to be. Why one time, I had to shoo them away from my peach orchard. They must've thought I was a crazy woman swingin' my broom and whoopin' like there was no tomorrow. Good thing I did. As it was, they got a good bellyful of green peaches. Had them sicker'n dogs for a day or two."

A smile tilted the corner of Elaine's lips. She could visualize a younger version of Craig racing through the peach orchard with a broom-wielding Mozelle close on his heels.

Mozelle glanced over her shoulder toward the door. "Why speak of the devil, there's Mr. Thibodeaux now."

Elaine's blood jolted through her veins and she reached a hand up to smooth her uncooperative hair before she turned.

"Ms. Smith, you up and about?"

At the sound of Joe Thibodeaux's husky voice calling to her from the porch, Elaine's heart skidded into a slower rate. "I'm up, Mr. Thibodeaux; come on in."

He pulled the screen door open and stepped into the kitchen. When he spied the two ladies sitting at the table, he scraped the floppy fishing hat from his head. He crushed the hat in one hand, pushed his other hand through his wild white hair and dipped his head in their direction. "Miss Smith, Ms. Reneau."

Mozelle popped out of her seat, fluffed her not-so-natural strawberry-blond hair and pulled a mug out of the cabinet. "I'm glad you took my advice and stocked this house with a matchin' set of dishes and silverware. Makes it mighty homelike for such a nice visitor as Miss Smith. Come join us for a cup of coffee."

Joe hovered by the door, frowned and stared down at his flip-flop-clad feet. "I just came to see if Miss Smith wanted help unloadin' her car."

Elaine jumped up from her chair. "Oh yes, thank you. I could use a hand. Some of the items are heavy. Students at the university helped me load the trunk and I'm sure I could unload it by myself. But your help would be greatly appreciated." Elaine's lungs gasped for air and she shook her head. What had gotten into her? She sounded as loose-jawed as the sweet Ms. Reneau.

"Joseph, are you gonna stand there, or come in and have a cup of coffee with us?" Mozelle stood with a mug in one hand and the coffeepot in the other, poised to pour.

"No, thank you. I have to get back to the marina. Got a fishing tournament to launch. Can you wait for an hour, Miss Smith? I'll be back to help then."

"Certainly." Elaine's gaze traveled around the room. "It'll give me time to figure out where I can put everything."

"Good enough." Joe nodded to Elaine and Mozelle and then backed out of the house. The door thumped loudly in its frame.

"Well, how do you like that? He took off outta here faster than a scalded cat. There's no gettin' into that man's head, now, is there? If he were any kind of gentleman, he'd have sat down with us for a cup of coffee. Those Thibodeauxs need lessons in manners. You'd think with their background and schoolin' they'd have learned a few by now."

Elaine leaned against the front-door frame and stared

at the marina a few buildings away. Indeed, the Thibodeauxs could use a set of manners. What with the one rushing out the door as fast as he could and the other running around half naked in a place of business.

With the rambling prattle of Mozelle in the background, Elaine allowed her memory to recreate the image of Craig standing behind the counter in the bait shop. As a scientist, she couldn't deny the kinematical perfection of the muscles rippling across his back when he flexed his arms high over his head.

With her lips compressed, Elaine mentally shook herself. But as a woman, she could certainly tighten the reins on her own chemical reaction to the man. He was not her type, and she had no desire to plunge into another relationship doomed to go nowhere. Her love of science would stand in the way every time. No use going there.

". . . I'll be glad when he settles down to one woman, me and every mother of unwed girls in the parish. What that man needs is a woman who can knock his socks off. You know, rock his boat until he can't see straight."

Elaine's attention jerked back to Mozelle. "I'm sorry, who were you talking about?"

"Craig Thibodeaux, as if anyone wouldn't know. He's hell bent on sleepin' with every woman who catches his eye. Has every addlepated female around vyin' for his attention."

The sudden disappointment settling over Elaine's sunny day startled her. Why should it bother her to hear every woman around wanted to crawl into bed with Craig Thibodeaux? She didn't even know the man.

"Well, I'd best be moseying along." Mozelle set her cup in the sink. "I have a bridge game over at my house in one hour. Join us if you have a hankering to play a hand of cards."

"Thank you, Mozelle." Elaine walked the older woman to the door. "And thank you for the muffins."

Fifteen minutes later, after a few accounts of how Mozelle had trumped Louella Landau in last week's bridge game, and a list of the ingredients she'd used in the blueberry muffins, and Mozelle finally made it through the door and on her way.

Elaine collapsed on the couch, winded by her encounter with the gregarious Mozelle Reneau. She couldn't help but smile, though. Her new neighbor's constant chatter and enthusiasm, while wearing, were also welcoming. For the first time since she'd arrived in Bayou Miste Elaine relaxed a little. Maybe this trip had been a good idea. The little cottage held a sense of home to her.

Not two minutes later, a tapping sounded at the door. Elaine pulled herself off the old couch. Joe Thibodeaux hovered on the other side of the screen, staring over his shoulder in the direction Ms. Reneau had disappeared.

"Hello, again."

"Thank God, she's gone." Joe swept his hat off his head and ran a hand through his thick white hair. "That woman could talk the ear off a fish."

A hound dog the size of a horse nudged the door open. Elaine smiled. "Does he belong to you?"

Joe turned and frowned. "Nope. He belongs to my nephew. Stay, Dawg."

"What's his name?"

"Dawg." Joe shot a stern look at the animal. "Stay out here and behave yourself." Joe muttered something else, but not quite loud enough for Elaine to hear.

To Elaine, it sounded like "I'll handle this." She shrugged. Now she was hearing things. "Just a minute and I'll get my keys."

Between Joe and Elaine, they had the supplies unloaded and stacked in the living room in less than twenty minutes. The entire time, Dawg lay on the front porch, chin on his paws, his soulful brown eyes the only part of his body moving.

Elaine could understand why. After the first five minutes, the heat and humidity had her sweating like a horse.

When Joe laid the last box on the floor, he straightened. "Need anything else?"

"I could use a little help setting up that folding table."

"Sure." While unfolding the legs of the table, Joe cleared his throat. "So, you got anyone back in New Orleans?"

Elaine's head shot up. "Excuse me?"

Joe's face flushed red. "You know, got a husband or fiancé back in New Orleans?"

Elaine studied Joe through her peripheral vision while shoving the brace into place on the table legs. "Why do you ask?"

Joe jerked the other leg out and smacked the brace before he answered. "Just curious. Not many young females come out this way by themselves. Seems kinda strange." Joe tugged at the collar of his T-shirt.

Elaine couldn't tell what he was getting at, but relented and answered. "No, I don't have anyone special in my life back in New Orleans." Boy, that sounded pathetic. She felt awkward in a small town where everyone was probably spoken for. And Elaine, from a city full of people, couldn't even claim to have a relationship with anyone. Yeah, she truly sounded pathetic. But what did it matter? She had her career, science, a cause to champion. What more could a woman want?

"My nephew, Craig . . ." Joe started.

Elaine's gaze swiveled back to the older man and she groaned inwardly. Why, when she thought she had her act together, did she continue to run into reminders of the half-naked Cajun with the coal-black hair and ice-blue eyes? Had it been so long since she'd had hot, steamy sex that the first attractive man she saw made her ready to jump his bones?

She recalled sex with Brian and shook her head. No, those experiences had been anything but hot and steamy. But here in the sultry swampland where beads of perspiration pooled between her breasts and rolled downward to the band of her trousers, all kinds of images slid through her imagination. All of them included gliding her naked skin against Craig Thibodeaux's smooth, incredibly sexy muscles.

"So, what do you think?"

Elaine stared at Joe for a few seconds. Was he asking her a question? "I'm sorry, what did you say?"

Joe's blush deepened to a ruddy russet. "Would you consider going out with my nephew?"

His words slammed into her gut and plummeted lower, where they had no business plummeting. "Go out with your nephew? Craig?"

"Yeah." Joe looked up and smiled, his expression as pleading as Dawg's had been out on the porch. "He really is a nice guy, once you get to know him."

"Let me get this straight. You're asking me to go out with your nephew, Craig?"

Joe nodded, twisting his hat in his hand.

"Not that I'm interested, but why doesn't he ask me himself?"

"Oh, he doesn't know I'm asking for him. And frankly, I don't think he'd be pleased to find out I had asked for him. But if he does ask you, will you give him the benefit of the doubt and say yes?"

Elaine's breath quickened at the thought of going on a date with Craig. "I'm going out alone on a boat with him tonight. Isn't that enough?"

"I know this is strange, but try to get to know him." Joe glanced at the mangled hat in his hands. "He's a little shy around the girls."

Elaine propped a hand on her hip. "That's not what Ms. Reneau said."

Joe frowned. "Mozelle is nothing more than a gossip. I wouldn't listen to her."

"She said you were the black sheep of your family. Is that true?" Elaine couldn't believe she'd asked such a pointed question, but she was so flustered by Joe's asking her to consider going on a date with Craig she'd spoken without thinking.

Joe's lips tightened. "She's got no right to be telling complete strangers my life history. What's happened in my family is my own business, not hers."

Immediately, Elaine felt contrite. She hadn't meant to pry. It wasn't like her to take any notice of gossip. She tried to get back to the issue at hand. "By the looks of him, Craig could date any woman he wanted. Why do you want *me* to go out with him?" Elaine tipped her head to the side. "And why does he walk around half-clothed?"

Joe gulped and tugged at his collar. "It's mighty hot around here in the summertime."

Elaine laughed. "I hope most of the men in Bayou Miste don't try to beat the heat in the same way. I'm not guaranteeing I'll accept an offer of a date from your nephew, but I'll definitely think about it."

Joe mumbled and turned toward the door. "That's what he gets for messing with a voodoo queen."

Did Joe say voodoo queen? Elaine shook her head. Perhaps she'd heard wrong. "What was that you said?"

"Nothing." Joe waved a hand over his shoulder. "I gotta get back to the bait shop. I left a motor running or something."

"Thanks for helping me unload." When Joe didn't turn or respond, she added, "I'll keep your request in mind."

The older man turned and smiled. "You won't be sorry."

She already was. If Craig wasn't the only guide she knew in the area, she'd keep as far away from him as possible. He unsettled her, and she didn't like to feel unsettled.

Elaine stood at the door for several minutes watching Joe amble down the road toward the bait shop. When he was halfway there, Elaine realized he'd left Dawg.

She waved her hand at the animal and nudged him with her foot. "Go on, Dawg. Go home." Dawg stood, his tail thumping against the wooden planks of the front porch.

The animal's eyes were so soft and beseeching, Elaine caved and opened the door to go back inside and unpack. "Fine. You stay on the porch. See if I care." She turned around to look back at him, but he'd gone. Elaine shook her head, marveling at the comings and goings around Bayou Miste.

She had a lot of work to do before evening and her rendezvous with the other Mr. Thibodeaux. At the thought of the Cajun hotty, the trail of perspiration between her breasts increased. Unfortunately, the temperature outside had nothing to do with the tingling sensations rippling through her body. Damn her hormones! She marched to the window air conditioner and turned it down several notches to chill her skin.

CHAPTER FIVE

"Craig! Craig!" The loud screech of the screen door heralded Uncle Joe's arrival at the marina.

Since he'd woken after sunup, all green and slimy, Craig had paced the floor. Well, as much as a frog could pace. He'd hopped a path back and forth across his little bedroom floor throughout the day. Like an idiot, he'd closed the door prior to his transformation into a frog. Once a frog, he was stuck in the bedroom until Uncle Joe came looking for him and let him out. His frustration level had topped out hours ago.

After his visit with Madame LeBieu, and before his metamorphosis, he'd sat down with Uncle Joe and covered all the bases if anyone came looking for him during the day.

His father was bound to demand to know his whereabouts and why he hadn't sealed the deal with Littington. His "working vacation" was supposed to be over in two days. With plenty of work piled on his desk and awaiting his attention, the family law firm would be less than thrilled if he extended his stay indefinitely.

If anyone asked for him from Bayou Miste, Uncle Joe was to say he'd been summoned to a nearby town and he'd be back late. Craig would call Jason Littington the following evening to arrange for a night meeting.

If his father or brother called during the day, Uncle Joe was to tell them he was taking some time to catch up on his fishing and would return the call that evening.

Meanwhile, he was stuck as a frog during the day, which had its own set of challenges. He hadn't eaten since the night before and he was getting desperate enough to eat a twelve-pack of flies. But the back bedroom was fly free and his froggy belly was starving. He'd tried to get his mind off his hunger by thinking about solutions to his little problem, but he'd come up short of any foolproof answers. How did you argue with a spell, or a voodoo queen, for that matter?

To get a woman to fall in love with him would be a piece of cake. But he didn't want the lady in question to think he was committing to anything other than a convenient relationship to break an inconvenient spell.

He hadn't had a committed bone in his body since Tracy, in law school. From that incident forth, he'd made it clear to the women he dated that he wasn't interested in a long-term relationship, which was one of the major factors in his decision to take this pseudo-vacation.

Ah, the lovely Cassandra, one of the newest partners in his family's law firm. Beauty and a razor-sharp intelligence were a killer combination. Craig shook his little green head. What a shame she'd only been hunting a diamond engagement ring. Like Tracy, it turned out she only wanted him for his family connections and money. For a brief period Craig had thought she was going to be different, but she'd turned out like all the rest. He wondered if she'd ever really loved him. Not that he wanted her to . . . until now. He should call her.

"Where are you, dagblast it?" Uncle Joe's voice called out on the other side of the wooden panel.

Craig hopped away from the door to avoid being pancaked.

"Craig?" The door swung open and his uncle towered above him. "There you are." Uncle Joe squatted near the floor. "That is you, isn't it?"

Craig nodded.

Uncle Joe grinned. "Takes a little gettin' used to, havin' a frog for a nephew. Almost thought I dreamt it all up." He clapped his hands together once.

The sound reverberated through Craig's head and he staggered backward.

"I've got good news. That scientist doesn't have any significant other hangin' around New Orleans waitin' for her to come back. You can ask her out. That is, as soon as you're up to it. Get it?" Uncle Joe laughed so hard he fell back off his heels and landed on his backside.

Craig wished he could take credit for knocking his uncle over. How could he make fun of his nephew when he was in such a dire predicament?

Now, what had his uncle said about the scientist lady? She was single? Craig cringed. As if he needed his uncle to set him up with women. He could do that on his own.

And the scientist looked like someone with relatively little experience in the field of love. She'd definitely expect more than Craig was willing to give. Her moss-green eyes would look up at him and beg him to love her in return. No, Craig needed a woman who fell easily in and out of love. One who would be heartbroken for all of a day, until Craig left Bayou Miste. Then she'd move on to the next man. Craig knew the type, and Elaine didn't strike him as it.

"I even softened her up for you."

Uh-oh. What did Uncle Joe mean by that?

"I asked her to consider going out with you and told her you were all right and not to listen to anyone who said otherwise."

Craig croaked and flopped over on his back. Just what he needed, a matchmaking uncle.

"Craig! Are you all right? Didn't get a hold of a rotten fly now, did you?"

Craig flipped over onto his haunches and shook his head.

"Good. Gave me a heart attack." Joe straightened. "Could you use some fresh air? I'll let you out the side door. Here, let me carry you."

Craig hopped out of range of his uncle's hand and made his own hoppity way toward the door.

"Okay, okay. I get the hint. You always were a determined cuss. Have it your way." Joe opened the door and allowed Craig to hop down the steps and out onto the grass.

Inside, the phone rang. Joe stared down at Craig and back to the bait shop. "Will you be all right out here by yourself? I'm going to answer that. Could be Littington."

Craig nodded.

Uncle Joe dashed back inside to answer on the fourth ring.

The overgrown grass needed cutting. Craig could barely see over the top of the jagged spears. He glanced down the road where Uncle Joe's rental house stood on the other side of Old Lady Reneau's. No one stirred outside in the midday heat.

He wasn't so certain being outside was a good idea. The world was a cruel place for a small green frog. Craig peered back at the bait shop. He could see beneath the porch. He never realized how dark and sinister the underside of the porch appeared. What dangers lurked there? He imagined a huge snake waiting to swallow him whole. Death by digestion. He shuddered.

"Woof!"

Craig jumped a full foot off the ground, his heart thumping against the thin wall of his chest. The grass cushioned his fall and he leaped to the side.

Behind him hovered a beagle, half the size of Dawg, but twenty times the size of Craig.

"Woof!"

The sound deafened Craig's ears and he raced for the steps to the bait shop. He didn't stand a chance of making it up the steps, but he could duck beneath. Suddenly, the underside of the bait shop didn't look so menacing. Next to the slobbering black, white and tan beagle, it was a haven, should he reach it before the dog decided to take a bite out of him.

Two inches from sanctuary, sharp teeth closed around Craig, locking him behind the canine bars of ivory. The smell of dog food and dead animals permeated his senses.

Craig freaked and puffed out his body. His skin oozed a natural coating of bitter-smelling oil. The dog gagged and Craig fell from its mouth to the grass below.

Craig staggered to all four feet and gazed up at the beagle. The dog foamed at the mouth and shook his head, obviously trying to get rid of the nasty taste of scared frog.

Huh! Serves him right. Eating defenseless frogs.

A deep-voiced bark sounded from the house down the street and Craig looked up in time to see Dawg barreling down the road toward him and the beagle.

The beagle stared at the much larger animal, tucked his tail between his legs and sped off in the opposite direction.

Way to go Dawg! That's putting the fear in him. When Dawg reached Craig, he ground to a halt, his back end swinging around the front of his body. He sniffed Craig and whined.

Craig could swear the dog knew him. If so, Dawg was a lot smarter than he'd ever given him credit for.

Dawg nudged Craig with a cool dry nose, knocking him over. Then a long wet tongue snaked out to rasp against his chest. The ground shook with rhythmic thumping. Craig's heart kicked into hyperdrive. Was it the voodoo drums? He righted himself and noticed Dawg's tail whacking the ground.

Damned wishful thinking. That old witch wasn't going to let him off the hook that easy. She wanted him to grovel and suffer for a while. To hell with that. He'd think of something or someone to get him out of this.

Craig glanced around. Yeah, but who and what?

Mo and Larry ambled down the street, two very large characters in a small town. They'd make great bouncers in a New Orleans bar.

Larry leaned down and scooped up a little green frog resting in the grass. Bringing his hand up to eye level, he whispered in a voice loud enough for Old Lady Reneau to hear, "Hey, Craig, is that you?"

"Of course it ain't him. Dat frog don' look nothin' like Craig."

"How you know what Craig looks like as a frog? Have you seen him yet?" Larry placed the frog in question back on the ground.

"Course not, fool! I think he'd look like a lot smarter frog den dat. Dat one's hoppin' away like it don' know me."

Craig croaked a laugh.

Larry cupped a hand to his mouth and yelled. "Craig!"

Both men wore the maintenance uniforms of Littington Enterprises, crumpled and dirty from a hard day's work.

"Hey, there be Dawg. You thank dat be Craig with him?"

Mo leaned down to stare at him. "Nah, this frog looks dumb too."

"Yeah, but you know how Dawg hangs with the boy like he ain't got any better sense."

Mo tipped his head sideways and frowned. "That you, Craig? If it is, hop twice."

Craig rolled his eyes, a technique infinitely easier as a frog. He hopped twice.

Larry grinned widely and rocked back on his heels. "What do you know? It is Craig."

"Yeah," Mo grumbled, "but he still don't look too smart."

Larry planted a hand on his hip. "Have you ever seen a smart frog, Mo?"

"Guess you got a point." Mo dropped to the step beside Craig. "Hey, man, Larry and I got this thang figured out."

Craig nodded his head, hoping to encourage Mo to continue.

"We thank we got you some ways out of dis problem."

All right already, spit it out! Would they go and plead with the old bat to free his body to return to normal? Would they sacrifice themselves to allow him to be free?

Larry plopped onto the stoop and pulled a folded sheet of paper from his pocket, carefully straightening it. "We made a list of candidates."

Candidates? Oh no, not them too? Between Larry, Mo and

Uncle Joe, they'd have him married off before the sun rose on a new day.

"Yeah, we figured you could use some help, being as you're a little short on time." Larry snickered. "Short, get it?"

Mo elbowed him. "Get on with it."

"Anyway, we thought of every single woman in the parish who might fall for you. Top of the list is DeeDee DuBois." Larry lifted a hand. "Just hear me out. She's twenty-four and available. Better still, she doesn't have any prospects."

"Larry put her on da list. Personally, I couldn't get past her slack jaw and pockmarks, but she'd be willing and would fall in love within da first fifteen minutes of a date. Hell, she'd fall in love with a warthog, she's dat desperate."

Craig used his front foot to make a gagging motion.

"No?" Larry looked down the list. "Maddie Golinski."

"She's too young. I thought we took her off da list. She's only fifteen. Give it to me." Mo snatched the list and continued down.

"How about Lisa LeBieu?"

Craig shook his head side to side in a swift motion. No way. She was the one who got him into this pickle in the first place.

"Guess not." Mo ran his finger farther down the list. "I'm sorry to say, but dis town don't have many unattached girls. All da good ones been spoke for. You gonna have to settle for one of da not so good ones."

Craig hung his head.

"Cheer up buddy. At least you be seeing dem at night. If you find a dark enough place, you can pretend she's pretty." Larry smiled. "Dat's what I do."

"You're a sad, sad little man, Larry."

Larry frowned and stood. "Am not!"

Mo rose, a full two inches taller than Larry. "Are too."

"Not!"

"Too!"

Larry's frown lifted and he stared down at Craig. "Hey, I just remembered. What about my sister, Josephine?"

Craig remembered a gangly preteen in pigtails. Josie, the little girl who used to kick him in the shins.

"You haven't seen Josie in eight years. She be all growed and not half bad to look at."

Mo crinkled his eyes into a narrow squint and touched a finger to his chin. Finally, he shrugged. "Hate to admit it, but Larry's got a point. She's just returned from beauty school."

"Yeah, she's learned a trade and everythang. 'Bout to drive Mom and the girls nuts doin' all their hair and nails."

Craig couldn't get past the image of the twelve-year-old Josie. And his best friend's sister. Since he didn't plan on a lifelong commitment, he couldn't get involved with a friend's sister.

Mo tapped the paper in his hand. "Dat's all we could come up with. You could go to another parish, but dat'll take time. Time you don't have."

Overwhelmed by his lack of a viable solution, Craig hopped away from Larry and Mo.

"We feel for you, man." Larry said behind him. "Can't begin to know what you're goin' through. Never been a frog before."

"Yeah," Mo agreed.

Craig could tell him. It stunk! Almost stepped on, chewed on by a dog, less than two inches high, no way to communicate . . . For a man with a law degree, his future didn't look so bright.

"Mo!" Uncle Joe's voice carried through the screen door

at the back of the bait shop. Mo jerked his head toward the door. "Does your uncle know 'bout da voodoo curse?"

Craig nodded.

With a grin, Mo yelled, "Yo, Uncle Joe, I be out here with your amphibian relative." Mo pushed himself off the steps and turned toward the door.

"Your grandmother just called. T-Rex is loose again, and your grandmother can't find Fifi. You better hightail it home or she'll make handbags and luggage out of that 'gator."

"C'mon, Larry. Craig'll figure dis mess out. He's da one with all da diplomas. Need you to distract Rex while I sneak up from behind."

"Why am I always the distraction," Larry groused. "That's just a fancy way of sayin' I be de bait for dat darn fool 'gator."

"Yep, but he likes the way you taste better'n me. We better hurry afore he makes a snack out of Grandma's poodle."

Craig tried to laugh at the hulk of a human worrying about his grandmother's toy poodle, but all he could do was croak.

"Yeah, Craig, we know." Mo smiled happily. "You don't have to thank us for all our suggestions. Just get to work on followin' through."

"I'll tell my sister you'll be callin'. Dat'll have da entire house in an uproar. Give dem somethin' to do besides gripe about Josie's beauty supplies all over the bathroom."

"C'mon, Larry," Mo said. "Good luck, Craig."

"Yeah, and watch out for snakes and 'gators." Larry waved a hand. "You ain't much of anythin' right now."

Larry and Mo hurried off in the direction of Mo's house where he lived with his gray-haired grandmother.

Craig shook his head.

Thirty-three-year-old Mo still lived with his mother's

mother. The old woman was a hoot. She'd shared her moonshine with them when they were hormonal teenagers full of themselves and bent on trouble. Mo thought the world of his grandmother and woe be upon the person who upset her.

But Larry's departing words sank deep. He wasn't much of anything. The simple phrase struck too close to home. How true it was. Not only in size, but also in direction.

When was the last time he'd done something he could feel proud of? Mo took care of his grandmother. Larry, for all his complaints about his eight sisters, loved each and every one of them. He wouldn't have offered to fix Craig up with Josie if he didn't think highly of Craig.

Larry's suggestion was a gesture of trust and faith in Craig to do the right thing. Only problem was, Craig wasn't looking for the long-term commitment that usually accompanied love. He wanted to find some love 'em and leave 'em woman to fall for him. He didn't want to do wrong by Larry's sister.

"Craig, I gotta service a few engines out on the dock. You're welcome to come with me." Uncle Joe paused on the steps. "Nah, you'd better stick close to home. No telling what could eat you by the water. Don't worry, it's not much longer 'til the sun sets."

Thank God. Although somehow the anticipated transformation didn't hold much appeal. Whether man or amphibian his situation seemed pretty hopeless.

Craig found a quiet spot beneath the step to wait and contemplate his choices. For the most part, he forced down the natural instincts to snatch the flies off boards, but a fat, juicy cricket managed to find its way past the shadows that hid Craig. The unsuspecting insect was toast with jam to his pallet, and why not? People ate cockroaches in some countries.

As soon as he turned back into a man, he'd make some calls, set up a couple of dates, test the waters of Bayou Miste. Like Mo said, he didn't have much time and he couldn't afford to be picky.

Perhaps he should ask Cassandra to come down from New Orleans. He could tell her it was some kind of emergency or other. She'd do it.

And with the pickings so slim in this part of the country, that choice looked more and more like the winner. But even if Cassandra said she loved him, would it be true? Craig didn't think Cassandra loved anyone but Cassandra. And could he afford to waste time on her?

Unfortunately, he couldn't afford not to. If he wanted his old life back, he'd better hope he'd misread the situation and she really did love him.

As the last wisps of sun sank over the horizon, washing the lush green swamps into gray, Craig hopped onto the steps. No sooner was he settled on the planks than the metamorphosis began. His skin pulled and stretched, the bones and muscles extending, flexing and growing. His body unfolded, straightening, pushing upward. Craig closed his eyes against the pain shooting through his nerve endings. Just when he though he would explode out of his skin, the pressure subsided.

He opened his eyes and his vision cleared. He towered above the steps he'd had difficulty climbing just moments earlier.

Steps? Craig glanced down at his naked body parts and darted a quick glance toward the houses neighboring the bait shop. Ms. Reneau stepped out onto her porch. As she turned toward the bait shop, Craig ducked in the side door.

"Whew! That was close." He'd have to plan his morphing location better next time. Apparently, there'd be a few more next times. But not many, if he could help it.

CHAPTER SIX

Elaine made her way to the dock with a large plastic bucket banging against her knees, a satchel containing her journal slung over her shoulder, and a large yellow flashlight clutched in one hand. She'd chosen to walk the short distance from the rental house to the pier thinking she'd stretch the kinks out of her legs. But if she were honest with herself, she'd admit she was procrastinating. The thought of spending a dark night in a boat on the water with a sexy man paralyzed her.

She didn't know which made her more uneasy—the man or the water. Either way, she'd plunged in way over her head. She had research to do and the source of the pollutants to discover. Wasn't that enough to worry about? Not to mention an irrational and debilitating fear of H_2O.

The thought of being surrounded by water made her stomach churn. Whatever happened, she couldn't lose her cool to a panic attack. This water was no different from what ran from her tap at home. And she would be safe in the boat, out of the wet stuff.

In the absence of streetlights the roadside blurred in the endless shadows of dusk. Elaine gladly wore her shiny new mud boots. If anything lurked in the gloom, the calf-high rubber protected her ankles. Unfortunately, the large boots didn't quite fit and she clumped her way toward the marina feeling about as graceful as a lumbering elephant.

Arms aching, Elaine hurried the last few steps to the bait shop, plunked her bucket on the porch planks and almost breathed a sigh of relief. Almost. Craig waited inside. Her heartbeat ratcheted up a notch. Perhaps if she repeated her mantra, she'd keep her wits about her and remain on track. "I am a scientist. I love science. I am a scientist. I love science."

She felt better already, even allowing a smile to curve her lips as she pulled open the screen door.

Like the night before, the bait shop stood in near darkness, the lights not yet turned on. Elaine's heart jumped into hyperdrive. The last time she'd come in here, she'd met Craig in the flesh, and not much else.

"I am a scientist. I love science."

The back door thumped and Elaine heard the soft shooshing of what sounded like bare feet on hardwood floors.

Bare feet. Ummmmm . . .

She pressed a hand to her chest and walked down a shadowy aisle. From the meager light filtering through the occasional window, she could make out a display of strings, hooks and lead weights.

"I am a scientist. I love science."

A tall shadow emerged in the doorway behind the counter.

"Mr. Thibodeaux? Oh, there you are—"

The rising moon chose that moment to tip over the top of the trees and shine in a window, illuminating him in a bright moonglow. All of him.

Elaine gasped and her mind shut down all other information-processing functions. A second after intellectual faculties ceased, every nerve ending in her body exploded in all directions. Her senses leapt into overload and her brain struggled to handle the volume of signals screaming along neural pathways.

Craig grabbed for the closest thing to him—a fishnet.

All his perfectly placed body parts were on display. Broad shoulders narrowed to a tight abdomen and a thin line of black curly hair lead to his . . .

"Oh, my!" Elaine froze, staring at the net and all it didn't cover.

Craig dropped the net and snatched a plastic bag of fake worms from the shelf beside him and covered his . . . package.

The trouble was, Elaine kept staring. Her mouth worked but the only words she could think of were, "I am a scientist. I love sex."

"What?" Craig asked, a harried smile tilting his lips.

"What? What?" She resisted the urge to smack her forehead with her palm. Stupider and stupider. Who'd have thought she'd attained a double major in chemistry and biology, a master's and a doctorate and graduated top of every class?

Craig pushed the hair back from his forehead with his free hand and leaned against a counter, crossing his bare ankles. His pose reeked of confidence, as if waiting on a customer naked constituted appropriate behavior—at least in Bayou Miste society. "Can I help you?" Craig asked in a voice completely at odds with his current state of undress.

"Oh yeeessss." Elaine's response was a breathy whisper.

When Craig shifted the fake worms to cover more skin, her gaze broke contact with his body and shot up to his eyes. Heat rushed into her face. The hotter her face grew, the faster her breathing became. She had to get a grip or she was going to hyperventilate.

Oh, how much easier to sink to the floor in blessed oblivion. But she didn't faint, much to her chagrin. She closed her eyes and breathed deeply, inhaling the potent smells of earthworms and fish. With her concentration shifted to the unattractive aromas, Elaine managed to rein in her galloping hormones.

Another deep breath and she opened her eyes, pressed her lips together and forced an eyebrow upward. "Do you provide such service to all your customers, or just me? This is getting to be a habit, Mr. Thibodeaux."

"Are you embarrassed by nudity? I thought all scientists approached the human body in a clinical manner."

"Yes, of course." She didn't look at him. She stared at everything but him—shadows in the corners, light fixtures on the ceilings, packages of fake worms. *Oh geez.* Her gaze returned to his face.

Craig's lips turned upward on one side and an eyebrow cocked as if daring her to say anything about his lack of clothing.

"Do you want me to wait outside? I don't mind in the least. In fact, I'll do just that." She backed down the aisle, but her bucket bumped against a shelf behind her, clipping the backs of her knees. Her legs buckled and she toppled to the floor in a heap of bucket, nets and notebooks.

Craig leapt forward, tossing the worms to the side, and reached out to grab her hand. "Are you all right?" He hauled her to her feet so fast she pitched forward and crashed against his chest.

Her fingers laced through his curly chest hairs and her breath caught in her throat. "I'm fine," she said, her voice a husky whisper. Then she noted something hard and stiff pressing into her belly. And it wasn't a package of fake worms!

What would it feel like to reach down and touch—

Elaine looked up into his face. Eyes as blue as a summer sky were hooded in shadow, but his lips curled up on the corners.

Embarrassment kept her close. If she backed away, he'd be on display. But if she stayed where she was, no telling what her crazed senses would do. Her analytical mind escaped her when she most needed it. She should be reviewing alternatives and examining all angles before coming to the most logical solution to her rising problem.

And rising it was.

A loud click split the air, and the fluorescent lights above hummed to life.

"Craig? You in here?" Joe Thibodeaux's voice called out.

Elaine's eyes widened at the sound. What would Joe think if he saw her in such a compromising embrace with his unclothed nephew?

Her face burned and she shoved against Craig's chest, ducking behind a cardboard display of sunglasses. "I'll just wait outside," she whispered. And with one last look at the gorgeous hunk of naked male standing before her, she ran for her life.

Once outside the bait shop, Elaine collapsed onto a weathered bench, pressing her hands to her fiery cheeks. She closed her eyes, but Craig's image burned in her memory. The muscled planes of his chest and shoulders, the narrow hips, tight abdomen and . . . and . . . that! All bathed in bluish purple moonlight and nothing else. How could she face the man when her body responded to him even when he wasn't standing beside her?

She really had to get a hold of her hormones. Elaine opened her eyes and looked around, realizing all her gear lay scattered across the floor inside the bait shop. With any luck, Craig would bring it out. She couldn't go back in there. No way, no how. Not the way her heart raced too fast to be healthy.

Two very short minutes later, Craig banged through the screen door. Blessedly dressed in jeans, a denim shirt and deck shoes, he carried all her equipment.

Elaine couldn't look at him without heat suffusing her cheeks. Thank goodness for the darkness of night and dim porch lights. She stood and held out her hands, looking at her stuff instead of his face. "I'll take those."

"No need."

"No, I insist. It's my gear, and I can carry it." Elaine couldn't decide whether to smack her palm over her mouth or to her forehead. Why couldn't she just shut up and let the man carry her things?

"Suit yourself." Craig set the bucket, satchel and bright yellow flashlight on the porch boards.

While Craig bent to accomplish the task, Elaine couldn't help but notice how his hair glowed blue-black, reflecting the light above his head. She really had to resist reaching out to touch the ebony waves.

He straightened and his gaze met hers. Briefly.

Her heart leapt to her throat and she dove down to gather her things. With her bucket looped over her arm, satchel over her shoulder and everything else gripped loosely in her hands, she followed him down the steps to the dock.

An unavoidable challenge.

Just as sexy clothed as naked, Craig's narrow butt twitched from side to side and his broad shoulders blocked Elaine's view of the water. Or was it that she only allowed herself to see him? In truth, if she'd looked up, she'd stare over the top of his head straight out into the swamp. But then, she couldn't decide what to fear most, this man or the water.

Or maybe herself.

She sighed, her thoughts an incoherent tangle of emotion and fear.

Craig turned left and Elaine got her first up-close and personal view of the inky black water not four feet away from her. She stood rooted to the planks, mesmerized by the swirling shadows created by lights reflecting off the smooth surface. Her already speeding heart threatened to jump out of her chest. Suddenly, Craig was a lifeline and she went after it.

Stomach in her throat, she ripped her gaze from the dark depths and locked in on the man she found completely distracting. Already, the distance between them seemed insurmountable. Much farther and she'd be paralyzed, incapable of following him.

Well then, get your buns in gear and catch up! Elaine forced her feet to move, stumbling toward the man, keeping her eyes on her goal. Looking ahead instead of down, she charged forward. Then her clunky boot caught on something protruding from the boards and she pitched forward.

With her arms too full to provide balance, she knew she was doomed. *Not again!* She tossed the bucket off her arm, chucked the flashlight, and threw her arms in front of her to brace for landing, praying she wouldn't fall into the water.

"Oomph!" Her palms connected with rough boards moments before her chest and head, absorbing only a little of the shock. Elaine squeezed her eyes shut and felt to either side for the reassuringly solid planks of the dock. When she was sure she wasn't dangling over the edge, she opened her eyes and lifted her head.

Her hair escaped its neat ponytail and swung into her face, blocking her view. When she pushed it aside and looked up, a pair of deck shoes stood inches from her nose. She let her hair fall back over her face, wishing it would hide her complete embarrassment.

Craig Thibodeaux squatted beside her and lifted the strands to peer under, concern written in his frown. "Are you okay?"

Elaine grimaced. "I think the only thing damaged is my pride."

Craig's smile seeped into her bones, warming her to her toes, tempering some of her humiliation. "Don't worry. I've tripped on that same board at least a hundred times. Don't know why Uncle Joe hasn't done something about it." He straightened and extended his hand.

Elaine reluctantly accepted the hand. Fear of the water outweighed her fear of her reaction to his touch.

With one strong tug, Craig brought Elaine to her feet and flush against his hard chest. His arms clamped around her, crushing her hips to his groin.

Elaine breathed in the soapy, musky scent of male, her heart skittering into her belly. Everywhere she touched him, electric shocks ran through her nervous system, traveling through her body to pool with pulsing intensity between her thighs.

"Oh my," she whispered. Pushing the hair from her eyes, she dared to sneak a peek at his face.

Craig's arms were steel bands around her back, but his

expression held a hint of laughter. "Are you going to make it from here to the boat, or do you want me to carry you?"

Startled at the tempting image his words evoked, Elaine shoved against his chest and stepped a few inches away, willing her heart to calm its erratic beat. "I can manage, thank you very much." Laced with irritation, her voice sounded ungrateful, even to her own ears. "I'm sorry. I shouldn't be so snappy. Thank you for helping me up. I'm not usually so clumsy."

"Must be that bucket you're so darn set on carrying." He raised a teasing eyebrow. "Or maybe it's just my charming presence."

Oh, it's you all right. She bit her lip to keep from speaking the words aloud. Instead, she gathered her bucket and satchel and scanned the dock for her flashlight.

The bright yellow torch had rolled to within an inch of falling off the dock. Her stomach sank to her knees at the thought of retrieving it. She couldn't ask Craig to get it and she couldn't leave the blasted thing. With a deep breath and fingers crossed, she inched toward the edge.

Before she came within two feet of the object, Craig leaned down and scooped it up. "Come on, we need to get going."

He pressed the flashlight into her hand and grabbed her elbow, hurrying her toward the boat. She felt as if she were caught in a river, headed toward the falls with no way to make it to shore. Her heart hammered in her chest and her hands grew slick. She wasn't ready for this. She couldn't do it.

As they neared the end of the pier, Elaine glanced around for the boat. Her expectations ran along the lines of a deck boat or maybe a pontoon boat. An ocean cruiser, if she thought it would work. What she found was a dinky metal skiff with an even dinkier engine mounted on the back.

Elaine's world tilted and turned all hazy around the edges. "Breathe," she muttered to herself.

"Did you say something?"

"No, not at all." She'd hoped for light and airy; instead she sounded completely flaky, like a woman ready to jump off the deep end of sanity. Which, frankly, was exactly how she felt. She closed her eyes and drew in a long slow breath, filling her lungs with air. *I can handle this.* She smiled and opened her eyes.

Larger-than-life Craig no longer loomed safely in front of her. He stood about a yard farther and lower in the tiny rocking boat with his hand outstretched.

Elaine swayed. Why did he have to be so far down, and surrounded by all that water? She refused to let fear stop her.

"Take my hand." Craig sensed the scientist's fear. Although she hadn't said a word, he felt it in the way her hand shook when she placed it in his. Was she afraid of him? Twice now, she'd landed in his arms and the experience had been . . . well . . . not unpleasant.

His groin tightened.

Okay, she'd sparked something carnal in him. He almost laughed out loud. Wouldn't she be appalled, if she knew?

He tamped down his lusty thoughts and tugged her gently to the edge of the pier. "Now all you have to do is step down. I'll do the rest."

Playing tour guide to a lab-rat scientist wasn't solving his problem, but what else did he have to do? Perhaps the solitude of the swamps would give him time to mull over his predicament.

Elle James

With her hand still in his, she stood staring down at the water. Her hair fell in soft curls around her face, softening her features, making her appear vulnerable. The glasses perched on the edge of her nose couldn't begin to hide her eyes. In the bait shop, he'd noted they were the color of Spanish moss.

When Elaine fell in the shop as well as on the dock, every one of his protective instincts shot to the forefront. And when he'd lifted her to her feet and into his arms, his body reacted immediately, every blood cell instantly alert. Thank goodness she'd pushed him away. Otherwise he'd have surrendered to the overwhelming urge to run his fingers through her hair and kiss her surprised pink lips.

Of course, kissing was the idea as far as Madame LeBieu was concerned. If he went along with her wishes, he'd have to woo someone into falling in love with him. Why not the clumsy but pretty scientist?

Craig stared up at her and shook his head. He'd come to Bayou Miste to secure another client for the firm, not to make a woman fall in love with him. When all was said and done, he'd return to New Orleans to represent spoiled and crooked clients in court. And he'd sure as hell return single.

Damn that voodoo witch!

Elaine stood frozen to the boards on the pier.

The look of absolute terror in her eyes forced Craig out of his own morose thoughts. "What's wrong?" He searched the boat, the dock, and the water. Nothing appeared out of the ordinary.

"Do . . . do you have a life vest?" she whispered.

"Yes, of course." Craig dropped her hand and reached under a seat for the regulation orange vest. He pressed it into her fingers, and leaned forward to grab her bucket and stow it in the boat.

When he looked back, she stood exactly as she had when he'd handed her the vest, staring at the water, her eyes wide and worried.

"What?" he asked irritably. Then he noticed that her hands holding the vest trembled. She was petrified.

"I don't think I can do this." Her voice was barely above a whisper.

"You don't have to. You could go home. I have other things to do."

His tone must have cut through her fear, because she shook her head and stiffened her back. Her lips drew into a tight line. "No. I have to do this."

"It's your choice. But if we're going, you have to get in the boat."

She stared down at the life vest and back to him.

"For Pete's sake." He climbed out of the boat. "Give me that." Grabbing the vest, he hooked it over her head and tied the strap beneath her chin. The subtle scent of flowers wafted in the air. Craig didn't know what he'd expected. Formaldehyde or rubbing alcohol, maybe. But not the hauntingly familiar scent of flowers. He withdrew his hands and noted her skin was as smooth and delicate as silk.

When Craig realized he was holding his breath, he forced air into his lungs. At that point he should have backed away. Yet his hands moved forward to lift her hair clear of the vest. The strands cascaded through his fingers to lie wild and soft against the orange fabric. He wanted to gather it up again and bury his face in the shiny tresses.

"Does this strap do something?" she said, her breath warm against his ear.

A river of awareness coursed through his veins and into his groin. He had to get a grip before he did something both he and Elaine would regret. She wasn't his type. Craig preferred the tough as nails, what's-in-it-for-me women. They could hold their own against his cynical views and lifestyle. Elaine, however, was . . . he grasped for the right word to describe his impressions of her. Soft? Vulnerable? Passionate?

The last word that sprang to mind struck him. Why would he think of her as passionate? Was it her full lips and wide eyes or was he only projecting his own carnal thoughts on her?

He gathered his diminishing faculties and set her away from him. Then he looked down at the strap in her hands. "That hooks around your waist." As he reached for the strap, blood sang in his ears. Before he could take it from her, he stopped. His sense of honor still warred with lust. If he touched her again, lust might win. He pointed at the strap and said, "It hooks around your waist and buckles there."

Craig performed an about-face and practically leapt into the boat, causing it to rock violently. He fought to stay on his feet, thankful for the distraction.

When he turned back toward Elaine, her face was white.

"Will it do that when I get in?" she asked.

"Do what?"

"That rocking thing." She swayed her hand back and forth, and her face paled even more.

Around boats all his life, Craig hadn't considered she might be afraid of the skiff. And all this time, he'd thought she might be afraid of him. He smiled up at her. "No, I'll hold it steady. You just hold my hand and step in slowly."

Reaching up, he grasped her hand and tugged gently.

At first she didn't budge. Then, one foot at a time, she inched toward the boat. When both her feet were at the edge of the dock, she looked down into his eyes.

As if he were her anchor, she kept her gaze fixed on his and stepped down into the little skiff.

The boat rocked gently and she threw her arms around his neck in a stranglehold.

Craig would have cursed, if he could breathe. He braced his legs wide, absorbing the sway of the boat until it stopped. With one arm around her waist, he reached his other hand behind his neck to loosen her grip. "It's okay. You're not going to fall. I've got you." His words soothed as he lowered her onto the hard metal seat.

Her arm around his neck only brought them closer when he bent over. His nose buried in her soft curls and he inhaled. Definitely flowers. He liked that it reminded him of springtime and wild roses in bloom.

Once seated, she released her grip on him, transferring it to her seat, her knuckles turning white. "I'm sorry." Her smile trembled and her green-eyed gaze darted around the boat.

"Why? Because you almost choked me to death?" He shook his head and grinned wryly, his heart going out to the frightened young woman. "Don't worry. I'm used to having women throw themselves at me."

Her eyes narrowed and a frown pushed her brows downward. "I was not throwing myself at you." Her voice sounded indignant and more like the self-assured scientist he'd met last night.

Craig breathed a sigh of relief. He could remain objective around the scientist. Just don't let the frightened mouse reappear or he wouldn't be responsible for his actions.

He turned in his seat, reaching behind him to pull the cord on the little outboard engine. After the second pull, it sprang to life, chugging and coughing smoke until it settled into a steady rhythm.

With the tiller in hand, he turned to face Elaine. "Ready?"

Her eyes widened and her hands clenched the cool metal on either side of her seat. She gulped, then nodded.

Craig eased the boat backward until it cleared the pier. He swung the bow around and headed into the murky swamp. All the while, he watched the expressions fly across Elaine's face in the little bit of light shining from the boat lamps perched on long, narrow rods at the front and back of the little boat. Occasionally, moonlight filtered through the dense trees overhanging the waterway.

"I'm sorry about all the fuss . . . getting in the boat and all," she stammered. "It's just that I don't know how to swim and I've always had an aversion to deep water." She glanced over the side of the boat, shuddered and then jerked her gaze back to his.

Craig tugged at the collar of his shirt with a lopsided grin. "That would explain the stranglehold. I'll try real hard not to tip us over."

She stiffened. "Is it easy?"

"Is what easy?"

"To tip the boat. Is it easy to tip the boat over?"

"Not if you're careful. Just don't lean too far to one side."

"Don't worry, I won't," she said, her expression serious. "Don't you have bigger boats?"

"Yeah." A smile tugged at the side of Craig's mouth. She probably wouldn't feel more comfortable unless the boat was a luxury cruise liner. He noted her fingers hadn't loosened their grip on the bench seat and his smile softened. She really was scared. "If you want to catch frogs, you have to do so in the shallow water. The bigger boats are for deeper water. They'd get bogged down where we're going."

Elaine fell silent, her gaze still locked on him.

Craig steered the skiff through the twisting channels, carefully avoiding overhanging trees. The little bit of a breeze their speed stirred kept the mosquitoes at bay. He made wide, sweeping turns so as not to tilt the boat and upset the scientist.

At first, her stare made him uncomfortable. He couldn't stare back or he'd risk running into a tree or small island, but he did glance at her from time to time. She wasn't bad to look at. Not at all like the flashy or suited women he spent his days with in the Big Easy. Her appeal was subtle. A quiet beauty you had to take a closer look to find.

"Are we going to where Bernie found the dead fish and alligator?" Her eyes lost their guarded expression, appearing more eager than frightened.

"Yes, ma'am." Craig nodded. "Why are you interested in dead fish?"

She hesitated and stared down at her feet, chewing her bottom lip.

Craig's years as a defense lawyer alerted him to her body language. And hers told him she was holding back. Interesting.

Finally, she looked up. Green eyes peered through wide, round glasses. "Can I trust you?"

CHAPTER SEVEN

Craig hesitated, his brow furrowing. "Can you trust me?"

"That's my question." Could she trust him? Besides being gorgeous in clothes and in the flesh, what else did she know about him?

"Yes, of course you can trust me."

She stared hard into his eyes and then heaved a deep sigh. "I'm not good at cloak and dagger stuff."

Craig responded with a nod.

"I received a sample of swamp water from an anonymous source. It was labeled *Bayou Miste*."

"And?" he prompted her.

"When I ran tests on the sample, I noted high levels of uranium, thorium and radium."

"How much?"

"Enough to threaten the ecosystem in this area, if it's not cleaned up immediately."

"Damn." Craig sat back and ran a hand through his hair.

"Exactly. If the water samples and animal life I collect

show the same toxin levels, the people and creatures in this area have a big problem."

At least Craig's reaction appeared to be genuine concern. Elaine had taken a gamble letting him in on what little information she already had in her possession.

"That's why you're studying frogs and fish." Craig stared over her shoulder, his gaze appeared to take in more than the six to ten feet in front of the boat. "This swamp is my uncle's livelihood. He's been here since before I was born."

"What about you? Have you lived here all your life?"

"No." He slowed the engine and nodded at her head. "Duck."

"Huh?"

"Duck." Craig reached across and pushed her head down. Something brushed against the back of her neck, snagged at her hair, and then let go. It skimmed across her cheek with a mildly abrasive texture. Visions of snakes and spiders leapt into her mind. A scream bubbled up in her throat, but she clamped her tongue between her teeth and rode it out.

Craig let go of her head and sat back in his seat, leaning to one side. A low-hanging branch weighted by heavy Spanish moss whipped past.

Elaine sent a silent prayer of thanks to the teeth god for holding her tongue. Craig already thought she was a klutz and a wimpy nut case. No use adding fuel to the fire with an earsplitting scream.

"You can sit up now; this area is fairly open."

She leaned back and stared at the man seated across from her. Studying him beat staring at the inky swamp water, and curiosity about the man helped distract her from her fears. "So, how long have you lived here?"

"Why do you want to know?"

On the spot, Elaine grasped. "Maybe I want to reassure myself you know where you're going."

A black eyebrow climbed upward. "Don't you think it's a little late to be worried about that?"

She shrugged. "I suppose."

His gaze connected with hers and held for a few moments before he looked ahead of the boat again. "I've been around these swamps for the better part of twenty years. My uncle had me guiding swamp tours and fishing trips when I was sixteen."

"Aren't you afraid of alligators or snakes?" A chill slipped down her spine.

"Nope, but I do have a healthy respect for them."

He smiled and she felt warm all over, as if she could conquer any alligator or snake as long as Craig smiled at her like that again.

"Why did you come to the swamps?" Craig asked. His attention focused on navigating, he didn't look at her.

"I told you, the water sample, toxins."

"I know all that." His gaze remained on the route ahead. "What I want to know is why you didn't send someone who isn't afraid of water to collect more samples?"

She stared out into the darkness. Perhaps because he wasn't looking at her, she felt more inclined to be open. "I guess I was tired of hiding behind my microscope. I wanted to challenge myself and my fears." And she had her ex-fiancé to thank for opening her eyes to what she refused to see.

Craig nodded and glanced at her, a half-smile lifting one side of his mouth. "Quite an adventurer. Didn't you do any fieldwork in grad school requiring you to get near water to gather samples?

"Yes, but not anywhere near expanses of water as large as this. I stuck to small ponds around farm fields." She grinned sheepishly. "I guess I sound pretty wimpy."

"No. I'd say you're pretty brave for facing your fears. That you're even in a boat surrounded by water is a testament to your sense of adventure and bravery."

Elaine rolled her eyes. "Now you're pulling my leg."

Craig winked. He turned to the motor and flicked a switch. The engine shut off but the skiff continued to slide through the water of the little lagoon illuminated in the boat lights. Silence descended for a brief moment before the cicadas picked up the beat and roared to life around them. Although the water remained inky black, she could discern the shapes of cypress and willow trees towering above them. Spanish moss draped from their branches, touching the water like feathery fingers stirring soup.

Without the noise of the engine, the swamp version of silence deafened her. What did she have to say to the nephew of a marina owner? Besides being exceedingly handsome, sexy and surprisingly intelligent, with blue eyes she could fall into, what did Craig have that other men didn't? And, more importantly, what could she possibly have in common with him other than a curiously sizzling attraction?

She'd felt his gaze on her and the beat of his heart when he'd held her close on the dock. Granted, she'd tried not to think about it, but she'd wanted to stroke his chest, to press her body closer to his.

Elaine gasped and stared down at her hands as if she'd find the answer to her inexplicable draw to Craig. What was it about this man that inspired her to such lusty imaginings? These feelings weren't something she could explain away as a chemical reaction.

She'd never considered love anything more than a chemical reaction to the body's need to reproduce. She'd always assumed her hormones would tell her when it was time and then she'd want to have sex. In the past, the chemical-induced urge had never come, and even with her fiancé she'd lost interest.

Was her body faulty? Were the chemicals out of balance? Is that why she couldn't get excited to the point of orgasm with a man?

Daring to look up, she stared into Craig's eyes. They were as pale as the night was dark. She felt a tug in her lower abdomen and a strange throbbing between her legs. Was this the chemical reaction she'd been waiting for? And if so, what an idiotic time to turn up!

The little boat slowed when they entered an open area half the size of a football field. Elaine eased around in her seat and stared to the far end of the lake. The light glinted off the silvery scales of floating carcasses.

"There they are!" she cried, pointing ahead, her fear of the water temporarily forgotten.

The stench of rotting fish and vegetation filled her nostrils to the point she almost gagged. Pulling her collar up over her nose, she stared ahead as the boat chugged closer to the pool of death.

"So many dead," she whispered, careful not to open her mouth too wide for fear of breathing in more of the unpleasant smell. She'd encountered her share of disgusting odors in the lab at the university, but this—

"How much of this stuff do you want?" Craig asked behind her.

"One of each species should be sufficient." She pointed out floating fish. "Can we get close enough to collect that fish as a specimen?"

"Do you have bug repellent in that bag?"

"Excuse me?" She turned back toward Craig.

"Bug repellent."

Buzzing tickled her ear and sent a quiver down the back of her neck. Elaine smacked at the annoying noise, hitting her neck. "I didn't think to bring any."

Craig shook his head, reached under his seat and pulled out a can with a green plastic lid. "Catch." With a flick of his wrist, he tossed the can to her.

Elaine let go of the seat and leaned forward to catch it in both hands. The boat rocked. The motion rattle her so much, she dropped the can and clutched the seat again. The cylinder clanked against the metal floor and rolled to Craig's feet. So much for being the grand adventurer.

"Here, let me." He grabbed the can and ripped off the top. Positioning the can in front of her legs, he sprayed a long steady fog around her ankles, knees and thighs.

The fumes gagging her, Elaine pulled her shirt collar more firmly over her nose.

"Scoot over," he said.

Elaine slid a little to her left on the bench.

Craig stood, twisted and sat next to her, his hip touching hers.

Breathing became an issue, with or without the dead fish and bug spray. Elaine's lungs worked in small jerky gasps, insufficient to provide oxygen to her brain. That would explain the disconnection with her powers of logic. All she wanted to do was to reach out and touch the thigh pressed to hers.

"Lean forward," he said.

She complied and Craig sprayed more of the smelly chemical across the back of her hair and down her back.

When she straightened, she looked up at him. Her gaze flicked from his eyes to his lips only inches from her own. "Is that it?"

"Not quite." For a moment he stared back. Then he

reached out with both hands. With his fingers skimming the sides of her cheeks, he leaned toward her.

He's going to kiss me!

Heart in her chest, Elaine hovered on the edge of a mighty abyss. She met him halfway, eyelids drooping, lips puckered, inexorably drawn to him.

His gaze coupled with hers and his cupped hand rose up the side of her face. Then he removed her glasses, pressing them into her hands. "Hold these."

Without the glasses, Elaine's green eyes peered at him, rounded and appealing in the light from the two boat lanterns. His gaze progressed from trusting eyes to full sensuous lips. Even slathered in smelly bug spray, the scientist tempted him. The sudden urge to lean forward and press a kiss to those lips nearly overwhelmed him. His hand tightened on the can of repellent and a waft of the potent chemicals blasted out, serving as smelling salts to his senses.

Holy cow! He'd almost kissed her.

Craig sat up straight, sprayed his hands and leaned forward again to wipe them against her cheeks.

The pungent smell took nothing away from those mystically green eyes or silky smooth skin. And the breast rubbing against his sleeve ignited nerve endings best left extinguished.

His fingers slipped beneath her hair to distribute repellent to the back of her neck.

Elaine's eyes hovered half closed. The rise and fall of her chest indicated the same difficulty breathing she'd had when he'd held her steady in his arms on the dock. The combination of silky hair against the backs of his hands, tender skin at his fingertips and lips mere inches from his set his heart racing.

Moonlight chose that moment to filter through the trees to the little lagoon. Elaine's face shone with an ethereal clearness, like an angel.

Her eyes widened, then blinked. With jerky movements, she leaned away from him until his hands dropped to his lap. Shaking hands smoothed through her wild hair. "How should we kiss the frogs?"

Craig frowned. From confusion over her words or from the sense of loss her movement created, he didn't analyze. "What did you say?"

Despite the dim lighting, Craig could see the rise of color in Elaine's cheeks. "How do we kiss—I mean, catch the frogs?"

Jolted back to reality, Craig shifted his weight to slide over to his seat. He dug a fishnet from beneath the bench, handed it to her and glanced at his watch. Eleven o'clock? With great effort, he stifled a groan. Six more hours to dawn and he'd moved nowhere closer to resolving his problem.

With a glance across at Elaine holding the net, he realized he'd only added to his problems by agreeing to take the good scientist out for a late-night fishing trip.

No, she wasn't the woman to break the spell. Unlike Lisa LeBieu, this one had a heart, one he'd surely break when he left this voodoo-ridden swamp.

The scientist glanced around from the safety of the middle of the boat and stared up into his face. "Can we get a little closer?"

Craig did a double take until he realized she meant closer to the dead fish. He lifted a paddle from the floor and dipped it in the water, propelling the boat forward.

Elaine twisted around in her seat, exposing the pale white skin of her neck.

The vision twanged Craig's growing awareness of her.

He knew how soft that skin was and thanked the stars it smelled of bug spray. He dipped the paddle again, and the force of his stroke turned them away from the fish and toward the shore. Moving to the other side of the skiff, he straightened the boat's direction with two compensating strokes. When they reached the fish, he dug the paddle in and slowed the boat to a stop.

"You have the net, scoop it up."

Elaine leaned forward ever so slightly, her neck craning to see the fish now bumping against the side of the boat. She scooted closer, the skiff dipping down on that side. When she could finally see into the water, she leveled the net and scooped the fish out, holding it high. A triumphant smile graced her lips. "I did it!"

Her exuberance brought a smile to Craig's face. "Very good. You caught a dead fish. Now, let's move on to the live frogs."

The excited smile turned downward and her nose wrinkled. She slid the fish into the bucket and closed the lid. "I've worked with a lot of stinky chemicals and samples, but this fish reeks."

"Happens when fish die."

Elaine's lips twisted and she shot a glance at him. "Where will we find the frogs?"

"Closer to the shore."

She turned to look ahead, her expression eager.

"That's also where we'll find the snakes and other swamp creatures, so keep your eyes open." He wanted to frighten her just a little with his perverse sense of humor. His words had the desired effect.

A shiver started at the top of her shoulders and wiggled down her spine. But she kept her back to him. Her spine stiffened and she focused her attention on the shore.

Craig shook his head. For someone afraid of the

swamp, she had spunk. Even when he tried to scare her, she remained on course. She had purpose, a selfless purpose, unlike the people he worked with in New Orleans. There, they would chew her up and spit her out for fun.

His eyes narrowed and he studied her closer. Or would they? Somehow, he could bet she'd hold her own if she believed in her cause.

"There! I saw one hop into the water." She turned, her face wreathed in an excited smile. "Did you see it, Craig? Can you get closer?"

Her use of his name caused his heart to skip a beat. Craig shook himself. Had the voodoo queen done more to him than turn him into a frog by day? Why was he mooning after this stranger? She wasn't anything near his type. Maybe another trip to the witch was in order. Surely his years as a skilled negotiator counted for something?

The skiff bumped against the shore, jolting Craig out of his musings.

Elaine yelped and held tight to her seat. When the boat stilled, she looked around. "I don't see any frogs and what happened to the noise?"

As if someone had a hand on the master switch, the natural clatter of crickets and frogs had shut off. Silence surrounded them.

"Be still and quiet," he whispered. "They'll return."

The two sat quietly, barely moving except to breathe. Then a cricket chirped, followed by another and soon the entire swamp roared with activity.

Elaine smiled up at Craig. A frog hopped into the water next to the boat. Her focus shifted to the water, Elaine held the net ready and leaned toward the edge.

With the smooth strokes of a natural-born swimmer, a frog the size of Craig's fist sailed on the surface. Elaine reached over the side and slapped the net at the frog.

When she pulled it from the water, it dripped empty. Her brows furrowed behind the rims of her glasses and her lips tilted in a pout. "Darn. He was a nice-looking one."

"Next time set your net in the water just below the surface and lift up when the frog swims over the top."

"Like this?" She leaned over the side and lowered the net in the water.

"Yes. Now hold still and wait for the next one."

Minutes passed. Elaine held still throughout, determination written in her pursed lips.

Soon a frog swam within range.

Elaine's body tensed.

When the frog swam over the top of the net, Elaine jerked the net up. Frog and net dripped water all over the front of her white blouse. "Wooohooo! I got one!"

Craig gulped. The smile on her face combined with the water across her chest sucker punched him in the groin. The lacy edges of her bra and the smoothly rounded globes beneath pressed against the transparent wet blouse.

Holding the net over the open bucket, she dumped the frog in with the dead fish, and then she slid the lid in place. The frog inside hopped, hitting the top with a bonk.

Craig flinched. He could relate to the frog. How frustrating to be so small and at the mercy of larger, carnivorous creatures. Not to mention, stuck in a container with a stinky dead fish. Craig's stomach clenched, and then knotted even tighter at his next thought. Dissection. "Are you going to dissect him?"

Elaine tilted her head to the side. "Of course. I have to study the effects of the pollutants on his skin, liver, heart and other organs."

With a sick feeling, Craig looked away. Was his fate to be someone's science experiment? If he didn't find someone to love him, that's what could happen. Either that or he'd be snake or alligator bait. Which would be worse—having his brains scrambled or digested slowly by a snake?

Perhaps getting the scientist to fall in love with him wasn't such a bad idea. As trusting and naive as she seemed, the chore shouldn't take long. He stared across at her. Would a few flowers and dinner in a nice restaurant work on a woman as smart at Elaine? And maybe after dinner they could make love into the wee hours of the morning.

The breasts shining through her blouse called to him. He could imagine his hands cupped over them, her dark, wavy hair splayed across a clean white pillowcase.

"What's wrong?" Elaine glanced up at him and followed his gaze to her blouse. "Oh my goodness!" She crossed her arms over her chest. "Why didn't you say anything?"

"I was enjoying the view."

Anger flashed from green eyes, and her brows dipped low on her forehead. She turned away and plucked at the material to lift it off her skin. Futilely she blew down at the wet fabric, but it didn't dry immediately. With a huffy breath, she kept her back to him. "I guess there's nothing to be done. If I want more specimens, I'll have to live with it." She threw a narrowed glance over her shoulder. "But you could have the decency not to stare."

Craig shrugged. "Sorry. I'm just a man. Can't help but admire a pair of right pretty breasts."

She swung her legs over the bench to the other side. But her heel caught the edge of the bucket, knocking it sideways. The lid flew off and frog and fish slid from inside.

"Get him!" Elaine dove for the frog at the same time as Craig. But the amphibious hopper leapt beneath the bench seat she sat on. "Can you see him?" Elaine lifted her feet and scooted back on the seat.

Craig could see one scared frog hunkered low. Just as he lunged for the creature, the frog hopped. Elaine toppled off the back of the seat, but Craig caught the escapee.

"I got him!" Craig scooped the dead fish back into the bucket and tossed the frog in after it, closing the lid down tight.

When he looked around, Elaine lay at the bottom of the boat, her shoulders shaking.

Craig reached out a hand. "Are you all right? Are you hurt?"

Her shoulders continued to shake, but she didn't answer.

Worried, he crawled over her seat and squatted next to her. "Did you break something?" His hands ran up her legs, checking for broken bones. When he reached her hips and waist, she exploded in uncontrollable belly laughter.

"What a funny pair!" She clutched her side and gasped. Tears streamed down her face. "My glasses . . ." More laughter. ". . . can you find my glasses?"

"No, oh wait, there they are." He plucked her glasses from her hair and handed them to her.

"I'm sorry, I can't help it. . . ." She held the glasses in one hand and swiped at her eyes with the sleeve of her other arm. "I can't get up."

Craig glanced around. Her ankles were still draped over the bench, as she lay sprawled in the bottom of the boat. He slid her feet off the seat and wrapped his arms around her. "Just hold around my neck. I'll get you up."

Elaine's arms encircled his neck, her glasses still clutched in one hand. With their faces only inches apart, he could see the way the tears clumped in her long black lashes. Her pink cheeks glistened with moisture and her hair framed her face like fine black lace. And those lips.

The bug spray should have been enough of a reminder to keep him away, but his gaze locked on her lips and there was nothing he could do to stop his next action.

Craig leaned forward and pressed his lips to hers. The satiny texture drew him closer. His tongue pushed past her teeth and entered her open mouth to taste her sweetness.

He barely acknowledged the clunk behind him when her glasses dropped to the bottom of the skiff.

With her hands threaded into his hair, she pulled him closer. Her wet shirt soaked against his dry one, drawing attention again to her breasts. How he wanted to see them, touch them and taste them.

He cupped his hand over a firm rounded globe, reveling in the warmth generated through the wet fabric. Dare he toss aside her blouse and take those luscious—

Elaine's fingers fumbled for his buttons, pushing aside the fabric to delve into his chest hairs.

Where had the prim and proper scientist gone? Who cared? As far as he was concerned, she'd just given him an invitation to reciprocate. *Hot damn, let the games begin!* His lips still locked with hers, he reached a hand between them and unbuttoned the front of her blouse. When he shoved the shirt over her shoulders, he leaned back to stare at the perfect orbs encased in silky white lace.

She reached up and unsnapped the center clasp, unleashing her breasts to his view. Dark, rosy brown aureoles puckered in the night air. He reached out to cup first one, then the other, tweaking the tips to hardened peaks.

Laying her back against the bottom of the boat, he leaned over her and took first one then the other nipple into his mouth. The smell of flowers assailed his nostrils—a scent vaguely familiar to him. With his hands massaging her breasts, he moved up to press a kiss to her temple. "Not enough," he whispered into her hair.

"Want more," she moaned, nibbling at his neck.

Craig loosened the button at the top of her khaki slacks and slid the zipper downward. His knuckles grazed the smooth skin of her belly to the top of her curly mound.

His own pants felt like they'd explode, he was so hard for her.

A buzzing sound pushed into his consciousness. He swatted at his ear, but the buzzing grew louder.

"What's that noise?" Elaine asked, pushing his hand from her breast.

Craig skimmed his hand down her torso to duck into the waistline of her pants. "What noise."

Elaine pulled his hand from her pants and shoved Craig off her. "That noise."

Craig sat up and listened. The buzzing he assumed was a mosquito had grown into a loud steady hum. "Sounds like a motorboat." He glanced down at Elaine, regret burning in his gut and lower. Beneath Elaine's staid exterior burned a passion as hot as Madame LeBieu's voodoo fire.

He reached out and pulled her to a sitting position. In a swift deft movement, he pulled the edges of her lacy bra together and snapped the clasp in place. His fingers lingered against her breasts. "We'd better go."

"What about the frogs?"

"We'll come back for more tomorrow."

Elaine's fingers paused in buttoning her blouse and she stared up at him. "More?"

"Frogs, damn it!" Craig practically leapt to his seat, rocking the boat in his hurry to get away from those eyes. Those trusting, sexy eyes. Eyes a man could easily lose himself in.

CHAPTER EIGHT

Still sitting on the floor of the boat, Elaine pushed the hair from her face. "What if the boat is the one dumping the poison into the swamp?"

"All the more reason to get the hell out of here." Craig flipped the switch on the motor and pulled a rope. The engine rumbled, but didn't start. He squeezed a rubber bulb on a hose and then pulled again. The engine sprang to life, idling in the water.

Elaine settled her glasses on her nose and carefully maneuvered to her seat. Instinctively, she leaned forward and touched a hand to Craig's knee. "We have to stop them."

"I read about some big shot company dumping pollutants into the swamps. People in the area said they'd hired thugs to take potshots at anyone who'd come near the dumpsite. No one was able to prove it in the courts, but the locals swore by it. Some criminals will go to all lengths to avoid being caught, even killing. I'm not willing to take the chance."

Craig stared down at her hand, his gaze intense.

Awareness shot all the way up her arm and down into her stomach. *Not a good idea, Dr. Smith.* She jerked her hand back to her lap, her fingers tingling. "We can't let them get away with killing the bayou."

Craig drew in a long, deep breath. His eyebrows rose and he made a show of panning the contents of the boat. "What do you suggest we stop them with? Have you got a gun in that satchel? Hell, you've got everything else."

Elaine shook her head, ignoring his sarcasm. "Everything but a gun. Can't we wait around and see who it is? Think about it. What better way to stop the polluting than to locate the source? We have to witness them in the act."

"Honey, if we can see them, there's a good possibility they can see us. We don't have time to ditch the boat, and I'm not so sure you want to crawl around on the little islands in the dark. They're full of snakes and alligators. Without a light . . ." He shrugged and, looking over his shoulder, backed the boat away from the shore.

A shiver wiggled its way down her spine. "Okay, next time I'll pack a gun."

Craig's attention shot back to Elaine. "You own one?"

She chewed her lower lip. "Actually, not. Does Joe sell them in his bait shop?"

"Yeah, but they're not like fishnets." He flipped a switch on the engine, the motor revved and the boat shot forward. "There's a wait time associated with buying guns. Have you ever owned one?"

"No." She hadn't thought about wait time. What did she know about buying a gun?

"And you've never fired one either, right?"

"No." Okay, so maybe he had a point. But did he have to be so superior? "How difficult can it be?"

"I can tell you right now, I'm not getting in the same boat with you if you're packing a pistol."

Her brows drew together behind the plastic rims of her glasses. Not that she wanted a gun, she'd never wanted one before. But his comment about not getting into the same boat cut to her pride. She'd worked with chauvinists who didn't think women belonged in scientific laboratories, as if they didn't have the brains God gave a gnat!

Just because she was a woman didn't mean she shouldn't be able to defend herself. She was as smart and capable as any man. Unless, of course, Craig was doing wicked things to her tongue or breasts. Then she had a hard time stringing two coherent thoughts together.

Her eyes widened. Why did she suddenly have a propensity toward lusty thoughts about a man? She'd never fantasized about one before Craig. She needed to focus on her work. Men were nothing more than a distraction. Especially this one. And her behavior—well she hadn't beat him off with a stick—or a net, for that matter. Elaine mentally kicked herself for the next five minutes. How could she let her hormones take control? She'd practically thrown herself at this virtual stranger.

At least with her new awareness of dangers in the dark swamp, Elaine quit worrying about the water and focused on what human threat might be lurking in that water. Alligators seemed to be the least of their troubles.

If the boat they'd heard belonged to the ones responsible for polluting the swamp, what would they do if they found Craig and Elaine fishing for evidence?

Her skin chilled in the damp heat. Were they capable of inflicting harm on those who discovered their crime?

Specifically herself and Craig? She glanced across at her sexy boat guide.

Sobering. Absolutely sobering.

She didn't want him hurt because she was too foolish to recognize a dangerous situation.

The remainder of the trip back to the marina passed in silent contemplation of the dilemma she'd dragged Craig into.

When the skiff slid up to the dock at Thibodeaux Marina, Craig jumped out while Elaine held on to the rocking boat. As much as she wanted off the water, the climb out of the boat seemed such a risk.

With Craig busy tying the lines, Elaine scanned the wooden dock for steps or a gangway. As far as she was concerned, even a six-inch gap loomed dangerously close to a chasm in her mind.

Then Craig stood before her, his hand outstretched. "Take my hand." His low, commanding voice cut through Elaine's rising panic.

She stared up into his eyes and stretched out her hand to his. Their fingers touched and electrical shocks singed her nerves, racing up her arm, into her chest. All thoughts of water seeped out of her consciousness. She focused on the ice-blue eyes in the dark, ruggedly handsome face.

Before she could say Atchafalaya, she'd been lifted out of the boat and pulled straight into Craig's arms. Pressed against his solid chest, she fought to breathe.

"I can't help myself," he whispered, and then he crushed her lips with his, forcing her teeth apart to allow his tongue entry. His hands slid up her sides to cup her breasts through her damp shirt.

Elaine's knees melted and she clung to Craig's shoulders, her arms finding their way around his neck. She felt sure the blouse steamed with the amount of heat generated by his touch. She fully expected the fabric to burst into flames.

Had she really deluded herself into thinking she could ignore this man? Yes. Would she rue the day she got involved with him? Yes. Would she regret this kiss? No.

All too soon he loosened his hold and backed away.

Rattled and embarrassed by her wanton response, Elaine straightened her collar and cleared her throat. "Well, now. Let's not do that again."

Stupid! Stupid! Stupid! What must he think of her when she uttered such inanities? She held her breath, waiting for him to crack a comment about not being interested anyway.

But Craig didn't say anything; he just smiled down at her in the faint glow cast by the lights dotting the pier. He lifted the back of his hand to her cheek and briefly caressed her skin.

Her eyes closed to his exquisite touch and opened again when the sensation disappeared.

Craig reached down into the boat and retrieved her bucket, flashlight and satchel before he turned to face her. "Ready?"

More than he could begin to imagine. If he hadn't turned and walked away when he did, Elaine would have embarrassed herself again by panting or throwing her arms around his neck.

This time, Elaine didn't argue with Craig about who should carry the bucket and he didn't ask. She followed him up the steps and out past the bait shop. Halfway across the road, Dawg joined them.

"Hey, boy." Without slowing, Craig reached down with his free hand and ruffled the dog's ears. "Been chasing any 'coons tonight?"

Dawg's tail wagged all along his body and he barked.

"I think you have a fan there," Elaine commented.

"He's a good dog." He patted Dawg's head. "Aren't you, boy?"

As she walked beside Craig, the thick night air wrapped around her like a comforting blanket. "He came to visit me earlier today."

"Did he bother you? If so, just let my uncle know and he'll tie him up."

"No, no, not at all. He created a great roadblock on my front porch. Which, come to think of it, could prove advantageous. Once I begin analyzing the specimens, I'll want my privacy. With him spread out in front of the door, I'm sure visitors will think twice."

"Maybe anywhere else but Bayou Miste. Unfortunately, the town knows Dawg and his habits. He's been at it for the past ten years. They'd just push him aside and charge on through."

Elaine smiled at the obvious affection Craig had for the lazy dog. And considering the number of times Dawg bumped into Craig's legs and wagged his body, the feeling was mutual.

She'd never had a pet. Her life centered on her work. Outside the university she didn't have much. Unless you counted her one creative outlet, her herb garden. Sadly, she didn't have anyone with whom to share it. Nor had she wanted to, until now.

A gentle breeze caressed her skin and she leaned her head back and sniffed the fragrant aroma of blossoming roses and honeysuckle. She glanced over at Craig. Walking with him in the early hours of the morning seemed right.

As they neared the porch of her rental house, she glanced at the luminous dial on her watch and yawned.

"I didn't realize how late it was getting. Thanks for taking me out in the boat."

He set the bucket on the porch, and then handed her the satchel and flashlight. When their fingers touched, Elaine snatched her hand away. Entirely too aware of him already, she wasn't sure she wanted to finish what they had started earlier. The man overwhelmed her with his sheer masculinity.

"Will I see you tomorrow?" she asked.

Craig stared down at her, lifted a tendril of her hair and tucked it behind her ear. "I'm not sure. Check with my uncle tomorrow at dusk. If I'm not available, my uncle will take you out."

Though disappointment burned in her chest, Elaine forced a smile. "That would be just fine." She wanted Craig to take her out again, not his uncle. Question was, did she want Craig to take her with the expectation of collecting more specimens or of stealing another moonlit kiss?

Elaine quivered, hoping Craig couldn't read the longing in her eyes. With a mission to accomplish, she didn't have time to act like some lovesick teenager bent on making out with the local bad boy.

She stuck out her hand. "Well then, thank you for your assistance."

He engulfed her hand in his larger one. Instead of shaking it, he tugged, bringing her up against him. With his free hand, he cupped the back of her head and brushed his lips to hers.

Logic completely shattered into so many ions blasting through her veins. Elaine stood on her toes to get even closer. Her hands slid up his chest to circle around the back of his neck and delve into his thick black hair.

How could his kiss be so wrong when it felt so right?

She pulled him closer, determinedly fighting off doubt and common sense. After all, when you have a chance to eat lobster, you don't settle for a peanut butter and jelly sandwich. She kissed her very tasty lobster, enjoying the sensations, knowing the satisfaction wouldn't last.

He was the local bad boy—she was a scientist. He lived in Bayou Miste—she lived in New Orleans. He loved women, had them falling all over him. She . . . well . . .

Elaine pulled back. *What am I doing?*

"Kissing me," he said, a smile curving his lips.

Heat rushed into Elaine's face, burning her cheeks. "Oh, did I say that out loud?"

"Yes." Craig's hands retained their hold, warming the small of her back, and his jeans zipper pushed against her tummy.

The cottage door stood closed behind her, a solid wood barrier between them and the ancient iron bed she'd slept in alone last night. What would it be like to invite a complete stranger into her bed? Did he still qualify as a complete stranger? They'd shared a boat ride, a kiss and she'd seen him naked. Twice.

All she had to do was unlock the door and invite him in. Let nature take its course.

Come to think of it, he'd probably run screaming as soon as he sampled her inexperience. She and Brian had done their fair share of kissing and making love, but their attempts had been anything but stellar. Staring into Craig's eyes, she couldn't imagine his lovemaking anything less than exciting, mind-blowing, turn-the-furnace-to-full-blast, rock-your-boat sexy.

The cool night air closed in around her, suffocating her ability to breathe. She pushed against Craig's chest and backed away until her ankles bumped into the porch steps. "Well, I have work to do."

"Don't you want to go to bed first?" His eyes twinkled in the light from her porch.

He was teasing her, and she didn't know how to respond. Her body warred with her mind and her mind won out. "I have to take care of the fish and frog before I can call it a night." She backed up another step. "Thanks again."

"My pleasure."

His warm words seeped into her pores, igniting the blood in her veins. If she stood there much longer, she'd be begging him to take her to bed. To hell with the fish or the frog, let's rock the bedsprings!

Elaine pressed a hand to her chest. *Ohmigod. What am I thinking?* She fumbled in her satchel for the keys, jammed them in the lock and raced through the door. "Bye!" she said without looking back into those mesmerizing blue eyes.

Perhaps having Craig's uncle take her out was a much better idea after all. All this sexual tension was turning her insides into a confused, raging inferno.

The door shut behind the intriguing Dr. Smith, yet Craig stood and stared at the small house, finding it difficult to leave. What was it about the scientist lady that riveted him to the spot?

He shrugged. Must be getting punchy with all that voodoo witch's talk of love. He had to remind himself Elaine was probably a woman who fell hard for a guy. Would it be fair to use her to get him out of this mess?

Her moss-colored eyes staring up at him from behind those disguising glasses left him feeling a little unsteady.

Should he go after her to break the spell or set his sights on a local girl?

The lights switched on one by one inside the house. He could see Elaine's shape silhouetted against the window shades as she moved around.

Craig needed more information about the scientist, if he chose to woo her. Not that he'd committed to that route. There were plenty of other fish in the swamp. He could check them out as well. But for now . . . he glanced at his watch.

His heart jumped in his chest. One o'clock. Four hours to sunup.

Craig strode to the end of the road and turned left into his uncle's yard. Much like every other house in the small community, the little clapboard structure had seen better days. A fresh coat of paint held the harsh effects of mold and humidity at bay. Two rockers sat on the porch in the moonlight, a quaint welcome to visitors.

Craig knocked on the door. No answer. He knocked louder, still no answer.

Where the heck could Uncle Joe be? He never stayed out late except on Saturday night.

For that matter, what day was it? Craig prided himself in controlling his schedule. Not knowing what day it was added another stick to his frustration bonfire. He rubbed his chin. What did he do yesterday? He'd taken Lisa out on Thursday, which would make that Voodoo Day. Friday, he'd spent the day as a frog, and that would make today Saturday, or early Sunday morning.

Craig shook his head. Had two days already passed since the voodoo queen cursed him? Two days out of the two weeks he had to undo the damage! Geez, time was running out.

Catching flies for the rest of his life was not an option.

Speaking of options, now would be a good time to contact Cassandra. He swung by his car for his cell phone. On the fourth ring, her answering machine picked up. Totally relieved Cassandra hadn't answered herself, Craig left a message he hoped didn't sound too bizarre.

Now for Uncle Joe. He had to be at his favorite honky-tonk on the outskirts of Bayou Miste. Craig debated driving his BMW, but the two-mile walk would do him good. Enjoying the feel of human leg muscles propelling him forward in an upright position, Craig walked faster and faster until he broke out in a run. Damn, it felt good to jog again. He hadn't exercised much since he'd arrived at Bayou Miste.

He missed his usual early-morning run through the streets of New Orleans. The brightly painted houses along his route and a post-workout cup of his favorite coffee always helped to jump-start his day.

He raised his arms and jabbed at the air. He couldn't do this as a frog. The best he could hope for was a decent leap without splatting into a wall. He had to get a handle on frog movements. Not that he planned to be one for long.

Craig heard the music before he'd come within two hundred yards of the Raccoon Saloon. The parking lot was jammed with nice cars, old pickups and a few rusty bangers. Yeah, the locals liked their beer and music. The die-hards turned out like clockwork on Saturday night.

Craig stepped into the smoke-filled bar and practically gagged. The smoke bothered him more than usual tonight. He scanned the room, looking for Joe's scraggly white hair. With the small bar so packed and hazy, he couldn't see him right away.

A meaty palm smacked him on the back.

Craig staggered under the force.

"Hey, Craig." Mo stood with a beer can in one hand

and a cigarette in the other. "Good to see you, man. Well, I mean, it's good to see you as a man, anyway." He tipped the can, draining the contents in two gulping swallows, then crushed the aluminum in his fist.

"Hi, Mo." Craig continued his perusal of the room's occupants. "Seen Uncle Joe?"

"Yup." Mo jerked his head to the left corner. "Back dere with Bernie and Oscar."

"Thanks." Craig squinted through the tobacco fog until he located the table. Three older men sat at the back of the room, as far away from the speakers as they could get.

"You know, Craig," Mo said. "Larry's right. You should go after his sister. She's had a crush on you since practically forever."

Craig's heart raced at the thought. Not out of anticipation, but panic. He liked choosing his own dates. The thought of Mo and Larry finding women for him curled his intestines. "I'm still thinking about it."

"Don't wait too long. Afore ya know it, dat full moon will be arisin'."

"Craig, honey." A thin hand slipped under Craig's elbow and a buxom breast pressed to his arm.

"Hello, Lisa." Lisa LeBieu, with her long straight black hair and olive skin, would turn any man's head, but Craig had been scorched once already. He didn't feel comfortable standing in the same room with her, much less with her lounging all over his arm.

She walked two fingers up his chest and tapped his chin. "I hear Grandma LeBieu put a hex on you."

Craig extricated his arm from her clutches. "Back off, Lisa."

She tried to hook his arm again.

With another backward step, he came flush up against

a wall. His head bumped a sconce, causing the light to shimmer.

"What's the matter, Craig?" She stalked him until her full breasts pressed against his chest. "Afraid of poor little me?"

"Yup." Her approach reminded him of a black widow spider. Black hair, red lips, all the soft feminine curves luring a man into her trap, and zing! "Do you mind? I'm here to see my uncle."

"I don't mind at all," she purred, running her fingers across his shoulders. Her hand stopped and she plucked something off his shirt. "What's this?"

Craig stared down at her hand. In the light from over his head, a long wavy hair glimmered. Elaine's hair. His mind conjured the image of her against the bottom of the boat, her hair spread wildly around her. Although he willed it not to, his groin tightened.

Lisa's eyebrows dropped in a v-shape. "Who is she?"

"I don't know what you're talking about." Inside, Craig cringed. God forbid Lisa LeBieu should get her claws into Elaine. The scientist wouldn't even know what hit her until Lisa had her stunned and cocooned. Protective instincts surged in Craig, something he hadn't felt toward a woman since his mother. Damn! What did he care about the owl-eyed professor?

Lisa's eyes narrowed and Craig could swear she read his every thought. The room closed in on him. He had to get away from her, find Uncle Joe and get the hell out of there.

With a smile forced to his lips, he tried to placate Lisa. "Sweetheart, I really need to see my uncle. Would you excuse me, please?" He laid his hands on her shoulders and gently pushed her away.

Then he ducked and ran.

Right into his uncle.

"Craig, there you are. Been wonderin' when you'd get off the swamp with that scientist lady."

Craig stifled a groan. As vindictive as Lisa was, all she needed was the identity of the hair's owner and she'd be wreaking havoc all over the parish. Craig turned to gauge her response.

Lisa stared down at the hair between her fingers, a corner of her lip curling upward, and not in a pretty, sassy way.

"Leave her alone," Craig warned.

Lisa's black-brown eyebrows rose on her smooth fore-head and her eyes rolled up to gaze into his. "A little too punchy, aren't we, frog man? What were you two doin' out on the swamp at night? Catchin' a little swamp nooky?"

A slow burn rose around Craig's collar and up the back of his neck. What had he been thinking when he'd asked Lisa out in the first place? Sure, she was cute, sexy and had a great body, but she was trouble with a capital "T." As his uncle had told him so eloquently when he was a young teen, "Think with your brain, not with your balls, and you'll stay right with the girls."

With Lisa and those cute curves, he hadn't been think-ing with his brain; that was apparent.

"Did you come lookin' for me?" Uncle Joe stepped in between Lisa and Craig.

"Yeah. We've got to talk."

"What's eatin' you, son? Besides that mangy beagle?" Joe snickered. When he saw the look on Craig's face, he coughed and straightened. "No, really, whatcha need?"

"Can we get out of here?"

"What, and miss the two-bit beer from two to four A.M.?"

Craig frowned.

"Okay, okay. The one day a week they offer beer at a tenth of the cost and you have to go and be a frog about it." Uncle Joe burst out laughing at his own joke, slapping his knee and bending double with the force of his guffaws.

At the moment, Craig saw no humor in his uncle's words. "I'll meet you back at the bait shop when you're finished cracking jokes."

"Did you walk?"

"Yeah."

Uncle Joe swayed and lurched toward the door. "I'll drive you home."

"No, I'll drive." Craig snatched the keys and stalked toward the door.

"Spoilsport. Won't even let a man have a little fun. Can't enjoy a good buzz without someone ruinin' it for me."

"My heart bleeds for you." Craig's voice dripped with sarcasm.

"No heart. None whatsoever. Drag me off in the middle of the night to talk to me and won't let me drive. It's not as if the Raccoon Saloon has two-bit beer every night."

"Only every Saturday night."

"The highlight of my week." His uncle belched.

"Come on, Uncle Joe."

Before they'd gone a mile, Uncle Joe lay fast asleep against the passenger-seat door, snoring loud enough to rival the cicadas.

Craig parked the truck in his uncle's driveway. When he got out and opened the passenger-seat door, the inebriated man almost fell out. With an arm hooked under an elbow, Craig helped his uncle into the house and to the kitchen table.

Uncle Joe slumped onto the speckled Formica tabletop and continued where he'd left off in the truck, snoring loud enough to shake the eaves.

"Uncle Joe?" Panic rose in Craig's chest. He needed Uncle Joe to wake up long enough to listen. "Uncle Joe!"

Joe lifted his head.

"Listen to me," Craig shouted loud enough to rattle the windows.

"Whadda you want?" Joe said, his voice slurred, his eyes barely open.

"You have to watch out for the scientist lady. I think she might be in danger."

He blinked. "From what?"

"Well, Lisa, for one. I don't like the way she looked at me in the bar. She's trouble." Lisa's evil smirk worried him. "Elaine's also investigating toxins in the swamp. There may be someone dumping stuff in there. If they find out she's snooping around, they might come after her."

"Whadda you want me to do?"

"Just keep an eye on her. Don't let her go out on that swamp alone."

"Okay." Joe's head slumped back to the table, hitting it with a thump.

Craig clenched his teeth and counted to ten. Then he hefted his uncle out of the chair and dragged him into the little bedroom, dumping him on the bed. When he slipped the shoes off the older man, Craig shook his head. The bait shop wouldn't open early this Sunday.

"Never mind. I'll keep an eye on her myself."

CHAPTER NINE

Elaine slept like the dead until the sun crept into her window and warmed her face. With her eyes still closed, she savored the feel of clean sheets, country air and a late-night kiss from a sexy Cajun. The mattress in the rental house was soft and comfortable. A bed made for lying in later than usual, preferably with the one you love.

Her eyes popped open. What was she thinking? As if love and Craig were at all compatible. They'd mix like oil and water.

Completely awake, Elaine sat up and swung her legs out of the bed. No time for fantasies, she had work to do. The fact that her mind had superimposed Craig's naked body in the sheets beside her had nothing to do with her rapid ascent from the bed.

Needing a little caffeine to help her maintain focus, Elaine trudged barefoot into the kitchen wearing a short nightie and not much else. Two scoops of coffee in the filter, water in the top and she was on her way to a luscious cup of go-juice.

Scratch. Scratch. Scratch.

Through the glass of the kitchen door, Elaine could see the screen door wobble.

Scratch. Scratch. Scratch.

Elaine crossed to the door and peered out. Dawg stared up at her, drooping brown eyes imploring her to let him in. She cracked the door and peeked through the screen. "What do you want?"

Woof! The dog tapped the screen door again with his toenails.

"You want to come inside?" Elaine opened the door wide enough for the dog to slip past. When she would have let the screen slam shut, the dog twisted around and stuck his nose in it.

"So what's it to be, in or out?"

The dog stood still, his nose holding the door ajar. Then a mottled green bullfrog hopped over the threshold and into the kitchen.

Elaine's gaze darted from the dog to the frog and back again. "Is this bullfrog a friend of yours?"

As if in answer to her question, Dawg wagged his tail all the way up to his nose and swiped his tongue over the frog, knocking the amphibian over on his side.

"Yeah, and with friends like you, who needs enemies? I get it." She knelt close to the frog and scooped him up in her hand, bringing him to eye level. "Can't say I've ever known a dog to have his own pet bullfrog, but I'm told anything can happen in the bayou." She shrugged. "Do you have a name?"

Woof! Dawg, nudged her hand, licked her cheek and wagged his tail so hard his body whipped from side to side.

"His name is Woof?"

Dawg nudged her hand again.

"Oh, you don't like me holding your friend, do you?" Elaine carefully placed the frog on the floor and patted Dawg.

The big dog lapped at her cheek and sat, pounding the floor with his tail.

"You're easy to please." Elaine shoved the dog out of her face and laughed, feeling light and carefree. Is that what a couple days away from the university could do for you? Was that what Brian was talking about? Had she gotten too carried away in her work and forgotten how to smell the stump water?

Elaine rose and stared down at the pair. A dog and a bullfrog. "You two can stay as long as you don't leave me any yucky presents."

Woof! Dawg gave his standard reply, licked her knee and flopped on the nearest rug as if all that wagging and woofing had worn him out. But the frog still stood where she'd set him on the floor. He seemed to stare up at Elaine's legs.

She could swear she saw a hint of intelligence in his little black eyes. Elaine frowned and shook herself. Bayou Miste was really getting to her. "If you're staying, you have to have a name other than Woof." She tapped a bare toe and tilted her chin. "Freddy?" She stared down at the frog. What was she expecting? A reaction?

The frog's head swayed from side to side.

Was that a "no"? She stared closer at the frog, never having known an amphibian to answer questions. Had she hit on some type of intra-species communication? Nah. "How about Bully?"

Again, the frog swayed side to side.

Elaine crossed her arms over her chest. This type of frog must have a natural swaying motion. "I can't believe

111

I'm talking to a frog." She shook a finger at the creature. "See what you're doing to me? I'm calling you Todd, like it or not."

The bullfrog didn't sway this time. Instead, its front legs jerked in a shrugging motion.

"Good. Now, I need to take a shower and get to work. Make yourself at home."

Craig tilted his little green head backward to take in all of a giant Elaine sashaying from the room. Her short, filmy pink nightgown did nothing to hide long, silky legs—legs smoother than whipped cream and probably as tasty. The cheeks of her buttocks peeked from beneath the hem of her gown, encased in black silk panties—a naughty contrast to the innocence of her top.

When she'd squatted next to him, all he could think of was licking her knees. Damned if Dawg didn't get the pleasure!

Dawg had stood by him at sunrise when Craig transformed back into the frog. He decided it was a good idea to have the dog close as protection against snakes and other creatures. Dawg proved even more useful when he'd helped Craig gain access to the scientist's house.

He'd hoped to get in and remain hidden so as not to be confused with one of Elaine's specimens. But Dawg came to the rescue again, by claiming Craig as his own. He wasn't so sure he liked being the dog's pet, but worse things could happen.

Note to self: Tonight, give Dawg a steak.

Elaine disappeared through the bedroom door and soon the rush of water could be heard from the bathroom.

Craig hopped around the room, hoping to get an idea of what Elaine was like by the things she'd brought with her. But all personal items were high on a couch or table. He couldn't see a thing.

He glanced toward the open bedroom door. Should he? Craig hopped by and shot a quick look inside. The light from the bathroom door shined like a beacon guiding a ship in the fog.

Maybe a quick tour of her bedroom while Elaine showered wouldn't hurt. Craig hopped into the room and began his search for some insight into this woman who talked to dogs and frogs. When he hopped around the side of the bed, he landed square in the middle of her pink nightgown.

He froze, wrapped in the tantalizing scent of a flower garden. The same aroma the voodoo queen had sprayed in his face. What kind of coincidence was that? The silky nightgown felt good to his sensitive frog skin. For a few brief moments, he languished in the folds, imagining Elaine still inside the short shift.

Water splashed in the bathroom, enticing Craig. More than anything, he wanted to sneak a peek. But what kind of man would he be if he did that?

Craig stared down at his green skin. He could argue that he wasn't a man at all. And as a frog, what harm would come of his seeing the scientist in the shower? She'd never know he wasn't a frog unless he told her, and he had no intention of doing that. But his conscience warred with his desire and won.

The water shut off and Craig heard the plastic against metal sound of the shower curtain rings sliding across the curtain rod.

He could imagine Elaine reaching for her towel, stepping from the tub onto the mat and wrapping the terry cloth around her body. His frog body tightened.

Quick, so as not to arouse her suspicions, Craig hopped out of her nightgown and made for the door.

"Hey, little guy," Elaine's soft voice called out behind him.

Craig stopped, frozen to the spot. Caught sniffing around a woman's bedroom.

"Did you get lost or something?" She stepped up beside him and crouched down.

Craig ventured a sideways glance and saw soft, creamy white feet with pink toenail polish. Her skin smelled of fragrant soap and radiated heat from her shower. Craig's cool amphibian body leaned closer to her warmth. Then he looked up.

Tight calves crooked at the knee to smooth, naked thighs. A fluffy white towel wrapped precariously around her hips and breasts did little to dispel Craig's rising frustration. He opened his mouth to yell.

"Gribbit!" Now that was about as satisfying as getting a splinter in one's webbed foot. He squatted next to a woman whose body could start a riot and all he could do was croak.

"It's okay, I'm not going to dissect you. You're welcome to stay here and visit with me. I'm just going to get dressed."

Elaine stood, her hands rising to the edge of her towel, opening . . .

Conscience overruled and Craig turned away, but not before he saw the rounded swell of her breasts. Unable to watch more, he beat a hasty retreat through the bedroom door. How much more exciting this scene would have been, were he a man. Then again, she wouldn't have let him past her bedroom door.

Guilt weighed heavily on his mind. He felt like a peeping Tom. Elaine deserved better. At least she was fighting for a worthy, unselfish cause—the environment. Craig was just fighting to save his own skin, and not of the green variety!

Was spying on her fair? No. Then why the hell was he lurking in the scientist's home?

Because he still needed to find someone to fall in love with him to break the spell and, as much as he was reluctant to admit it, Elaine was a prime candidate. Damn the situation! And damn that voodoo priestess!

Dawg rose from the rug and trotted over to Craig.

Woof!

I know, I know. I got myself into this situation. If I had taken the women I dated more seriously, I wouldn't be where I am today.

Woof!

Dawg trotted past Craig to the door.

Knock, knock, knock!

Woof!

"Now who could that be?" Elaine walked out of the bedroom, tugging a pale blue, snug-fitting shirt over a lacy white bra and down to her khaki shorts. Her hair was combed straight back from her forehead, and hung in loose, wet ringlets down past her shoulders to the middle of her back. Her brows dipped low over her moss-green eyes. Then she slipped her owl glasses over her nose and reached for the doorknob.

"Well, now, what have we got here? Good morning, beautiful." The oily, cocky words oozed out of the one person in the parish Craig had always wanted to smash in the nose, Randall Pratt.

Elaine's back stiffened and she tipped her head down, looking through her glasses like a stern schoolmarm. "Excuse me, should I know you?"

Randall pushed past her into the small living room.

"Absolutely, you should know me. I'm the most eligible bachelor in the parish, Randall Pratt. And you are?"

Elaine raised one eyebrow, and crossed her arms over her chest. "Not impressed."

Chalk one up for the scientist. Craig liked her more and more every minute. She wasn't quite as naive as Craig had originally thought. And she could spot a snake when he slithered through her door.

"Tsk, tsk." Randall walked around the small room, fingering books on the coffee table. "We don't want to start out on the wrong foot now, do we? I came to see if I could help you with anything. Unloading your car, moving furniture in the bedroom. You name it, I'm your man."

"Unless you like handling stinky dead fish and dissecting frogs, I don't think so."

Randall looked up, his nose wrinkled. "That's an exciting occupation for a woman. What are you, some kind of frogtologist? Or are you dreaming up new recipes for a cookbook?"

"The cookbook. Definitely, the cookbook." Her voice dripped with sarcasm.

Throw the bastard out, Elaine. Craig wished he could do it for her. If he were in human form, he would.

The snake drifted over to her worktable and stared down at her microscope. "What's this, a microscope?"

"No, it's a frying pan." Elaine marched over to stand between Randall and her equipment. "Yes, it's a microscope. If you're through with your inspection, I have work to do."

Yeah, buster, beat it. Craig hopped over to stand next to Elaine.

Randall leaned closer and touched a finger to her collarbone. "Why don't you and me go by Maggie's Café for a bite to eat?"

Elaine slapped his hand away. "I'm not hungry."

"Oh, come on, you have to eat sometime." He tucked a lock of hair behind her ear. "How about for dinner tonight?"

Craig's blood boiled. If the man didn't get his filthy paws off the scientist, he'd . . .

He'd . . . what? Croak?

"No thanks," Elaine replied, ducking around Randall to march over to the door. "Besides, I already have a date."

Craig shot a glance toward Elaine. She had a date?

Randall frowned. "With who?"

Yeah, with who? Craig couldn't think of a single man good enough for Elaine in the entire parish, barring yours truly. He didn't like that she'd agreed to go out with someone else. The thought curled his insides. He didn't like the idea at all.

"Whom I go out with is none of your business." She opened the door and motioned for him to go through.

Randall swaggered toward her, stopping short of the door. "I make everything that goes on in this town my business."

Yeah, Randall had a knack for getting into everyone's business, all right. A couple years younger than Craig, Randall had been a pest growing up. He'd found pleasure in tagging along behind Larry, Mo and Craig. Whenever he had the chance, he got them in trouble. Like the time he'd sunk the fishing boat at the marina. Since Craig and Larry had been the last to use it, they'd taken the blame. Later, they'd caught him with the plug in his pocket.

"Mr. Pratt," Elaine said.

"Call me Randall."

"Mr. Pratt," Elaine repeated with more emphasis. "Please leave."

Craig and Dawg hopped and trotted to stand beside

Elaine. The dog growled low in his chest. Craig found himself wishing the old voodoo queen had changed him into a dog, instead of a defenseless frog. He could have sunk his canine cutlery into the jerk to speed him on his way.

"I don't take no for an answer. I'll be back." Randall leaned forward and kissed Elaine's surprised lips.

She reached up and slapped him in the face. The smack of palm to cheek rang loud against the walls.

Woof! Dog stalked forward.

Randall pressed a hand to his cheek and backed toward the door. The shocked look on his face was almost comical. "You shouldn't have done that."

Elaine stood taller, her lips pressed into a straight line. "No. You shouldn't have kissed me."

"I'm not through with you, lady." Randall's voice promised retribution.

But Elaine held firm. "Leave."

Before Randall's heels cleared the door, Elaine slammed it shut.

She stared at the door as if it had committed the offense instead of the man who'd gone through it. "The nerve!"

She swung around, almost stepping on Craig, and paced across the room. With an angry yank, she pulled the glasses from her face and waved them in the air. "I can't stand a pushy creep who thinks he owns the place." She scrubbed her fingers over her lips. "And he kissed me! Yuck!"

Craig hopped out of the way of her next pass. Twin flags of pink flew high on her cheekbones. The moss green of her eyes deepened and sparked like a forest fire. Tendrils of dry hair drifted up from the wetter strands and danced around her face.

Damn, she was hot when she was mad.

He'd risk making her mad just to see her reaction—exciting and sexy as hell. Where had she been hiding all that passion? If she could get this riled over a stolen kiss, imagine her passion in bed. Craig's little froggy heart couldn't take much of this. When the hell was dusk?

Just as quickly as she'd started pacing, she flopped onto the couch and leaned her elbows on her knees. The fire died from her eyes and she stared at the books on the table.

Dawg left Craig's side and trotted over to Elaine. He nosed the hands clasped in front of her. Her fingers parted and the dog stuck his nose between them.

Craig hopped toward the scientist, wondering what had happened for her to stop ranting so suddenly. Like Dawg, he sensed her sadness even before a tear slid down her cheek to fall on the dog's nose.

"What's wrong with me? Am I really rigid?" She leaned forward and wrapped her arms around the dog's neck. "Can't I be kissed and not treat it as an assault?"

No, you were right. The guy deserved your slap. Craig wished he could take her in his arms and hug away her hurt expression.

Woof! Dawg pulled out of her clinch.

"See, even you don't think I'm loveable. Perhaps you're right. Who could love someone with frizzy hair, who looks like a schoolmarm and hides behind her microscope? Brian didn't."

Who was Brian? Craig had a mind to pummel the jerk's face for making Elaine cry.

"How can you date someone for four months and never really see them?" She flopped onto her side and tucked a throw pillow in her arms. "It's no use. I'm afraid of water, I'm afraid of relationships. All I have is science. Which makes for a cold bedfellow."

Woof!

119

"You said it. It's a rough life." She rolled into a sitting position and punched the cushion into the corner. "But I'm here for a reason and I might as well get started. I can work on my love life later."

Elaine pushed off the couch and strode to the refrigerator. She pulled a large lump of silver wrapped in plastic from the freezer and took it over to the table.

"At least frozen it doesn't smell quite as bad, huh Dawg?"

Dawg sniffed at the fish in her hands and nuzzled the plastic.

"Sorry, fella. You don't get to eat the evidence yet. Let me take some samples from it first. Although the thought of eating this should turn your stomach. Oh." She glanced toward Craig. "And you might want to let your frog friend outside before I start dissecting his cousin."

Craig's empty frog belly clenched as he imagined a sharp scalpel cutting through the tender skin. She was right. He wasn't up to seeing a fellow frog sliced open for science. She found it necessary; he found it way too frightening.

He'd leave her to the specimen samples and find something else to do.

Like figure a way out of his predicament?

As time slipped away, he didn't feel any closer to resolving his difficulty. If he didn't move fast, the full moon would seal his fate and he might end up under Elaine's microscope, just another cell to analyze, or a heart muscle to slice a cross section from.

Could he make Elaine love him and subsequently get him out of this mess? Her mention of Brian-whoever indicated the relationship might be over. That made her a prime candidate, didn't it?

The image of the lone tear trickling down her cheek

seared a path from his mind to his heart. What kind of bastard was he to think he could make her fall in love with him, when he had no intention of ever returning her love? And why the hell did he have this overpowering urge to pummel Brian's face for making her cry?

He needed to find someone a little less vulnerable. Someone who wouldn't look at him with genuine tears in her eyes when he told her it was over. Was there such a woman?

Lisa. But Lisa couldn't love anyone but herself and she knew about the spell.

No, he had to find someone to love him and it had to be real or he risked being a frog forever.

CHAPTER TEN

"Uncle Joe!" Craig strode into the bait shop from the back room just after dusk. He'd made good his escape from Elaine's cottage when Dawg whined to get out. Transformation caught him on the back step of the shop again. This time, Ms. Reneau hadn't been anywhere in sight. Thank God! "Uncle Joe!"

"You don't have to yell, for Pete's sake. I ain't deaf, you know." Uncle Joe squinted one eye and touched his hand to his head. "Did you get the number of the truck that hit me?"

Craig shook his head at his uncle's scruffy clothes and bed hair. "Try Mad Dog 20/20."

"Oh, yeah." Uncle Joe turned toward the commercial refrigerator and yanked out a bottle of water. "I need a couple dozen painkillers."

"Prevention is much more effective than the cure. You should avoid the Raccoon Saloon on Saturday nights."

Uncle Joe lifted a hand, Boy-Scout style. "I'm swearing off, I promise."

Craig grinned. "I've heard that before."

"Right now, even the thought of booze turns my stomach."

"Good, keep it that way." Craig walked to the window and stared out. His gaze gravitated to his uncle's rental house. He wondered when Elaine would arrive at the bait shop. "Heard anything from Littington?"

"Yup. Got a meetin' set up for tonight at nine at the Lake View Restaurant in Morgan City."

"Good." Although he would be glad to finish his business with Littington, Craig found he'd rather be with Elaine out on the swamp.

Uncle Joe ran a hand through his hair, making the long white tufts stand on end. "Bad news is, I got a call from your father."

Craig shot a sharp glance at his uncle, familiar tension settling in his neck and shoulders. His father was already pushing to acquire this deal. Life was all about the business—no time to enjoy family and friends. Craig inhaled and held his breath. "Is he coming down here?"

The older Thibodeaux looked up, his eyes bloodshot. "God forbid, no."

Whew! All he needed was his father's interference at this point to make the situation a complete nightmare. As if a voodoo hex, pollution and funny feelings about a scientist weren't enough. "I thought you said it was bad news."

Joe scratched his chest. "Just hearing from your father gives me the hives. He can be such an ornery fool, acting like he's got a corncob shoved up his—"

"Yeah, well . . ." Craig interrupted his uncle's colorful language. With his back to the wall and one foot crossed over the other, Craig struck a casual pose, his gaze never leaving his uncle's face. "I take it he's still trying to get you to clean up and work for the firm again."

"Never a call goes by without him pluggin' for me to come back."

"Why don't you?"

Uncle Joe lifted his palms upward. "And give up all this?"

Craig looked around at the shop's interior. "What? A beat-up old bait shop and marina?"

"You may see it as nothing but a rundown bait shop. But I look at it as my salvation." He winced and dug around under the counter until he came up with a bottle of ibuprofen. "Ahhhhh."

"Why did you give up law?" Craig asked.

"Had my reasons." Uncle Joe uncapped the bottle and shook four tablets into his hand.

"Name one."

"I don't want you gettin' no ideas about quittin' the firm. Your father would skin me alive. It's bad enough one of the family dropped out. Can't have another Thibodeaux desert the ship."

"Come on, Uncle Joe. You can tell me anything. I'm not walking out on the firm. I'm aiming for partner within the next two years."

Uncle Joe tossed the pills into his mouth and swallowed a swig of bottled water before he replied. "Let's just say I had a change of heart."

Craig's eyebrows rose. His curiosity wouldn't let his uncle alone. "It was a woman, wasn't it?"

"Now don't go puttin' words in my mouth." Joe walked a few steps away. "I never said it was a woman."

"It was a woman." Craig smacked the wall next to his

hip. "Exactly the reason why I haven't shackled myself to one. They're trouble."

Uncle Joe stared into his nephew's eyes. "You'll sing a different tune when you find the right one, boy. And if you're anywhere near as smart as you profess, you'll fight for her, no matter what."

Craig stared back into intense blue eyes, very similar to his own. "Is that the problem? You didn't fight for her?" he asked softly.

The older man turned his back to him. "Go away, boy, I got work to do."

"Okay, but we're not through talking."

"If you know what's good for you, you'll let this sleepin' dog lie." Uncle Joe grabbed a broom, and with short, sharp strokes, swept his way toward the front of the store.

"One other favor, Uncle Joe."

"Ain't you had more than your share for the day?" Joe muttered.

"I need you to stall the scientist until I get back from my meeting with Littington."

"No need. I could take her out myself, if I have to."

"I thought you didn't do night tours?"

Uncle Joe shrugged, his face reddening. "I just told her that 'cause I had a card game with the boys that night. I'll take her."

"No." A jolt of unexpected panic seized Craig. He'd told Elaine Uncle Joe could guide her, but the thought of her and the older man out on the water without his protection chilled him. No telling what would happen if whoever was dumping the toxins found them snooping around. "I want to take her out. Frankly, I'm concerned about the entire situation."

"Afraid she'll take more than her limit of frogs?" Uncle Joe snorted. "I believe there's enough frogs in that swamp to supply a whole slew of universities." He scratched his chin. "Although, more and more of 'em seem to be going belly up lately. Bernie came by again, yesterday with news of more dead fish around that same lagoon."

"It's not so much the frog supply I'm worried about. It's who else is out there on the swamps at night."

"You're getting punchy, boy." A frown pulled his brows low. Joe crossed his arms over the tip of his broom. "People fish at all hours on the swamps. No crime in that. Done it myself for the past thirty years."

"Maybe so." Craig turned and stared out at the night, rolling his shoulders to ease the tension. "Times are changing, and not everyone out there has fish on his mind."

Uncle Joe stood his broom next to Craig. "There something you're not telling me?"

"Let's just say I'm looking into it. Leave the scientist to me." He turned back toward his uncle. "Stall her, tell her I'll be late, but don't take her out there without me."

A smile curled at the edges of the older man's lips. "Sounds like you got a hankerin' for the gal."

Craig stopped in mid stride, turned and looked out the window again. "Call it whatever you like, but wait for me to get back," he responded in low, clipped words.

"Okay, okay, you don't have to bite my head off."

Craig glanced at his watch. "Damn. I better get moving if I plan to meet with Littington."

"Yeah, that's another thing."

"What?" Craig asked without turning away from the window.

"Your father asked about the Littington deal."

Craig shot a glance at Uncle Joe. "What did you tell him?"

The old man shrugged. "You're workin' it."

"Good." With a nod, Craig looked out at the swamp one last time, then headed for the door. "All I need is for him to race down here and find out what a mess I'm in."

"Spare me. I'd make a deal with the devil himself to keep your father from comin' down."

"Be careful what you say. That voodoo queen just might be the devil incarnate. Don't give her more ideas."

"Believe me, I don't want to be in your skin. Human or amphibian."

Just as Elaine gathered her gear for another night on the swamp, the phone rang. Having only left the number with the dean's secretary, she wondered what was wrong at the university. Her heart skipped a beat. Why else would the university call? "Hello."

"Elaine?" A familiar male voice crackled over the line.

"Brian?" Elaine's apprehension diminished, replaced quickly by annoyance. "Are you on a cell phone? I can barely hear you?"

"Yeah, it's me," he answered cheerfully, as if their last words had been nothing out of the ordinary.

"How did you get this number?" she asked, her words abrupt.

"The dean's secretary gave it to me. I told her it was a family emergency."

"So you lied to Annette."

"I consider you family. Pretty romantic, huh? I had to talk to you. I don't like the way we ended our last conversation. I'm sorry. I miss you and want you to come back."

Elaine held the phone away from her ear and rolled her eyes. When she placed it back against her head, she spoke in slow, deliberate syllables. "Brian, we not only ended the conversation that day, we ended our relationship."

"I wanted you to know I was wrong about Cynthia and she means nothing to me and—"

"She dumped you."

"Actually, she didn't tell me she was married."

Elaine emitted an unladylike snort. "So you called second stringer Elaine to fill in while you find another secretary to bounce?" Wow, she had been naive.

"No, that's not it at all." He sighed. "I guess I was pretty harsh and I understand if you're still mad, but I did call to apologize."

"No need to apologize." Elaine almost felt sorry for the man. He really did sound sincere. Although she questioned what she'd ever seen in him in the first place. "I think you did me a favor."

"Really? How?"

"You opened my eyes to my appalling lack of a life outside my work."

"I did that? Glad I could help," he said. "So, when are you coming home?"

"Not until I've completed my research." The thought of going home didn't hold as much appeal as it had the first day. Could one tall, sexy Cajun have anything to do with her current feelings?

"How much longer will your research take?" Brian persisted.

"At least a couple more weeks." Fourteen more nights with Craig in the dark, just the two of them. Too bad it had to be in a boat.

"Two weeks?" Brian's voice rose slightly. "That long? What if I come down next weekend? We could spend some quality time together. You know, sit on the porch and sip mint juleps or whatever the locals do on their day off."

"Brian, we're through." The idea didn't bother her nearly as much as it had two days ago. Frankly, she couldn't imagine what she'd seen in him in the first place. With understanding gleaned from meeting a man who could knock her socks off, Elaine realized she'd only been attracted to Brian because he'd paid attention to her for a while.

"Come on, Elaine. I made a mistake. Since the argument, I've had time to think." He sighed. "I really miss you. How about if I come down there next weekend?"

"Look, I'm busy with my research. I'll be working through the weekends." With the distance between them, she found it easy to put him off. When she returned home, would she take up where they'd left off? Did she want Brian back in her life?

Sure they'd had some nice evenings watching his favorite shows in her living room. They had quiet, pleasant sex on the rare occasion. Brian had been everything she'd thought she wanted in a relationship. He had been comfortable—and generally predictable.

One fiery kiss from a black-haired Cajun in the Louisiana bayous changed all that. She'd tasted the excitement. Her blood had burned through her veins, igniting her senses. Elaine had never felt that way with Brian.

"You're still mad." Brian broke into her erotic musings.

A couple days ago, she'd been mad and very disappointed. Now, she actually felt relief.

"Think about it." Brian went on. "I don't mind making the trip. It could be fun."

"I'll think about it." Elaine stalled, although she knew she'd never trust Brian again. They had no future.

A pair of light-blue eyes swam into her thoughts. She wasn't sure of her feelings for Craig. But with fourteen days of research left, she might have more of a clue by then.

"I'll take that as a yes," Brian said. "I'll talk to you later in the week. Take care and watch out for snakes."

"But Brian—"

The line went dead.

Great. Now she had to convince him she didn't want him there. Elaine set the phone in its cradle and tapped her fingernails against the counter. She'd call him tomorrow and tell him not to come. Her relationship with Brian was truly over, and she suffered no disappointment and only a minor bit of regret for not having seen the truth earlier.

How liberating. She deserved better than comfortable.

Her surge of energizing euphoria slipped a notch. Was Craig, the ladies' man, any better for her? With his striking looks, he could have any woman in the town. Why would he be interested in a frizzy-haired scientist for anything more than a fling? For that matter, why would Elaine willingly continue a relationship knowing it wasn't going anywhere?

Okay, one revelation at a time, one hurdle to cross at a time. She had work to do. Elaine gathered her bucket, nets, satchel and flashlight.

Night cloaked the land as she clunked along the road to the marina. Would Craig be waiting impatiently? Or had he gotten his uncle to fill in for him, after all?

The back door to the marina opened and a tall dark figure emerged in a tailored suit. He marched to a shiny black sports car, climbed in and spun out of the parking lot. Something about the way he moved seemed familiar. Elaine shook her head. Who did she know in Bayou Miste who'd wear a suit or drive an expensive sports car?

Elaine's heart kicked into overdrive when her hand touched the door handle to the bait shop. Would Craig be waiting in the shop? Would he be naked? She found herself silently wishing a "yes" answer to both questions.

What was she thinking? The man was way too sexy for her own good.

With her mouth watering, she entered the building. Lights lit the aisles and shelves. No deep shadows to hide naked men.

"Mr. Thibodeaux?" Elaine didn't see anyone moving about. The place looked empty.

"Yo! Back here!" Joe Thibodeaux's voice called out and he emerged from behind the back counter. "Can't find a damn thing in this place."

"Hello, Mr. Thibodeaux. Are you taking me out in the boat this evening?"

"No. Craig'll be takin' you when he gets back." Joe ducked below the counter again.

"Oh, he's not here." A lump settled in her stomach.

"No, just left."

"Was that him in the sports car?" Somehow, she hadn't pictured Craig owning a sports car on his income.

"Yeah." Joe answered from behind the counter. He surfaced with a box. "He had an appointment to keep before he could take you out on the swamp. He'll be a couple hours."

Disappointment warred with relief. "Couldn't you take me out, Mr. Thibodeaux?"

"Nope." Joe set the box full of assorted fishing paraphernalia on the counter. "Don't do much fishin' in the dark. Gave it up on account of my night vision pretty much stinks. Don't worry, he said he'd be back." He rifled through the box without looking up. "Can't find my favorite filet knife."

Elaine reached into the box and pulled out a long thin knife. "Is this it?"

Joe shook his head. "If it had been a snake, it woulda

131

bit me." He looked up. "You're welcome to hang out in the bait shop until he gets back. Although I'm not much entertainment."

"Thanks, but I have work I could be doing back at the cottage. Mind if I leave my things here for now?"

"Not at all. Set them behind the counter." Joe pointed with his knife.

Elaine piled her bucket, nets and satchel on the floor and turned to leave.

"Craig treatin' you right out there on that swamp?" Joe shaved a fingernail with the filet knife.

Warmth spread up her neck and into her cheeks as she relived the feel of Craig's hands on her breasts and the touch of his lips to hers. "Oh, yes. We're finding specimens."

"Good, good." Joe peeled off another fingernail, then looked up. "Did the boy get around to askin' you out?"

Elaine's cheeks burned. "No. Of course not. I'm not here to date; I'm here to conduct research."

"Yeah." Joe wielded the knife without looking up. "A woman as smart as you has gotta be pretty dedicated to her work. Not much time for fun and dating."

Ouch. His description hit the nail square on the head. Actually, it made her sound just as Brian had described—boring. "I like to have fun." Damn, she sounded defensive. She didn't want to give Joe the impression she was a pathetic recluse.

"Craig's been known to be serious about his work, something you can appreciate. But he's got a sense of fun buried in there. He, Mo and Larry used to pull some pretty wild stunts around here during the summers." Joe hands stilled and he glanced up. "Not that he does that anymore."

"No?" A smile curved Elaine's lips. She could picture a younger Craig racing through Ms. Reneau's peach orchard. Even then, he had to be a complete heartbreaker with those dark good looks and ice-blue eyes. "Does your nephew always wait on customers in the . . . a . . ." Elaine coughed, suddenly embarrassed.

"The what?"

Elaine's gaze searched the corners of the shop and her face heated. "Nude. Does he always serve the customers in the nude?"

"Huh?" One eyebrow rose into the white thatch of hair hanging over Joe's brow.

With a shrug, Elaine shook her head. "Never mind."

The old man's face split in a grin. "Don't know if he serves customers in the nude, but Craig does have a way with the women."

Elaine's smile faded. "I bet he does." Women. Plural. As in, more than Elaine. "So he's dated a lot of women, then?" Elaine couldn't help asking.

"Yeah, but the boy needs to settle down." Joe ducked his head and whittled at another nail.

"He does? Why?"

"He needs someone to love him." Despite Joe's attention to his hands, the conviction came through in the tone of his voice.

What was the old man up to? Why was he trying to get her to go out with his nephew? "And are you saying I'm the one who should?"

"Yeah. He needs a serious settled woman to ground him in reality."

Elaine coughed to hide her immediate denial. Settled woman? That made her sound old and not at all sexy. With her ego beaten to a pulp, her opinion of herself began to smell worse than the dead fish in her freezer. "If your nephew is such a ladies' man, why would he want to 'settle' with a woman like me?"

133

"Because the other girls don't matter to him. They never did."

"Then why should I?" Elaine couldn't believe she was discussing Craig with his uncle.

"Because, despite what he might think, he needs someone like you."

"Settled," Elaine added, her voice flat.

"Yeah, settled." Joe's words slowed and his brows wrinkled into a frown. "Not in an ugly way. What I mean is, not flighty."

"Sounds more like he needs a mother, not another date." Elaine turned toward the door. "You can count me out of this equation."

"Miss Smith." Uncle Joe laid a hand on her arm. "I'm afraid you got me all wrong."

Elaine stared into Joe's face, an eyebrow raised. "Your nephew sounds like a womanizer incapable of committing to a relationship. Any sane woman would run screaming from such a man."

The older man's hand dropped to his side. "Maybe so, but he's changing his ways." In a low mutter he added, "He has to."

"And you want me to help him change his ways?"

"Yeah." An implied "please" emanated from Joe's anxious face.

"I don't have time to tame a wild man, Mr. Thibodeaux." Although the idea had its appeal. Her heart jolted before she could rein it in again. "I'm here to study the swamp, not your nephew."

"But he really is a nice young man."

Elaine crossed her arms in front of her. "And a ladies' man who can't take women seriously."

Uncle Joe grimaced. "Did I say that?"

"Pretty much."

His lips curved downward. "That's not exactly how I meant it to come across."

"Nevertheless, I'm not interested in your nephew, his women, or his needs. I'm interested in the swamp." She turned toward the door. "Now if you'll excuse me, I'll go back to the cottage until Craig shows up to take me out."

"I screwed up, didn't I?" Joe's eyebrows sagged and the corners of his mouth dipped.

Elaine couldn't be mean to the well-intentioned man. He reminded her of a sad basset hound. She smiled despite herself. "Depends on what you were aiming to accomplish."

"I want you to go out with my nephew."

"Okay, I will."

Joe glanced up, hope clear in his expression.

Elaine continued. "I'll go out with him in the boat. But I won't go out on a date. Frankly, he's not my type." Who was she kidding? That was exactly the reason why she gravitated toward him. That bad-boy aura intrigued her.

"Now, don't let my words turn you off. He's got a good heart."

"I'm sure he does." But he was a charmer. A man who could probably have any woman he wanted. How could she compete with the others? And did she want to? "Mr. Thibodeaux, I'm not interested in your nephew." *Liar!*

"Maybe you aren't right now, but if he asks, will you at least think about it? That's all I'm going to say. I'll keep my big mouth shut from now on."

Elaine stared at Mr. Thibodeaux. She could see how much he meant his request. Craig would never ask her out, so why not make the older man happy? "I'll think about it."

CHAPTER ELEVEN

"I want a firm I can trust to represent my interests both here in Cypress Springs and in New Orleans." Jason Littington tossed his napkin on his plate and sat back.

"That's why I'm here, Mr. Littington." Craig twirled the stem of his wineglass. "I've read about Littington Enterprises. You've built quite an empire in oil refineries in southern Louisiana."

"Yes, it hasn't been easy. Maintaining a delicate balance between the EPA, tree-huggers and local unions gets tricky. Do you realize the Cypress Springs factory employs more than four hundred locals? That's four hundred possibilities for lawsuits from Bayou Miste to Morgan City."

"I like to think of it as one of the largest and most responsible employers in the surrounding parishes." Craig's eyebrow rose, challenging the other man to dispute his words—he didn't. "Why did you choose our firm?"

"Your father and I went to Tulane together. We were roommates. I still consider him a friend."

Craig nodded. "He would have come himself, but he's tied up in several high-profile suits in New Orleans." He tipped his head slightly to one side. "Are you having any legal difficulties at this time, Mr. Littington?"

"Oh, the usual. An occasional disgruntled employee, meeting emissions standards with the cost of legal waste disposal rising. Face it, people want jobs, they need gas to run their cars, but no one wants the refineries in their backyard. With all the state and federal regulations, it's hard for a corporation to make a profit."

With a slight nod, Craig tried to appear sympathetic. Littington didn't look like he suffered financial constraints. His Armani suit and Rolex watch showed no signs of wear.

Craig stole a glance at his own watch. He'd already been with Littington for an hour and a half. Normally, he spent that and more if the client's financial worth warranted the effort. But tonight, he could only think of Elaine and going out on the swamp.

Time crawled. Littington gave him the same background information he'd heard a hundred times from other wealthy clients. Started with nothing, built a huge empire with the help of a few political aces played along the way. Yada, yada, yada.

With a stifled yawn, Craig glanced at his watch again. "Mr. Littington—"

"Call me Jason."

"Jason." Craig smiled. "I can have the paperwork drawn up by Wednesday. Do you mind if we meet at the same time and place? I'm unavailable during the day."

"Not at all. Evenings work better for me, as well." Littington pushed away from the table and stood. "Tell your father I said hello."

Craig rose and shook hands with his father's friend.

The older man's smooth white hair, tailored suit and manicured nails reminded him too much of his father. Almost a carbon copy. Would Craig look like that in twenty years? Would the bottom line be all that mattered? He shook aside his wanderings. "I'll see you on Wednesday, Mr. Littington."

The drive back to Bayou Miste raced by in a blur. The smooth-running engine and sound insulation left Craig twenty uninterrupted minutes to think. And what did he think about?

Elaine.

Barring the frog-curse crisis, they'd come to Bayou Miste for completely different reasons, the irony of which was not lost on Craig.

He'd come to secure a deal with a wealthy client bent on lining his pockets and finding loopholes in EPA regulations, possibly leaving his refineries open to dumping more pollutants into the environment.

Elaine had come to Bayou Miste to research pollutants and save the environment from would-be killers. And she thought he was nothing more than the uneducated nephew of the marina owner. What would she think of him if she knew the truth?

Craig's foot lifted from the accelerator and the car slowed. A hard, sickish lump formed in his gut. Did her opinion matter? He'd only known her two days, for Pete's sake.

His foot jammed the gas pedal to the floor and the BMW shot forward, taking the curvy roads much faster than was legal or safe. Craig didn't care. Some situations called for breaking the rules.

He had to stop thinking about a certain dark-haired scientist with her heart in her work. He should be worrying about how to solve his amphibian dilemma.

Note to self: Concentrate on your priorities.

With a mental kick in the butt, Craig forced his mind back on track, straightened his shoulders and focused. Who were the likely candidates? He didn't have a lot of time left to make someone fall in love with him.

DeeDee DuBois, Maddie Golinski, Lisa LeBieu, and Josie Ezelle. Craig breathed out a huge sigh. DeeDee and Maddie gave him the hives, they were so . . . so . . . well, not his type. Lisa chilled him to the bone with her voodoo grandmother. Which left Josie.

Craig tipped his head to the side. He hadn't seen Josie in eight years. She'd been a leggy teenager with braces and a laugh like a hyena. But still, she was nice and not bad-looking.

How would her brother, Larry, feel if Josie fell in love with Craig? Did Larry understand Craig had no intention of getting married and settling in Bayou Miste? Once the girl admitted she loved him, the curse ended. Done, finished, kaput! Craig would be out of Bayou Miste so fast the town would wonder what had hit.

Was that fair to Josie? Would Larry hold it against Craig? Not that Craig came to the swamp that often, but he did value the memories the two shared. He, Larry and Mo had been friends for a long time.

Maybe he'd better run it by Larry first. But as far as the list went, Josie was the only reasonable option.

If you choose to ignore Elaine.

Damn. Craig wished his inner thoughts would give it a rest. He refused to go after Elaine. She'd just been dumped by one boyfriend. What kind of cad would knowingly do it again in such a short time?

No. He couldn't.

On the other hand, what if she went into a relationship with her eyes wide open? If he told her he didn't want anything long-term, would she still fall in love with him and accept the consequences?

Representing high-dollar divorce and corporate law cases seemed a snap compared to finding someone to love him. Spending his days as a frog certainly didn't help circumstances. He was a man for the few hours a night when most people slept. How could he woo someone so quickly in the narrow time slot allowed?

For one, he could get that someone into bed as soon as possible. If his love candidate could be lured under the sheets, he could keep her awake into the wee hours, getting her to know and love him. That seemed like a much better plan than hanging out in bars or all-night diners hoping to meet an insomniac. Which meant he'd have to go for Josie or Elaine. Josie it was.

With the decision made, Craig felt a little more in control. He'd start the next night on his campaign to woo Josie. If Larry had no objections.

Craig parked the BMW at Uncle Joe's house and trotted back to the marina where he slipped out of his suit and into jeans, a long-sleeved denim shirt and deck shoes. He emerged into the bait shop.

"That you, boy?" Uncle Joe called out.

He and Bernie sat at a rickety card table with a chessboard between them.

"Elaine come by?" Craig asked.

"Sure did, about two hours ago." Joe's fingers lingered over a black knight as he studied the board. He moved the knight forward and to the left, removing a white pawn from the game. "She left her things behind the counter. Wanted you to come get her when you got back."

"Thanks." He located the familiar bucket, satchel and net, swept them up in his hands and headed for the front door.

"What's this about you serving customers in the nude?" Uncle Joe called out. "Can't afford a sexual harassment suit against the marina."

Craig's face warmed but he kept going. "Don't worry about it, we'll talk later."

When he cleared the door, he trotted down to the dock and tossed the items in the boat. Adrenaline shot through him as he walked up the steps to the road and aimed for Elaine's cottage. Memories of their last kiss and Elaine in a towel replayed in his mind.

In human form, the correct body parts responded, causing him significant discomfort. If he didn't get a grip before he got to her door, further movement would prove difficult. He'd be tempted to throw her to the floor and—

Don't go there, buddy. Remember Josie? Your plan? Is Elaine anywhere in your plan?

No.

Regret formed a tight knot in his chest and he questioned his decision to exclude Elaine from the list. Of all the candidates, she interested him the most—which scared him down to his toes. Perhaps he had a masochistic tendency to deny himself pleasure.

Lights from the cottage windows shone into the night, illuminating his steps. He searched through the panes until he spotted Elaine's silhouette in the living room, bent over something.

As he knocked on the door, blood pounded in his veins. To get his physical reactions in check, he shook his head, rotated his shoulders and stamped his feet. His upper lip broke out in a sweat like it had on his very first date at the tender age of sixteen.

At the ripe old age of twenty-eight, these chemical reactions shouldn't be so prominent. Elaine was just a woman, a woman with a to-die-for body disguised in khaki. She was the only female Craig knew who'd go out on a boat in light-colored, ironed slacks.

The door opened and Elaine stood there in her neatly pressed white oxford shirt and khaki slacks. Although Elaine was covered from head to foot in starched clothing, Craig could still envision her in the bath towel, her hair in neat, wet waves down her back, a rosy hew to her freshly washed cheeks.

"Ready?" he asked, staring into moss-green eyes barely hidden by the tortoiseshell owl glasses.

"Yes," she said, her voice a breathy whisper.

"Me too." Craig turned away before she could see how ready he really was.

Elaine sat back in the boat, smearing bug repellent on her neck, hands and ankles.

Craig hadn't spoken more than two words since he'd helped her into the boat. He kept a distance between them, and made their brief contacts short and impersonal.

Now he sat in brooding silence, guiding the small skiff through the black waters, his attention fully focused on the channel ahead.

Elaine couldn't stand the silent gap widening between them. "I identified the frog we caught yesterday as a *rana sphenocephala*."

A frown dipped between Craig's brows.

The frown made her all the more determined to get him to talk. "It's more commonly known as a southern leopard frog."

He looked at her briefly. "How can you tell them apart?"

Not exactly a warm response, but open-ended. Encouraged by his question, she hurried to answer. "We can identify the different species by location, coloring, shape, and sounds. The leopard frog, found in southern

Louisiana, is an orange-brown color and has a low-pitched guttural sound, similar to a chuckle."

A smile tilted the corner of Craig's lips. "Laughing frogs. Did you stay up all night waiting for the leopard frog to chuckle?"

Elaine returned his smile, warmed by his response. "No. But did you know Dawg has a pet bullfrog?"

Craig's body stiffened and he shot her a glance. "Oh?"

Confused by his tense reaction, she leaned forward. "Does that bother you?"

"No, not at all. Dawg makes friends with everyone. It really doesn't surprise me that he's made friends with a frog." Craig negotiated a turn before he spoke again. "Are you going to dissect him?"

"Dawg?"

"No, the frog."

"No, I don't think Dawg would appreciate my cutting into his pet frog." She shook her head. "Funniest thing I've ever seen, though. A canine protecting a bullfrog."

"Like you said, strange things happen in the bayou."

"Did I say that?" She knew she'd said those very words to Dawg earlier that morning, but not to Craig.

"Must have heard it somewhere else." Craig nodded ahead of them. "Duck."

This time out in the skiff, Elaine didn't hesitate. She ducked. The same drooping Spanish moss scraped across her back and over Craig. They'd entered the same lagoon where they'd found the dead fish.

When Craig cut the engine, the boat skimmed silently through the water.

Elaine strained her ears to listen. "Hear that?"

"What?" Craig lifted the oar from the bottom of the boat and dug into the water to slow the craft.

"Exactly. Nothing. I don't hear another motor. I hope

we'll have plenty of time to collect as many specimens as we want."

"Get your net ready, we're about to bump into a small island."

As the boat slid into the bushes and vines crowding the shore, Elaine braced herself. A rounded bump in the water loomed ahead of her. Her heart skittered to a stop. "What's that?"

Craig shone a flashlight beam at the dark brownish-black knob about the size of dog's head. "You're a scientist, don't you know a cypress knee when you see one? They grow out of the roots of the cypress trees here in the swamps."

Heat rose in her cheeks as she realized how stupid she must appear. But her chagrin was short lived as frogs hopped into the water, diving deep to escape the massive beast of a boat disturbing their evening song.

With her heart pounding in her chest, Elaine readied her net and leaned over the side of the boat. Her face stared back at her in the reflection of light from the boat lanterns. The inky black depths mesmerized her until her head spun and her vision blurred. The familiar panic associated with her fear of water rose up into her chest, threatening to overwhelm her calm exterior.

Craig leaned across and touched a hand to her knee. "Do you want me to do it?"

With conscious effort, she ripped her gaze from the reflection and stared down at the hand warming her skin through the khaki fabric. When she didn't respond, she felt his hand squeeze gently.

"Elaine?"

She glanced up into eyes so blue she fell right in, drowning in their depths. He'd called her by her first name. How resonant and beautiful his voice made it sound.

"Do you want me to help?" He smiled into her eyes and

144

warmth spread from his hand up her thigh to throb gently in her groin. Molten blood coursed through her veins, scorching her insides and making her body tingle with awareness, awareness she'd sworn to ignore. "No."

"No?"

She straightened away from him. "I can do this." All she needed was to focus on the task. She stared at the water again, and completely forgot why. All her consciousness centered on the dark-haired Cajun mere inches away. Like a celestial body drawn to the sun, her body gravitated toward him.

The boat tilted as Craig shifted to straddle the bench seat. A leg appeared on either side of her and she leaned back against his chest, his heat enveloping her.

"I want to help," he whispered into her hair, his breath stirring the tendrils around her ears. "Don't deny me the opportunity to be macho."

Elaine stilled, her body an engine heating to dangerously explosive levels. She'd never felt this alive and aware of her own sensuality.

"Look." Craig reached around her and pointed to a frog swimming in the water close to the skiff. He wrapped his fingers around the hand with the net and leaned into her until the mesh rested in the water. Together, they waited until the frog moved closer.

Unable to breathe for fear of moaning, Elaine enjoyed the solid muscles pressed against her back. A brawny arm wrapped around her middle and his hand cupped hers, guiding the net through the water.

Even through the pungent odor of bug repellent, she could smell his aftershave and minty-fresh breath. Closing her eyes, she imagined him pressing a kiss to her temple. With the image so real, she could almost feel his lips brush her skin in a butterfly-light kiss.

Elaine's eyes popped open as she felt the caress again. He kissed her temple!

What should she do? A girl could get lost out here. Lost to her purpose, lost to her self. And with a man like Craig? A man who probably cut a notch in his bedpost for every woman he bedded and left heartbroken.

Elaine jerked away. Craig's warmth burned her like the moth in the candle flame. If she hovered too close, she knew her wings would catch fire. Fear born of self-preservation urged her to struggle.

"Whoa, steady now," Craig said, as if gentling a spooked horse. He spread his arms and legs wide to still the rocking boat.

Without his arms to hold her back, Elaine lunged for the other seat. But the rocking motion threw her off balance. Teetering near the edge of the boat, she flung out her hand toward Craig. Then the boat tipped and she toppled over the side.

The legendary slow-motion switch kicked in gear. Elaine absorbed the details of the overhanging trees, marveling at the long strands of moss stretching three, sometimes four feet in length. Craig stood, his mouth forming around her name. His fingers reached for hers, tips touching tips, with no purchase found.

Craig's beautiful blue eyes were the last image she committed to memory before water embraced her, sucking her down to the silt and aquatic vegetation on the bottom. Liquid filled her nostrils and throat as she opened her mouth to scream.

Afraid of the water, she'd never learned to swim, so she sank like a rock. Her lungs starved for air felt ready to burst and her head grew light.

Water churned beside her. Strong arms grasped beneath

her shoulders, hauling her up. Up to the surface, to air and light. When her face broke through she struggled to crawl higher up the torso holding her. Panic filled her and she floundered, afraid she'd sink beneath the surface again.

A grunt was followed by strong arms clamping hers to her sides. "Stop kicking, woman."

She coughed and spluttered, "Can't swim."

"You don't have to," Craig said, his voice calm and steady. "Stand up."

Elaine kicked and flailed to keep her head from submerging again.

"Damn it woman, stand up!" He turned her in his arms to face him, holding her tight against his chest. Where she floundered in the water, he stood solid and still. "Try it. Put your feet on the bottom. It's only about chest deep."

"Can't swim," she whispered, tears trickling down her cheeks.

"You don't have to, Elaine." He stared into her eyes for a second more, then leaned forward and claimed her lips with his.

Shocked into stillness, Elaine clung to Craig. Her arms wrapped around his neck, her breasts pressed against his hard-muscled chest.

With her lips locked to his, her feet found the bottom and relief swept through her. Relief quickly transformed into desire as she returned his kiss, her tongue meeting his thrust for thrust.

When they came up for air, Elaine stared into his eyes. "You saved me."

"No, the water wasn't very deep. You could have saved yourself." He reached up to brush her cheek with his fingers. "However, if we don't get out of here soon, we'll be alligator bait."

Fear charged through her veins again and she practically crept up Craig's body, wrapping her legs around his waist. "Ohmigod, where are they?"

"They could be anywhere. And as much as I enjoy you crawling all over me, I don't relish the idea of being dinner to a reptile."

"Oh, yes, of course. I'm sorry, I'm acting like a blubbering baby. It's just—"

"It's okay. Just loosen up on my neck so I can get you back in the skiff."

Mortified and still shaking from her traumatic experience, Elaine shut up and let him lift her back into the boat. She clung to the seat as the boat dipped down into the water when he pulled himself aboard.

When they were both settled on the metal benches, Elaine let out a sigh. *Thank God.*

"Look over there." Craig pointed to the water about ten feet from the boat. Light reflected red off two golf-ball-sized bumps on the surface. Elaine peered closer and saw the water swirl in long waves behind the bumps. "What is it?"

"Alligator."

"Wow." Her stomach flip-flopped. "That was close."

"Yeah. And that's a big one."

"Could it have . . ." she gulped, ". . . killed a grown man?"

Craig nodded, his expression grim. "One that size could. He must be fourteen feet long."

A chill coursed down her spine and set into her bones. Her teeth chattered so loud, the sound echoed between her ears.

Craig looked over at her. "We need to get you back to the house."

"But we didn't catch anything." What about her research? She hadn't caught a single frog or fish. The evening was a complete loss. Except for one fiery kiss.

"It doesn't matter. You need to get out of those wet clothes and into something dry or you'll get sick."

"I'm okay," she insisted. Another shiver shook her entire body, belying her words. *Why am I arguing?* All she could think about was that alligator. Maybe a hot shower would warm her body and erase the smell of swamp water from her hair and skin.

"Yeah, you're okay." He turned to pull the rope on the motor. He tugged with such force, the engine leapt to life.

Elaine hunkered low as he turned the skiff and headed out the way they'd come. The wind from the boat's movement cut through her wet clothes, making her even colder.

Craig stared over at her and caught her shivering again. He slowed the boat to almost a complete stop, reaching his arms out to her. "Come here." His words were a command, but spoken with tenderness.

Elaine placed her hands in his and allowed him to pull her across to sit on the bench beside him. He wrapped his arm around her and, with the other hand, increased the speed on the boat and navigated them back toward Bayou Miste.

Was his embrace a prelude to something more or just a friendly attempt to comfort her? Although she felt warm and secure, Elaine knew she was in way over her head with Craig.

CHAPTER TWELVE

When the boat bumped against the dock, Craig jumped out and tied it in place. Then he reached down and pulled Elaine up to stand beside him. He rubbed her arms and turned her head so he could see her face more clearly in the faint dock light.

Her teeth were chattering and her lips were a sad shade of purplish blue. She looked like a pathetic drowned rat with big owl eyes. Nothing to stir a man's desires. Yet he wanted more than anything to taste those full lips and share his warmth with her.

A mighty tremor racked her body and she stared up at him with an apologetic frown. "I'm sorry. I just can't stop shaking." A tear trickled from the corner of her eye. The single drop traced a path down her cheek and became Craig's undoing.

Without a word, he scooped her into his arms and marched across the pier and up to the road.

Elaine squealed and hooked an arm around his neck. "You don't have to carry me. I can walk."

"Hush," he said, breathing hard after the climb.

"Craig, put me down," she said in her matter-of-fact voice.

"Just shut up and let a man be macho, okay?" He tempered his words with a brief smile. Then he concentrated on breathing all the way to her cottage. When he reached her porch, he set her on her feet and doubled over, making a show of gasping for air.

Elaine's mouth quirked upward and she fisted her hands on her hips. "You sure know how to make a girl feel all feminine and petite.

Craig straightened and winked, no worse for the wear after his uphill trek.

After a failed attempt to shove a cold hand into her wet pocket, Elaine muttered, "I can't make my fingers work to get the key out."

"Here, let me." Craig moved up behind her and pushed her cold hand aside, sliding his into the soggy opening.

Elaine leaned back against him, her shivers creating small vibrations against his chest and groin. Even with her damp clothes pressing against his body, he felt warmth spread downward from where her back touched his chest.

When his large hand snagged on its way in, he wiggled it free and pushed deeper.

Elaine gasped, and her body stiffened.

At last, Craig's fingers touched metal. With his hand cupped over the keys, he could feel her thigh through the thin lining of her pants. His grip tightened, and he pulled her snug against him, reveling in her feminine form and the feel of her backside rubbing his front.

151

A soft moan escaped her lips, her shoulders relaxed and her head dropped back against his shoulder.

Fire raced through Craig's veins, and he felt the moisture in his clothes steam. He jerked the key free and shoved it into the lock.

With his arm around her, he guided her inside and closed the door behind them. When he stared down at the trembling waif of a scientist, all he could think of was making mad, passionate love to her.

Why?

"You need to get out of those wet things and take a hot shower." He said the words, but he made no move to leave her.

Elaine reached up to unfasten a button, her fingers shaking and stiff. After several attempts, her arms dropped to her sides and she looked up with half a smile. "Maybe I'll just shower with my clothes on. Thanks for save—getting me out of the water and carrying me up to the house. You didn't have to."

"Don't mention it." He should have left, but Craig found himself reaching out to flip the top button of her blouse. "Here, let me help."

Her hands came up to rest atop his. When he hesitated, she caressed his forearms, all the encouragement he needed.

Craig loosened the next button, and the next, until he reached the waistband of her dripping khaki slacks. He slipped his fingers beneath the big button and pushed it through, then slid the zipper down.

A gentle tug freed her shirt from inside the trousers. With his hands poised over the edges of her blouse, he finally looked up.

Behind the rims of her glasses, Elaine's moss-green eyes darkened to a forest-green hue. Her lips, having regained their natural rosy tint, parted and her tongue snaked out to wet them.

"Need more help?" he asked, his voice gruff with the effort to control his instincts. He wanted nothing more than to rip the shirt from her back, toss her over his shoulder and carry her off to bed. Was he possessed? Had the voodoo witch cast a love spell on the scientist?

"Please," she whispered.

That's all it took.

Caught in a haze of desire, Elaine stared up into Craig's eyes as he shoved the blouse over her shoulders. His gaze raked over her and she trembled, wondering if he liked what he saw.

Slowly, she reached up behind her and unclasped her bra.

Craig smoothed the straps over her shoulders and down her arms until her breasts were bare and free of constraint. The bra dropped to the floor.

The hunger in Craig's eyes sparked a similar need inside Elaine. When he lifted a hand to cup one of her breasts, she leaned into him.

Craig frowned when his warm fingers touched her skin. "You're still cold."

"I'm getting warmer by the second," she said, her voice low and husky.

"You still need that shower." His hands dropped to her waist and he pushed her slacks over her hips and slid them down her legs, trailing his knuckles across her thighs, calves and ankles.

Elaine shivered.

"See? You're still shaking."

She didn't bother to tell him she wasn't shaking from cold. She stepped out of her slacks and stood in front of him dressed only in her lacy white bikini panties, feeling incredibly feminine and sexy. She pulled her glasses off and set them on the table. Everything was soft and fuzzy around the edges.

Now what should she do? Her skin warmed from within, her attraction to Craig sending heat shooting through her body. Would Craig follow through? Elaine hoped he'd continue his he-man tactics and sling her over his shoulder, carrying her off to bed where they'd shake the cottage's very foundation. Whatever move he decided to make, he'd better make it quick, before Elaine chickened out.

But Craig raked a hand through his hair and backed up a step.

No. He couldn't be getting cold feet now. Elaine's body was ablaze, and he was the one who'd lit the match. "Don't stop now," she whispered and closed the distance between them. Had she ever been so bold?

"I don't think we should," he said.

"Then don't think." Her words shocked herself. Since when had Elaine Smith ever *not* thought? Since Craig Thibodeaux appeared naked in front of her, that's when.

He looked into her eyes. "It can only lead to hurt."

She slipped a button loose on his shirt, spread the fabric apart and kissed his chest. "I'll take my chances."

"I'm not one to commit." He leaned forward and pressed his lips to her forehead.

He lingered until the imprint seared a permanent place in Elaine's memory. A slow burn knotted her stomach. She'd always known Craig was a ladies' man, but frankly, she didn't care at this moment. She wanted him. "I'm not asking for any promises." With a flick of her finger, another button worked free.

His hands stopped hers and he held them until she looked up into his eyes. "I don't want to make you cry."

She stared up into his light-blue gaze and wondered at her ability to push all else aside for a brief moment of pleasure. But push she did. "I'm a big girl. I can handle this. Now, will you shut up and lose the clothes?" She wound her fingers into his hair and pulled him down to her lips. Before she kissed him, she whispered against his mouth, "I want you, Craig."

He crushed her to him, slanting his mouth across hers. Her lips opened wide enough for his tongue to slip through and taste her sweetness. He traced a line of kisses across her jaw to her earlobe, sucking at the tender skin.

Elaine moaned. Her hands flew down his chest, urgently popping buttons free and tugging his shirt from his trousers. He shrugged out of the garment and stood bare-chested in front of her.

For the second time that night, he scooped her up in his arms.

Ahhhh . . . wishes do come true.

Then he carried her to the bathroom and set her on her feet. With a few quick movements, he had the water steaming and the rest of his clothes lying in a heap at his feet. He stood proud and naked in front of her and this time, Elaine took a moment to study every feature of his magnificent body. From his wavy black hair to broad muscled shoulders, down the hard planes of his tight stomach, to the stiff evidence of his desire.

Ohmigod. She gulped. His desire for her! A strange sense of power surged through her veins and a smile curved her lips. She hooked her thumbs into the elastic of her panties and slid them down her legs. Then with a wink at him, she ducked behind the shower curtain.

Craig followed her in.

They both reached for the soap at the same time. Elaine's hands wrapped around the pink bar of Caress, and Craig's hands wrapped around hers. Together they worked up a lather, staring into one another's eyes.

Elaine set the bar back on the edge of the tub and started at Craig's shoulders, working her way down his chest to his stomach, avoiding his protruding member for the moment. She wanted to make him as hot as he made her.

While she lathered his front, Craig wrapped his arms around her back and lathered her shoulders and down her sides to her buttocks. He cupped her cheeks and pressed her pelvis against his hardness.

Electric shocks jerked through Elaine's veins, all culminating at the juncture of her thighs. She wanted nothing more than for him to ram himself into her and satisfy her needs. But he poured shampoo into his hands and turned her around to lather her hair.

Ummm. Nothing felt better than someone rubbing your scalp, except . . . *Don't go there, honey,* Elaine warned herself.

He rinsed the suds from her hair and lathered his hands with soap again. He pulled her shoulder blades against his chest and washed her belly, sliding his hands upward to cup her breasts. He pinched and tweaked until her nipples stood at attention and she thought she'd fall apart. Then his soapy hands slid downward to tangle in the mound of hair between her thighs. His fingers slipped between her folds and touched her nubbin of desire.

Elaine forgot to breathe. Her hands covered his as he flicked and fingered her to a fevered pitch. "Ohmigod. I'm on fire."

The water heater picked that moment to run out of hot

water. The temperature changed from steamy to luke-warm in a matter of seconds.

"Better hurry and wash the soap off," he whispered against her ear.

Welcoming the cooling effect, Elaine rinsed quickly, the pelting cold water barely tamping the rising heat within.

Craig reached past her and twisted the faucet knob. With infinite care, he turned her around, cupped her face in his hands, and lowered his mouth to hers. She tasted the water on his lips, and slid her tongue across his teeth to delve in and tangle with his. Her hands roamed over his back in a frenzy, angling downward to cup his buttocks and pull him against her.

"I want you," she whispered into his mouth. "I want you inside me."

Craig lifted her off the ground and backed her up against the wall of the shower. The cool, hard ceramic tiles shocked her skin, a sharp contrast to the heat generated between their bodies. Craig wrapped her legs around his waist, while she locked her arms around his neck. Then he lowered her onto him, penetrating slowly until she took all of him.

"Oh, shoot." He jerked her off him, and winced.

"What?" Fear of a looming rejection swirled around her when her feet touched the bottom of the tub.

"Protection. I forgot about protection."

Elaine relaxed and smiled. "Is that all?" She kissed his collarbone and laid her wet cheek against his chest, feeling the pounding of his heart beneath her ear.

"Is that all? Geez, woman, you test my endurance." His hands smoothed up her sides to cup her breasts. Bending low, he took one into his mouth. "I can't get enough of you." He pulled hard, sucking the tip between his teeth.

Elaine clutched his head, holding him close. The cool tiles against her back did nothing to chill the molten energy roiling inside. "You're a guy, don't you carry one in your wallet, or pocket or something?"

"Let me check." He slapped the shower curtain aside and dove for his jeans. In the back pocket, he found his wallet, held it up and leafed through the wet papers and leather. "Oh, thank God!" He held up a foil pouch and pressed a kiss to it.

Elaine stepped from the tub and wrapped a towel around her, suddenly a little shy. In the throes of passion, being naked with Craig felt natural. With the interruption, the passions cooled slightly. How did you rekindle? She ached to finish what they'd started, a need throbbing low in her belly.

Don't lose it now! Good Lord, how many opportunities did she get to rumble with a sex god? She risked a glance at his naked form, hope swelling in her chest. Obviously, he still wanted her. All she had to do was show him how much she wanted him.

With the edges of the towel clutched in her hands, she turned toward the bedroom door.

Craig followed.

When she reached the bed, she swung around and drew in a deep breath. Never in her life had she wanted to be with a man like she wanted to be with Craig. She dropped the towel. Oh, how liberating to stand nude and not feel self-conscious.

The look on Craig's face scorched her naked skin. Moving with the grace of a predator stalking his prey, Craig growled low in his chest and swept in on her, tossing her to the mattress. Climbing on the bed, he straddled her hips.

Elaine squealed and giggled, feeling strange about

laughing while making love. Brian had taken sex so seriously. "You're an animal."

"You bring it out in me." He lapped at her neck and nibbled his way to her breasts.

His hands and lips worked their magic down to her stomach. With his knee, he nudged her legs apart and lay down between them.

Unused to this, Elaine leaned up on her elbows and watched him as he scooped his hands under her buttocks and buried his face in her femininity. When his tongue touched that certain spot, Elaine fell flat on the bed and arched her back. Her world burst apart in a cataclysmic explosion.

His tongue flicked again and she moaned. "Ohmigod, you're killing me."

Craig lifted his head. "Does that hurt?"

"Don't stop!" Elaine screeched. Reaching down to clutch his hair, she pressed him back to the task he'd begun. "Ah, geez, don't stop."

He tongued and licked, sending her over the edge again. One long finger slid inside her, swirling the moistened opening.

Her body spasmed, jerking and exploding with sensation, lifting her higher and higher. "Now," she gasped. "I want you inside me, now."

Craig tore open the aluminum pouch, slid the condom over himself and pressed the tip of his swollen member to her opening. He hiked her knees up and planted a hand on either side of her. Swooping low, he stole a kiss and moved into her, slowly, steadily, until he filled her. He pulled halfway out and paused.

Impatient beyond reason, Elaine wrapped her legs around his waist and brought him home.

In, out, he pumped against her. She matched him thrust for thrust, rising off the bed to take him all the way into her. She'd never felt so complete, so full, and so right. For a split second, her eyes widened. Ohmigod, this was what they meant by orgasm.

Now that she knew, she couldn't go back. Brian was firmly part of her past—a lackluster, black and white past. Craig was vibrant, Technicolor, here and now.

His body stiffened, he threw back his head and he moved into her one last time. Balancing on his hands, he held steady for a long, exquisite moment and then collapsed on top of her.

For several seconds she couldn't breathe, and didn't care. She could die like this and have no regrets.

But eventually, Craig rolled to his side, taking her with him, refusing to sever their intimate connection.

Elaine sighed and snuggled against his chest, allowing the curly hairs to tickle her nose. She inhaled his scent, a mixture of her soap and his musk, a heady combination. "Ummmm. I could lie like this forever."

Craig held her in the crook of his arm and sighed.

Forever.

Suddenly, his body sprang into alert posture. An adrenalin rush poked his heart into overdrive and he breathed like a marathon athlete at the finish line. Self-preservation mode had kicked in.

As a high-dollar attorney for hire, he'd represented the gamut of divorce cases. He'd witnessed what he'd thought were reasonable adults do cruel and ugly things to each other in the name of revenge and greed.

Disillusioned, Craig had sworn to avoid the "D" word the only way he knew how . . . by thoroughly avoiding the "M" word. With his job and his lifestyle, he couldn't picture any one woman sharing his life for longer than half a year—max. And then what? Divorce, raked over the coals, dragged through the quagmire of he-said-she-said court.

No thanks, not for him.

He studied Elaine in the light from the bathroom door. Her face glowed a creamy pink, warmed by the heat generated from skin-to-skin contact. Incredibly long lashes brushed her cheeks.

Craig lifted a hand to the smooth line of her jaw. Her skin, soft and smooth, did funny things to his stomach. His breathing slowed to match the steady puffs of air stirring the hairs on his chest.

Funny. He couldn't picture her standing up against him in a divorce court. Closing his eyes, he tried to envision her in a tailored suit, a briefcase in one hand, and a divorce lawyer by her side. The only image he conjured was Elaine in a lab coat, her glasses perched on the end of her nose, a smile curving her lips as she looked up at him from her microscope.

With little more effort, he envisioned them at sixty, lying in bed. His hair would be gray or gone. Hers would be a frizzy mass of salt and pepper. Her green eyes would look up at him, crinkled at the corners.

Instead of repulsing him, the image warmed him. Suddenly overcome with fatigue, he pulled Elaine closer and drifted off to sleep.

On the edge of consciousness, three quarters of the way to dreamland, Craig heard the steady beat of a drum.

CHAPTER THIRTEEN

Elaine stretched, rolled onto her back, and slung an arm across the pillow next to her. The empty pillow.

Her eyes flew open and she sat up. Where'd he go? A quick scan of the room and through to the small living area revealed nothing. No dark-haired, blue-eyed, hunk-a-hunk-a-burnin'-love roaming around naked in her little cottage.

The Cajun sex god had flown the coop.

With a groan, she flopped flat on her back, the sheets against her bare skin a sensual reminder of the mattress acrobatics she and Craig had performed into the wee hours. Elaine punched the pillow. How could she be so foolish to think he'd stay? He probably hopped in and out of so many beds he didn't know where he was half the time.

The scent of Craig drifted up from the pillow. Without thinking, Elaine hugged it to her breasts and inhaled deeply. A soft sigh escaped her lips, and the twisty-gurgling feeling in the pit of her stomach settled into a hungry rumble.

Why should she be annoyed with his disappearance? Hadn't he said he wasn't into commitment? She'd gone to bed with her eyes wide open.

Then why did it hurt so much that he'd disappeared?

You're a big girl, Elaine; get over it.

With a glance at the clock on the beside table, she realized it was well past noon, which explained his absence. Craig probably had to go to work sometime today. Out of courtesy, he'd let her sleep.

Cheered by the deduction, she shoved aside the blankets and trotted to the bathroom. The small white-tiled room looked like a tornado had hit. Jeans and shirts littered the floor along with an empty foil packet.

Craig left without his clothes?

Elaine scooped up the items, heavy with moisture and smelling strongly of swamp water. No wonder. He probably slipped out in the dark so as not to embarrass her or himself in the light of day.

She flicked open the shower curtain. The soap bar lay in the bottom of the tub, a fragrant reminder of the two of them sliding together beneath the warm spray, slicked with suds.

With a nervous jerk, she closed the curtain and leaned in to turn the faucets on without looking. A cold shower ought to dispel any lingering fantasies.

While the water pattered against the plastic shower curtain, Elaine stared into the mirror at the reflection of a stranger. With her hair mussed, eyes glowing, and cheeks flushed pink, she looked more alive than she'd ever imagined. The sight of beard burn across her breasts only increased her agitation. An image of Craig sucking one rosy tip at a time into his mouth sizzled in her mind. Her nipples hardened into turgid peaks and fire seared into her belly.

Elaine opened the medicine-cabinet mirror and grabbed for toothpaste. With clean teeth and fresh breath, she could conquer the world.

With speed born of desperation, Elaine accomplished her morning ablutions and a brief shower in less than ten minutes. A miracle for any woman. The thought of spending another moment in the bathroom they'd shared drove her out quickly.

Dressed and ready for anything, she gathered the damp clothing and stuffed it into the washing machine hidden behind louvered doors in the kitchen.

Now what?

She scanned the miniature lab scattered across the tables erected in the living room. One would think that after two trips into the swamps she'd have a larger selection of specimens to work with. One dead fish and a frog. Not much. But a start, nonetheless.

Elaine rolled up her sleeves and went to work.

Two minutes later, a scratching sound at her front door alerted her to a visitor.

Setting aside a slide, she walked across the living room and opened the door to Dawg.

"Good morning," she called out, forcing cheerfulness she didn't feel.

She leaned down and ruffled the dog's ears. "Why take my sexual frustrations out on a dog? Huh, boy?" With a glance around she noted his frog wasn't with him. "Where's your friend?"

Woof!

The mottled green bullfrog of the day before hopped into view from around the door.

"There you are. I thought maybe you'd decided to ditch the dog."

Dawg's tail thumped the floor, and he slurped the frog with a long juicy tongue.

Elaine laughed out loud when the frog fell over, completely slimed in dog saliva.

Woof!

"You are a special case, aren't you? If you two don't mind, I have work to do."

Considering that the world outside the cottage doors loomed as a dangerous jungle to a bullfrog, Craig contented himself watching Elaine.

Completely absorbed in dissecting her specimens, she studied samples of tissue beneath her microscope and scribbled notes in a journal all afternoon. She barely noticed when Dawg flopped down on the floor against her feet. But when he laid his head against her legs and looked up at her with an open-mouthed yawn, she finally paused for a moment.

"Am I boring you?" She reached down and patted the dog's head. Her stomach rumbled and she glanced at the clock over the mantle.

"Lordy, already four o'clock and I haven't even had breakfast." She glanced back at Dawg. "I don't suppose you're hungry too, are you? How about a peanut butter and jelly sandwich?"

Ummmm . . . a peanut butter and jelly sandwich sounded like heaven to Craig.

Dawg rolled his eyes up, and his tail thumped his agreement.

Elaine walked the few steps across the room to the little kitchen area.

The dog lurched to his feet and followed Elaine to the kitchen. Craig hopped over to stand close by.

"I'm sorry, but I'm fresh out of flies for Todd."

Good. Craig would rather starve than eat another fly. He'd have to fill up on human food at night.

Armed with a sandwich and a glass of ice water, Elaine sat at the Formica table. "I'm not liking what I'm seeing, Dawg."

Dawg nudged her leg and pounded the floor with his tail.

Elaine tore a piece of crust off the side of her sandwich and absently handed it over to the dog. "The toxin levels are dangerously high in all the samples. Frankly, I'm surprised the leopard frog was alive when we found him. His liver was only half the size it should have been. Remind me to ask Craig about factories in the area, will you?"

The dog's mouth dropped open in what resembled a grin and his tail swished across the floor, knocking into Craig.

Craig steadied himself and looked back up at Elaine.

She had a distant expression on her face. Her fingers plucked at the crust on her sandwich, but she didn't eat. "Do you think Craig will avoid me now?"

Taken off guard by her change in subject, Craig felt as if he were eavesdropping on her private reverie.

"I mean, after all, I'm no prize catch when it comes to looks." She slipped her glasses off her nose and tucked a loose curl behind her ear.

Ummm . . . Craig recalled nibbling on that ear. And what did she mean, not a prize catch? Seemed the good professor didn't even know what she had hiding beneath her lab coat. His gaze followed her hand down the side of her long, creamy white neck.

"I wonder why he's so afraid of commitment?" Elaine

slipped the glasses back on her face. "Not that I'm interested in a lasting relationship with the man. Besides," she
stared down at Dawg and Craig, "what do we have in
common?"

Craig opened his mouth to answer, but snapped it shut
before he croaked and embarrassed himself. What did
they have in common? Was she kidding? They fit perfectly, him inside her, her snuggled up against him in bed.
Heck, the woman had enough passion to light the skies
on fire. He'd never been with someone so instinctively
natural and . . . and . . . sexy. And she had no idea.

Elaine shook her head. "Okay, okay, so we have one
night of incredibly hot sex in common."

Yeah, you know it. Craig's chest swelled with the knowledge that he'd given her as much pleasure as she'd given
him. When he looked down, he realized not only had his
chest swelled, but his neck swelled too. He opened his
mouth and belched out a loud croak.

"You know, Todd, I think you're right." She crossed her
arms over her chest.

Huh? All he'd done was croak. How right could he be?

"Being with Craig makes about as much sense as a dog
keeping a pet frog. Last night was a mistake." She paced
across the room, tapping a fingernail to her bottom lip.
"Maybe I'm just on the rebound from Brian."

Rebound? If last night was rebound material, he deserved to be a frog forever. No way all that passion was in
response to being dumped by another man. No way.

Elaine spun and pinned Dawg with a direct gaze, then
transferred her attention to the frog beside him. "Perhaps
if I invite Brian to Bayou Miste next weekend, I'll see how
much more suitable he is for me and I'll get young Mr.
Thibodeaux out of my system."

Next weekend? Her ex-boyfriend was coming next

weekend? Craig tapped his webbed foot and steamed through his leathery skin. All this time he'd worried he was going to break Elaine's heart, she'd been in love with another man. A man who'd dumped her and now wanted her back. How could she be so willing to take the creep back? She'd cried the day before, for Pete's sake.

"In the meantime, I have work to do. I don't have time to worry about my love life. If I'm going to make a difference in the swamp, I'd better get cracking." She knelt beside the dog and Craig. While she ruffled Dawg's neck, she gazed down at Craig and chucked a finger beneath his green chin. "Can't have all your cousins getting sick out there and dying because some idiot is dumping pollution into the water."

She plowed back into her work with a vengeance, barely looking up for more than a minute until the sun disappeared behind the treetops on its descent to the horizon.

Throughout the rest of the afternoon and early evening, Craig watched for a chance to escape the tiny cottage, but Elaine got so wrapped up in her work, she even forgot to put out Dawg. And the lazy canine stretched out on the braided rug in front of the couch, completely content to sleep the day away.

As the sun crept out of the sky, Craig grew increasingly nervous. If he didn't get out of the house quickly, he'd transform in front of Elaine. He couldn't afford to do that. If she was the one, she couldn't know about his condition.

Was she still a valid candidate to solve his problem? If her ex-boyfriend showed up, would she go willingly into his arms? A heavy weight settled on Craig's chest, and he fought to shake it.

He glanced at Elaine. What idiot would think she was

rigid? The woman was completely uninhibited in bed. Knowing what he knew about her zeal for lovemaking only made him hot.

She stood in front of her microscope, the floral dress brushing her calves, her delicate ankles peeking from beneath the hem. For the past four hours, she'd sliced, prepped and studied the specimens, making notes in a journal beside her.

Elaine displayed passion not only in bed, but also in her work. She cared about finding the source of the pollutants and determining the damage such an infraction could have on the ecosystem of the swamp.

Craig stared at Elaine, her hair pulled back into a ponytail, her attention focused on the slide under the microscope. She had what he lacked.

Passion.

Passion to fight for a cause she believed in. Passion enough to challenge her crippling fears to discover the truth. Passion to root for the underdog—or underfrog, in this case.

And what did Craig have? A place in his family's law firm, defending clients with more money than brains, vindictive people who didn't care about anything or anyone but themselves.

People like himself.

The clock on the fireplace mantel rang eight times, piercing Craig's depressing musings. His body tensed, and he shot a glance to the clock and then to the window.

The sun hid behind the trees, sliding its way through the forest to the hidden horizon.

Damn! Only a few minutes stood between him and Elaine discovering the truth. He had to get out of the cottage and quick.

He bounced up and down on Dawg's floppy ear.

The dog twitched but didn't budge.

With a mighty leap, Craig hopped straight up in the air and came down on Dawg's forehead. *Time to wake up, boy.*

Dawg opened an eye, spotted Craig and thumped his tail against the floor.

Craig butted his head against the dog, trying to nudge him to his feet. *Come on boy, get up.*

The dog lumbered to all four feet, stretched and yawned his mouth so wide he whined.

"Hey Dawg." Elaine scribbled something in the journal, then looked up. "Nice to see you're still with the living. You slept so long, I thought maybe you were dead."

With another hop, Craig bumped into Dawg, hoping to steer him in the direction of the door.

But Dawg had other ideas. He trotted over to Elaine, sat down and stared up at her with his soulful brown eyes.

She reached down to pat the dog's head. "Did you work up an appetite, sleeping for so long?"

Woof!

"I'll take that as a yes. Come on, I've got some leftover lunch meat." She led the way into the kitchen.

The dog followed her without a backward glance at Craig.

Traitor.

What was he going to do? His little heart pattered hard against his chest. His damp clothes were in the washer in the kitchen, with Elaine.

Craig's ears rang and his skin tingled. Uh oh. He shook so hard he swayed, the tremors moving from the tip of his nose to all four feet. Damn, the change was happening. With three giant jumps, he landed just inside the bedroom door before the transformation gripped him.

His bones and skin stretched, the chemicals in his body

burning like billions of miniature electrical shocks. Slowly his body unfolded, reshaping until he stood tall and straight.

The room tilted. Craig braced his feet and turned to stare across the room at the mirror on the wall. He was back. Thank God.

Knocking sounded at the front door, jerking him out of his muzzy-headed state. Who the hell was visiting Elaine after dark? He ran for the bathroom and snatched a towel to wrap around his waist.

"Do you think it might be Craig coming back for his clothes?" Elaine hurried past the open bedroom door, Dawg close at her heels.

Did her voice sound eager or nervous? He wondered if she regretted their romp in the sack.

Craig hid behind the bedroom door and waited to see who it was. He'd watch for a chance to use this distraction to make good his escape.

Elaine opened the front door. Mo filled the entry, his broad shoulders seeming to stretch from one side of the doorframe to the other. He wore his factory work clothes, but his shirt hung loose from the waistband. With a shy smile, he stuck out his hand. "Hi, I'm Maurice Saulnier. You don't know me, but I'm a friend of Craig Thibodeaux. Do you know where dat boy be?"

What the heck was Mo doing here? Craig needed to leave, but his curiosity got the better of him, and he leaned closer, straining to hear and see.

With her back to Craig, Elaine shrugged. "Actually, I don't. But I expect we'll go out on the swamp again tonight. Do you want me to give him a message?"

"*Oui*, tell him to come see his old friend Mo."

"Is it an emergency?" Elaine's voice was polite and inquisitive.

"I guess in some ways dat what it be."

"Anything I can help with?" She leaned toward Mo and placed a hand on his arm.

"Just tell him I arrange him a date with DeeDee DuBois for tonight. She'll be waiting at Catfish Haven at nine."

Elaine's back stiffened. "Oh."

Craig cringed. *Thanks, Mo. You have the insight of a moose.*

"I have de night shift at de factory, otherwise I'd tell him myself."

"I understand." Her voice sounded strained.

If Craig had entertained ideas of showing up naked in Elaine's room and picking up where they left off the night before, he squashed those ideas now. Some serious damage control had to be done in the wake of Hurricane Mo.

The big Cajun clod backed away from the doorway. Elaine followed him out on the porch, with Dawg close at her heels.

While Mo and Elaine stood outside the front door, Craig found his shoes in a corner and slipped them on. He snuck around the bedroom door and dashed for the back kitchen entry. No time to grab his clothes, the towel would have to do.

With all the speed of a hurdle jumper in Olympic competition, Craig flew through the backyards of the neighboring houses, hell-bent for the bait shop.

As he passed the house next door, he spied Mozelle Reneau sweeping off her back porch. She stopped and stared out at him, her mouth dropping open.

Heat burned up his neck to his cheeks. Heck, what did you say to an old woman when you streaked by her in nothing but a towel? "Hi, Ms. Reneau!"

"Craig, what do you think you're doing, running around in nothing more than your birthday suit?"

"Can't talk now," he yelled, leaping over her azaleas into the next backyard.

He didn't slow down or look back, but he heard Mozelle's exclamation, "Good Lord! What's the world a-comin' to?"

When he finally stood in the safety of the little room off the back of the bait shop, Craig hauled in deep breaths. The situation had reached the point of ridiculous.

He had to find someone to love him, and soon, or he'd go stark-raving mad. Perhaps a date with DeeDee DuBois would be the trick. Surely, she would be desperate enough to fall in love with him on sight.

Climbing into a clean pair of jeans, Craig paused. A vision of Elaine asleep that morning, her hair spread against the pillow, her mouth full and tender from a night's kissing, plagued his mind.

Get over it. She's not your type.

Elaine Smith was out of the question. The idea of breaking her heart made his own chest ache.

CHAPTER FOURTEEN

So Craig had a date with DeeDee DuBois. Elaine shouldn't have been so surprised. He'd told her he wasn't the commitment type. And she more or less said she didn't care. Then why did she feel so rotten?

Elaine sat at the Formica table, her hands curled around a cup of tea. Normally, she'd be heading over to the bait shop at this time, ready to go out on the swamp with Craig.

Given the circumstances, why bother? He had a date with DeeDee. That would take a couple hours at the least. If they didn't decide to have dessert at her place.

The knot of pain tightened in Elaine's belly. She pushed aside the tea and dropped her forehead to the table. Hopeless, that's what she was. Her track record with men stunk. She'd dated Brian for comfort level. With Craig, nothing about comfort entered her mind. He made her burn all over.

"Why am I such a fool?" She banged her forehead on the smooth, speckled tabletop.

A knock at the screen door made Elaine turn her head sideways against the table.

The screen opened and Craig stepped through, a perplexed look on his face. "Are you okay?"

Elaine jerked up her head, her cheeks flaming. "Who, me? Of course I'm okay. Why shouldn't I be?" *Just because you have a date with DeeDee shouldn't make me want to crawl under a rock.*

"I got worried when you didn't show up at the shop. Aren't we going out on the swamp tonight?"

The clock on the mantel chose that moment to bong nine times.

"Did your friend Maurice find you?" she asked.

"No."

"He dropped by here earlier with a message for you. He said you had a date with DeeDee DuBois at Catfish Haven. Shouldn't you be there by now?"

His lips curved upward and his oh-so-blue eyes twinkled. "I had the same message from DeeDee. I called and told her I had a prior engagement."

Sudden joy surged through Elaine's upper body. She quickly squelched it. Craig played the field. He was a ladies' man and she was only one of his ladies. The fact that he'd cancelled his date with DeeDee didn't mean anything.

Did it?

"If we're going, you better change. The mosquitoes would have a heyday on your body in that outfit." His gaze roamed over her shoulders and down to her legs.

Warmed by his perusal, Elaine averted her eyes. "I'll only be a minute." She leaped from her chair and dashed to the bedroom. After closing the door behind her, she collapsed against the wooden panel, her heart pounding in her chest. *He's here! He's here!*

Three feet in front of her stood the white iron bed they'd shared the night before, the sheets still tangled from their lovemaking. She hadn't been able to face making it after he disappeared that morning.

Now the sheets called to her and her braless breasts tingled against the fabric of her sundress. Wickedly sensual possibilities raced through her mind, and her breathing quickened. What would Craig do if she opened the door and invited him in for an encore?

But he hadn't come to make love. He'd come to take her back out on the swamp. No mention had been made of their passion-filled night. Elaine pressed a hand to her stomach.

Had what they'd shared meant nothing to him? She'd thought their passion magical. Didn't he? Had Craig been bored with her like Brian? As the ultimate failure hit her square between the eyes, tears welled. Good God, she was boring in bed! More than anything she wanted to run and hide. Just as she'd done to get away from Brian.

A single tear leaked out the corner of her eye and trailed down her cheek. When the lone droplet reached the edge of her chin and dripped on her hand, her foggy brain kicked into gear. *What the hell am I doing?* Was her spine made of swamp goo?

No.

Elaine scrubbed at the tear and straightened. She reminded herself why she'd come to this podunk town in the first place. Not to run away but to help solve the mystery of what was killing the swamp at Bayou Miste. Not, repeat, NOT to sleep with Craig. Her only logical course of action was to ignore the man completely.

With a decisive sweep of her arm, she stripped the sundress over her head and tossed it across the room. In a few efficient movements she'd slipped into jeans, a long-sleeved white blouse, socks and tennis shoes. Thus *fully* covered, she felt more equipped to face the incredibly hunky Cajun waiting to take her out for a little boat ride.

After a deep breath, she flung open the door, ready to march into battle.

Craig stood in the middle of the living room in his tight jeans, long-sleeved chambray shirt and a smile hot enough to initiate a core meltdown in her nuclear reactor.

The wind sucked out of her sails, Elaine almost ducked back into the bedroom. How could she avoid responding to him? No woman in her right mind could ignore such a perfect male specimen.

"Are you ready?" Elaine forced a flippant tone into her voice. "As far as I'm concerned, the sooner we get to the bed, the better."

A chuckle from Craig made Elaine reevaluate what she'd just said. Damn, she'd said 'bed'! Slow-burning fire moved up her neck into her cheeks. "Boat! I meant boat."

His nod and slightly curled lip didn't ease her embarrassment. Not only did he find her boring in bed, he thought she was funny to even suggest they jump back in the sack.

Mortified but determined, Elaine grabbed her bucket, nets and satchel and stomped to the door. When he didn't follow, she turned back with one eyebrow quirked up. "Well, are we going or not?"

His lips widened into a full-fledged laughing grin. "We go, *chère*."

Elaine charged ahead two feet in front of Craig. As she passed Ms. Reneau's house, the old woman stuck her head out the door and shouted, "Watch out for that pervert, Elaine. He's up to no good. I can tell you that. I'm gonna have a good long talk with that uncle of yours, Craig." She waved her fist at him and ducked back inside.

Elaine slowed and looked at Craig, then back at the empty porch. "What's that all about?"

He shrugged and spread his hands wide. "I have no idea. None whatsoever."

A sideways glance at his slightly guilty expression confirmed he lied. Typical male.

Still angry and with no really good reason, Elaine clung to her ire, choosing to walk several feet in front of Craig all the way to the dock. Once her feet hit the boardwalk, she stopped and stepped aside to let Craig lead the way. Anger could be carried too far. No need in setting herself up for a fall into the water.

When they sat safely ensconced in the skiff, Elaine realized she wasn't as petrified of the boat or the water as the first day. Instead of sitting on the bench seat facing Craig as she usually did, she turned her back to him and watched where they were going. As they slid through the murky swamps, the gentle breeze stirred by their progress caressed her face.

She closed her eyes and imagined Craig's fingers curling around her jawline and down her neck.

"Duck."

Elaine opened her eyes in time to see the willow branch laden with Spanish moss. Dodging to the left, she avoided being slapped in the face. Not until they cleared the overhang and entered the polluted lagoon did she see a light gleaming from the bow of a much larger deck boat. Two men wrestled a barrel to the edge and shoved it over.

Elaine leaned back and placed her hand on his leg. "Craig, there's someone out there," she whispered.

As the barrel sank into the water, so did the realization of what she'd just witnessed. "Ohmigod!" She clapped a hand to her cheek. "These are the guys polluting the swamp."

Just then, one of the men looked up and spotted their little boat. He turned to his partner and pointed in their direction.

Craig swung the skiff in a tight circle.

"Where are you going? We have to stop them!"

"No, we have to get the hell out of here before they dump us in with that last barrel."

Elaine glanced back at the deck boat. One man jumped into the driver's seat and revved the engine. The other slid in next to him. The boat swung around and aimed for the tiny skiff.

"Hurry, Craig," Elaine shouted. "Oh no! They're coming straight for us!"

"Keep your head low. They might have guns."

Her eyes widened as the boat gained on them. "Would they shoot at us?"

A popping sound penetrated the steady hum of the motor.

"Get down!" Craig yelled.

Elaine bent double, her heart in her throat. "What are we going to do?"

"Do you think you can flip the switch on the front light?"

"I can try." Elaine dropped to her hands and knees on the floor of the skiff and inched forward, swaying with every sweeping turn. Cool water soaked through her jeans, chilling her until her teeth clattered together. When

179

she made it to the front of the boat, she ran trembling fingers up the metal pole until she encountered the switch. *Click.* The light went out.

Craig flipped the switch on the back light, plunging them into darkness.

"We don't stand a chance of outrunning them," he shouted over the whine of their overburdened motor and the quickly approaching deck boat. "We have to find a place to hide."

Meager moonlight trickled through the dense canopy. Elaine strained to make out what was ahead, wondering how Craig could see enough to steer.

A branch loomed in front of her and she leaned sideways. "Duck!" she shouted.

Elaine hoped the little branch would be more of a hindrance to a much larger vessel. She glanced back to see if their pursuers would slow.

The deck boat, lights a-blazin', blasted through the leaves.

Craig steered the skiff into a smaller waterway. Elaine kept a close eye on what lay ahead to keep from getting knocked from the craft, while glancing back to gauge the distance between them and the gun-toting villains on the deck boat.

As the channels narrowed, the deck boat slowed. Several gunshots cracked the air. Something whizzed by Elaine's ear and hit the water a few feet away.

"Get on the bottom of the boat. Now!" Craig shouted.

With her heart pounding in her throat, Elaine dove for the floor, bumping her knee on the bucket. "But what about—"

Another shot rang out.

Craig's arm jerked off the tiller and the skiff wallowed to a stop.

Why was he slowing? A glance behind them sent her heart skittering down into her stomach. "They're getting closer!"

Craig grunted and shifted to the other side of the bench seat. With his other hand, he grasped the handle, gunned the motor, and whipped the skiff around a bend in the maze of islands. Trees blocked them from the deck boat's view, but Craig didn't let up speed until they could no longer hear or see the light from the other craft.

Uncomfortable against the metal ribs and rivets, Elaine lifted her head and peered behind them. No deck boat, no villains shooting bullets their way. She swiveled to look ahead.

The skiff angled slowly for what looked like a willow tree. Before she could open her mouth to cry out, the bow parted the slender leaves and they entered a natural grotto. The leaves fell back in place behind them, blocking out the meager light from the moon.

Craig cut the engine and the skiff drifted to a stop.

Elaine sat up in the bottom of the boat, feeling around like a blind man for the bench seat. "Do you think we're safe?" she whispered.

No answer.

With her eyes opened wide to let in any light whatsoever, she spotted his outline hunched at the rear of the boat. "Craig?"

He shifted and muttered, "Damn."

"What's wrong?"

"Nothing." A grunt gave lie to his words.

"Yeah, right." Elaine hauled herself up to the bench next to him and felt her way up to his shoulders.

Elaine's right hand connected with something warm and sticky.

Craig flinched.

"You're wounded!" Her heart threatened to choke off her air supply. Geez, those goons may have killed him. A heavy weight settled in her chest and she scrambled to find the light.

Craig gritted his teeth to keep from groaning. His shoulder burned like the devil. "It's nothing. The bullet grazed me. I'll be fine."

The back light flashed to life. The reflection off the water bounced against the canopy of leaves transforming the grotto into a greenish-yellow cocoon.

When Elaine turned, her face blanched and her eyes rounded. "Ohmigosh."

"Really, it looks worse than it is. The bullet grazed the skin." He flexed his arm, wincing again at the pain. "No damage to the muscles or bones."

"Let me get a better look." With shaking hands, she unbuttoned the chambray shirt and gently pushed it over his damaged shoulder. "You're right. It just grazed the skin; however, we need to stop the bleeding. Did you bring any towels?"

"Use the knife in the tackle box to rip off a piece of my shirt."

Elaine dove for the box next to his feet and surfaced with the knife. Instead of cutting into his shirt, she pulled her shirttails from the waistband of her jeans and unbuttoned the front. Thinking she'd take a piece off the bottom, Craig was surprised when she slipped the whole shirt over her shoulders and held it in her lap. Dressed only in a lacy white bra and jeans, Elaine sliced through the fabric of her blouse.

Craig gulped and tried not to stare at her full, rounded breasts. Breasts he'd nibbled on the night before. "Careful with that thing. I use it for filleting fish. It's sharp."

"Hush and let me take care of you." Grabbing the sides

of the sliced blouse, she ripped it in two. With a few quick movements, she slit and cut it again into a smaller piece. Then she folded the corners of the smaller square and pressed it against the wound.

His wince drew an apologetic smile from her. "Can you hold this and apply pressure while I make a strap to hold the bandage in place?"

With his tongue too dry to articulate, Craig reached up with his good hand. She guided his fingers into place, and then bent to the task of cutting the rest of the shirt.

Armed with a long strip of cotton material, Elaine wrapped the makeshift bandage over his shoulder and under his arm.

When she circled around the back of his shoulder, her breasts pressed firmly to his chest and her hair brushed against his cheek. Craig inhaled her fragrant floral scent. Blood pumped through his veins to the rhythm of voodoo drums.

Wow, I must not be that badly injured if I can't keep my mind—and hands!—off Elaine.

Once she'd knotted the strip over the wound, Elaine started to lean back.

But Craig caught her bare back with his good hand and pulled her against his chest. "*Mon Dieu*, you drive me wild, woman."

She made a pitiful attempt at pushing against him. "Craig, you're in no shape to do anything."

"I'd happily bleed to death." His mouth closed over hers, his tongue pushing past her teeth to deepen the kiss.

The silky lace of her bra tugged at the hairs on his chest. Craig found the back clasp, and he worked the hooks free. With slow deliberate movements, he slid his fingers under the strap and slid it from one shoulder, then the other, freeing both her breasts.

With a groan, he tried to bend to take a rosy tip into his mouth, but pain shot through his shoulder. "Ow!"

Elaine backed away and stared into his face. "We can't do this."

"The hell we can't." He grabbed her wrist and pulled her over to sit in his lap, bringing her breasts within lip range. "Ummmm." He kissed a peaked aureole. "Better."

Her fingers laced through his hair and pressed him closer. "I didn't think you found me attractive," she said between several breathy gasps.

Craig stopped short of sucking her breast fully into his mouth and lifted his head. "Come again?"

Cheeks aflame, she muttered, "Nothing," and tugged his head downward.

"Not find you attractive?" He leaned away and stared down at her body. Her thigh pressed hard against his crotch, the warmth fueling deeper fires within. "Are you out of your mind? What's not to love?" Had he really spoken the "L" word? Did she notice? Craig stole a glance at her face.

Her brows furrowed. Not a good sign.

How could he gracefully take it back?

"If you don't find me incredibly hideous, why did you leave before morning?"

Oh geez, she'd blamed herself for his ducking out. He wanted to tell her he'd been with her all day, but he couldn't. Craig thought quickly. "What would Ms. Reneau say if she saw me sneaking out of your house early in the morning?"

"I don't care what Ms. Reneau says. I do, however, care what you think." She looked away, biting her lip. "I think."

His heart warmed. "Well, I care what Ms. Reneau

thinks. She can be . . ." He paused for the right word. "Well . . . determined when she thinks you're doing wrong."

Elaine smiled and traced a finger across his lower lip. "And you've had occasion where she thought you were in the wrong?"

"Once or twice." With a swift move, Craig snagged her finger with his teeth and sucked it into his mouth.

"Can't be all bad. You survived. Therefore, I'll take my chances." Elaine plucked her finger from his lips and leaned down to press a kiss to his temple. Then she guided his mouth back to her breast.

With a sigh of relief, he pulled her nipple between his teeth and flicked his tongue over the puckered tip. Oh, how good she tasted. Thank goodness she hadn't probed further into his "L" word slip. Unsure how he really felt, he didn't want to discuss it.

Craig transferred his attention to the other breast. He'd just kissed it when Elaine twitched.

Then she jerked her head and twitched again. "Um, Craig?"

"Yes, darlin'," he answered, his focus on the luscious mound in front of him.

"I think the mosquitoes found me."

Later that night, Craig slipped into his jeans and bent to kiss Elaine. He paused when the meager glow of the half-moon shone through the cottage window.

The bluish light caressed her pale cheeks, highlighting an errant curl that lay across her jaw and lips.

When Craig smoothed the strand behind her ear, Elaine turned her face into his hand and moaned softly, a fraction of the sound she'd emitted a few short hours before. She stretched her arm across the bed, the sheet shifting to reveal a full, creamy breast.

Craig's groin tightened and he reached for the zipper on his jeans. He wanted to rejoin her in the bed for one more moment in her arms and between her silky thighs.

The clock in the living room chimed the hour. Six o'clock. If he didn't hurry, the sun would rise and he'd be nothing more than a frog to this woman. Sweeping low, he pressed his lips to hers in a gentle kiss. With a final glance, he slipped out the back door and stole silently through the predawn shadows.

The little room at the back of the bait shop felt smaller and more confined than he remembered, the single bed a far cry from the comfort of Elaine's. He'd never been concerned over his sleeping arrangements before.

Pink and orange fingers of light shot through the dense undergrowth of trees as the sun crested the horizon.

Craig's vision blurred and he dropped to the floor, his transformation begun.

CHAPTER FIFTEEN

The lingering scent of Craig's aftershave assailed Elaine's senses, lifting her from her dreams. *Ummmm.* She smiled and sat up, letting the sheet fall to her waist. The cool morning air soothed her skin, tender from hours of lovemaking.

Craig Thibodeaux was fast becoming a very addictive stimulant. Although she knew he'd be gone, she couldn't help scanning the room, just in case. Disappointment tainted the sunshine streaming into her window, but she hugged the night's passions close, recalling in vivid detail—

A knock sounded at the front door, jarring Elaine from her recollection. Who the heck would be at her door at . . . a glance at the clock revealed she'd slept past noon. Not in the mood for guests, she flopped back down and buried her face deep in the pillow, pushing the sides up to cover her ears.

The knocking only grew louder.

So much for basking in the morning afterglow.

With an impatient jerk, Elaine tossed the sheets aside and swung her legs to the floor.

Persistent pounding reverberated through the house and her head. She had no choice but to slip into slacks and a T-shirt. By the fifth round of pounding, Elaine catapulted from mild annoyance to outright anger. She grasped the door handle and yanked it open. "Where's the fire . . . ?" The last word trailed off when her gaze collided with the Cajun siren standing with a hand on her hip.

The female was every woman's nightmare. Creamy mocha-colored skin radiated youth and vitality. Midnight-black hair fell in loose waves down to the middle of her back. A petite body sported perfectly proportioned breasts, a tiny waist and a smoothly rounded bottom.

The young woman wore a black leather miniskirt with silver chains looped low on the front, and a black tube top barely covered her perky braless boobs. "Hi, I'm Lisa. Got any coffee?" Lisa pushed past Elaine and entered the little cottage.

What was it with people barging into her personal space? "Excuse me? Do I know you?" Elaine didn't bother disguising her irritation.

"No, we haven't met." Lisa's gaze panned the room and then returned to Elaine. "I just wanted to come over and meet the competition."

Like a loose shoe in a clothes dryer, Elaine's thoughts tumbled. "Competition for what?" She could picture a contestant runway at a Bayou Beauty Queen contest. She had better odds for winning an alligator toss or swamp-vine-swinging contest against this woman.

Lisa turned in the middle of the living room and raised an eyebrow. "Competition for Craig, of course."

Elaine's heart plummeted into her empty stomach.

She'd always known Craig was too good-looking to be a one-woman man. But to have one of his other conquests barge into her house smacked her in the gut.

Lisa and her perfect everything served as a grim reminder of the impermanence of Elaine's hold on Craig. How could she compete with Miss Cajun Princess, whose face and body could stop a ship? Elaine glanced down at her wrinkled clothes disguising any feminine curves beneath. Her body would only sink a ship with disappointment.

Coffee. She needed coffee. Elaine stumbled for the kitchen.

The sex kitten moved around the room, lightly touching books and equipment. "Are you from N'Awlins, too?"

"Yes." Elaine concentrated on scooping coffee grounds into the filter.

"That's where I'm going as soon as I can shake this place," she said, her tone more of a spoiled teenager than an adult.

"What about Craig? Aren't you going to hang around and see who he chooses?" Must be lack of caffeine. Did she really ask another woman, a complete stranger, that question?

"Craig?" Lisa's dark brows crinkled. "No use waiting around for him. He doesn't believe in commitment."

The Cajun beauty's matter-of-fact tone reinforced Elaine's observations of the day before. Why did someone else voicing the truth make her stomach muscles clench?

"I've known Craig for years," Lisa continued. "He likes playing the field. If you know what's good for you, you won't let yourself fall in love with the jerk."

"He's not a jerk." Despite Craig's disappearing act, Elaine didn't believe he deserved Lisa's name-calling.

189

"And I have no intention of falling for him. Even if I did, it wouldn't be any of your business."

The black-haired woman shrugged. "Did he tell you we went out?"

Elaine's heart bottomed out in her shoes. The man knew how to pick them.

"No? Tsk, tsk. He's such a naughty boy." The way Lisa said "naughty boy" made Craig sound like a sex offender.

In Elaine's case, he'd been anything but offensive. "Look, I don't know why you came over here, nor do I care. But I certainly don't want to hear any details about your relationship with Craig Thibodeaux. I'm not now, nor have I ever been in love with him."

Lisa's mouth curled upward on the corners, but the semblance of a smile didn't quite reach her eyes. "Oh, I'm not warning you or anything. I'm just saying it'll be a waste of time. The man is a confirmed bachelor. Women are nothing more than playthings."

Elaine knew everything Lisa said was true, but at some deeper, more hopeful level, she'd ignored reason. And although every logical cell in Elaine's body screamed for her to hold her tongue, emotion won out. "Did you ever think that maybe he hasn't found the right woman yet?"

Lisa's eyes narrowed. Her gaze ran the length of Elaine's body from the top of her frizzy brown hair to the tips of her unpolished toes. One of the Cajun woman's plucked eyebrows winged upward. "And you think you got what it takes to capture Craig's attention. Sweetie, if I couldn't keep him, what makes you think you will?"

She jutted her breasts out just a little more as if to emphasize her point. Then she tossed her glorious black mane over her shoulder and sauntered to the door. With her hand on the knob, she paused and glanced back. "Oh, I wouldn't mention this conversation to Craig. He doesn't like to talk about his old girlfriends with the girlfriend of the day."

Lisa's parting words left Elaine with a depressing image of thirty-two flavors of women at an ice cream shop. She stared at the door for several minutes after Lisa left. The magic of what she'd experienced with Craig the previous night seemed . . . tawdry now.

Lisa's words echoed in her mind. If the dark-haired Cajun beauty couldn't hold Craig's attention how could Elaine expect to? Yet as much as she tried to tell herself it didn't matter, she knew it really did. With Craig, she'd felt beautiful and accepted, not a geek to be laughed about later.

"You're not going to take any bunk from that bayou bimbo, are you?" Ms. Reneau stood framed in the screen door. "Mind if I come in?"

Elaine blinked and shook her head. "Please do."

"That girl's trouble." Mozelle turned to stare at Lisa climbing into a turquoise '67 Mustang convertible. "I said the same to Craig less than a week ago. But would he listen? No sirree. Went ahead and took her out, he did. What's this world a-comin' to? Young people disrespectin' their elders. Humph!"

Sadly, Mozelle's words served to confirm Lisa's claim. Craig had gone out with the Cajun vixen less than a week ago. Did he take her to bed, too?

The older woman stepped through the door and into the small cottage. She peered closely at Elaine before shaking her head. "You feelin' okay?" Mozelle placed the back of her hand against one of Elaine's cheeks. "No fever, but you don't look so good. What did Lisa say to you?"

Elaine looked away, unwilling to share her disappointment with her kind neighbor. "Nothing."

"Nothing, ha!" Ms. Reneau walked closer and lifted Elaine's hands. "She said hurtful things, didn't she?"

A traitorous tear snuck out the corner of Elaine's eye and trailed down her cheek. "I'm a geek. I'll never attract a man."

"No you're not. You're a very lovely and intelligent woman. Come here." Ms. Reneau pulled her into a tight hug.

It had been six years since Elaine's parents passed away . . . six lonely years without someone to hug her and tell her everything would be all right. With Ms. Reneau's arms wrapped around her, Elaine let the floodgates open and cried her heart out. She cried for all the years of trying to fit in. She cried for the death of her parents when she'd only been twenty and in the middle of her graduate degree. She even shed a tear for Brian's betrayal, but most of all she cried because she knew she didn't stand a snowball's chance in the bayou with Craig.

Ms. Reneau patted her back and whispered, "It'll be all right, honey. It'll be all right."

When the storm passed, Elaine lifted her head and sniffed. "I'm pathetic. I shouldn't feel so sorry for myself."

"You got every right to." Ms. Reneau pushed her back and stared into her eyes. "But there's no use wallowin'. Whatcha gonna do about it?"

"What can I do?" Elaine scrubbed a hand over her damp face.

"Fight for what you want." The older woman dropped her arms from Elaine's shoulders and planted her fists on her hips. "Iffn' you want Craig bad enough, ain't he worth fightin' for?"

"Craig?" Elaine blushed. "Who said anything about Craig?"

"Girl, it's written all over your face. You're crazy about the boy."

Elaine gasped, and her eyes widened. "Is it that obvious?"

"As plain as the nose on my face." Ms. Reneau crossed her eyes and stared down the length of her nose. "Why do you think Lisa felt threatened?"

A frown drew Elaine's eyebrows together. "Lisa . . . threatened? No, no, you've got that backwards."

Ms. Reneau's eyebrows rose. "Why would she come over here and feed you full of a bunch of hooey-balooey, if she didn't feel threatened by you?"

"I don't know. But she's so much more beautiful than I am. How could Craig possibly be interested in me? She's so sexy and perfect. I'm . . ." she stared down at her baggy T-shirt and frowned, ". . . just me, a scientist. I don't even know how to act like a girl."

"You don't?" Ms. Reneau tipped her head to the side and glanced toward the bedroom. "I'm not blind. I saw Craig sneakin' out of this house in the early morning hours on more than one occasion. If I'm not mistaken, he's more than a little interested."

"Yeah, but I'm not interesting enough to hold his attention. I don't have gorgeous hair like Lisa, and I don't even know how to flirt!" Elaine's shoulders slumped and she turned away.

"We can do something about the hair and I can help you with some tips on flirting."

"It won't help." Elaine's head drooped. "Once a geek, always a geek."

"Hmmph! That's no way to act." Mozelle touched a finger to Elaine's chin, lifting her face. "How did you get through all those degrees?"

Elaine's brows drew together. "What's my education got to do with this?"

"You didn't get through all that schoolin' by quittin' when the going got tough, did you?"

"No."

"You persevered and tried harder, didn't you?"

"Yes, but—"

Mozelle planted her hands on her hips. "No buts. You just have to set your mind on it and go after what you want. Iffn' that's Craig, you have to load your guns with the right ammunition."

"Huh?" Elaine blinked. "I don't understand."

Mozelle rolled her eyes. "Get your pocketbook and keys. You're drivin'."

"Where are we going?" Elaine grabbed her purse and car keys.

"You'll see."

Like a lamb to the slaughter, Elaine allowed Ms. Reneau to lead her out of the cottage and to her car. Once they were inside, Elaine turned to ask, "Where to?"

"There's a little shop in Morgan City with just what we need."

Not at all reassured by Mozelle's mysterious words, Elaine set the car in motion and pulled out of the driveway. She had plenty to do with her experiments, but she knew if she stayed at the cottage, she wouldn't be able to concentrate. Definitely a first. Elaine had always prided herself on her ability to focus on work, no matter what.

The dense foliage of southern Louisiana flashed by in a blur of green. Mozelle kept up a steady stream of chatter the entire way; about what, Elaine couldn't begin to remember.

When they reached the edge of Morgan City, Ms. Reneau pointed to a sign strangely fitting for the Atchafalaya basin. The background was a mixture of tiger stripes and jungle foliage with the words SHEAR SAFARI BEAUTY SALON looped across in vines.

Elaine stared at the establishment, her stomach knotting. Whenever she'd taken time to have her hair professionally styled, she'd felt even more inept. She'd walk away without a clue of how to recreate what the beautician had mastered. Within hours, her hair reverted back to the same unruly mop. "You have your hair done on safari?"

"No, but it's about time I started. One of my dearest friends works here and she's been after me for years to try something different."

"And you're going to do it on my account?" Elaine glanced at her with misgiving. "I don't know if I want to carry that kind of responsibility."

"Fooey! I'm responsible for my own actions and I choose to change. What about you?"

The gauntlet had been tossed to the ground. Would Elaine pick it up and rise to the challenge? Or would she wimp out and run back to hide behind her microscope?

Craig's blue eyes and the hard contours of his body seared through her memories. "It's not just about hair. What could he possibly see in me?"

"Honey, if you can't see it yourself, how do you expect him to see it?"

"Still, I don't know if I'm ready for radical change."

"Suit yourself, but I have a hair dye with my number on it. I'll see you inside." Mozelle jumped out of the car and strode into the little shop.

Which left Elaine sitting staring after her, feeling like the dinghy cut loose from the ship.

She was here, she might as well get a trim. Elaine got

out of the car before she could change her mind and shoved her keys into the bottom of her purse.

Then she hesitated and stared up at the jungle-printed sign. Did she really want to have her hair done by someone with jungles on her mind? What would she do? Blow it up with an elephant gun?

Elaine raised a hand to her ponytail. What was the worse they could do? Her hair couldn't look any less attractive than it did already. Could it? She was entirely too consumed by her own appearance. Her mind should be on the task at hand.

What was she doing, anyway? *Reacting to the threat of a beautiful woman who'd once had Craig's attention. That's what.* Oh, and like a new hairstyle would improve her chances with the man? Was she out of her mind? Out of her league, yes, but did she have to lose her marbles as well?

Elaine spun to unlock her car door.

"Oh, don't leave! We get so few visitors in this town, I'd do your hair for free just for the practice!" The sweet southern drawl called out from the glass doorway of the salon.

Heat suffused Elaine's cheeks and she turned toward a young woman with big, bleached-blond hair. "I changed my mind."

"Well, change it again, honey!" The woman's voice was pleading and welcoming, all wrapped up in a friendly smile.

Elaine hesitated. "I don't think . . ."

"That's just it. You're not supposed to think when you go to the salon. You're supposed to relax and leave the thinking to the pros."

Accustomed to using her brain all day long, Elaine couldn't string two coherent thoughts together to make a sensible protest. Why not let someone else do the thinking?

On second thought, the blonde's bleached tresses and thick makeup didn't instill confidence in Elaine. Why would someone wear her hair poofed out so big? Having battled natural curl all her life, Elaine couldn't imagine anyone *wanting* big hair. The woman's short leopard-print skirt and black tube top hardly seemed appropriate for daytime attire. No, this was a really bad idea.

The beautician stepped out and hooked her arm through Elaine's, giving her no choice but to follow. "Come on, I promise not to do anything drastic. A cut and maybe some highlights. That's all."

The pungent scent of perm solution and hairspray assailed Elaine's senses the moment she set foot in the salon.

"Mirna Mae, look what I got!" the blonde yelled across the room.

A thin, older woman of indeterminate age, probably in her fifties, stood behind a black vinyl chair, brushing the tangles out of Mozelle's brassy honey-colored hair. Mirna raised her arms in a touchdown motion. "Wooohooo! Way to go, Josie! Got yerself a live one."

"What's yer name, honey?" Josie propelled her toward a chair.

"Elaine."

"Aren't you the scientist been goin' fishin' with Craig?"

Elaine nodded, not at all excited about discussing Craig with yet another woman, especially after Lisa's visit. She just wanted her hair done. No questions asked.

Josie sighed. "Girl, what I wouldn't give to be in yer shoes."

"If I were twenty years younger, I'd take a crack at him myself," Mirna Mae, in a skintight leopard-print jumpsuit and wrinkles camouflaged in five coats of base makeup, called out. She led Mozelle to a sink in the back.

Elaine knew she'd made a mistake. Her hair was fine the way it was. She leaned forward to get up, but a hand pressed her firmly back against the black vinyl.

Trapped, her heart kicked up its pace into pre-panic mode, similar to the way she felt around water. In a salon filled with other women, she recognized she was in way over her head. Beauty shops were for girly girls, the ones who spent hours at the mirror fussing with makeup or hair. Such machinations were a complete mystery to Elaine. No, salons were not for serious scientists or social outcasts like herself.

Josie turned her to face the mirror and pulled out her ponytail. With deft fingers, she fluffed the long strands out and around Elaine's shoulders. "You've got a lot of lovely natural curl."

Elaine's eyebrows rose, and she stared at Josie's reflection in the mirror. "Kinky, curly, unruly mop would better describe it. My hair is hopeless. I should just shave it."

The bottled blonde's eyes widened. "Are you kidding? I have a dozen clients who'd give their left breast for hair like yours. Right, Mirna Mae?"

"Both breasts." Mirna Mae shut off the water and slung a towel over Mozelle's hair. "Wouldn't you give both breasts to have Elaine's hair, Mozie?"

Mozie sat up in the shampoo chair and nodded across at Elaine. "In a New Orleans minute."

Elaine heaved a sighed. "Is there any hope of taming the beast?"

Josie glanced up and smiled. "What? Your hair or Craig?"

Warmth spread up Elaine's cheeks into her hairline. "My hair, of course. I have no interest in Mr. Thibodeaux."

"In that case, the hair is doable." Josie fit a plastic cape around Elaine's neck and Velcroed it snugly against her skin. "The man is an entirely different matter."

"You got that right," Mirna Mae agreed.

"Come on." Josie grabbed Elaine's elbow and urged her out of the chair. "It's off to the shampoo bowl for you."

Mirna Mae switched on a blow-dryer, aiming it at Mozelle's hair. The noise drowned out any chance of small talk. Thank goodness.

With the spray of water sprinkling her forehead and the cool porcelain sink against the back of her neck, Elaine relaxed. Josie hadn't brought up the subject of Craig during the entire shampooing process. Maybe she wouldn't discuss him for the rest of the makeover.

Fat chance.

The blond beautician draped a towel over Elaine's hair and patted it dry. "I useta have the biggest crush on Craig Thibodeaux when I was thirteen." She smiled dreamily and her tone held a hint of nostalgia. "With that coal-black hair and ice-blue eyes, he was a god a girl could easily sacrifice her virginity to."

"Did you?" Elaine could have slit her own throat as soon as the words popped out of her mouth. What had she been thinking to utter such a personal question? Perhaps the flash of jealousy scorching her veins had a little to do with her outburst.

"Oh heavens no." Josie led Elaine back to the swivel chair and pulled the towel from her hair. "He was my big brother Larry's best friend. Larry threatened to tell Mom if I so much as flirted with him." She sighed. "But he couldn't stop me from dreamin'."

Yeah, Elaine had had a few of those dreams herself. Some of which weren't only dreams. *Think ice. Think ice.*

She concentrated on quelling the rising warmth in her belly and face. Revealing her current relationship with Craig to this woman was no way to win friends in this part of the state, as evidenced by Lisa's little visit.

Josie checked the labels on several cans on the counter and lifted one marked *conditioner*. With a flick of her wrist, she sprayed a liberal dose into Elaine's hair. "You know what's crazy?"

Elaine shook her head rather than answer. She could pick any number of crazy things that had occurred lately.

"After all those years of tellin' me to back off Craig, recently Larry's been pushin' me to go out with him. Makes me wonder what he's up to."

Elaine watched her own brows draw downward. Her fingernails flexed against the arms of the chair. She knew she had no hold on Craig. But this was the second woman in the past two hours to talk about going after Craig. Craig, the man she'd slept with for two nights straight!

"I don't know what's got into that boy." Josie set the can on the table and ran her fingers through Elaine's hair. "Maybe he figures I'm all grown up now and Craig's a mighty fine catch, after all. What do you think, Mirna Mae? Should I go for him?" Josie never looked up, just kept on smoothing conditioner through Elaine's hair.

Elaine held her breath. Whether or not the beautician went after Craig shouldn't bother her in the least. Hadn't she told Craig his lack of commitment wasn't a problem with her?

Then why did it suddenly feel like a problem?

Josie sighed and stepped in front of Elaine to examine the front of her hair. "A guy like that could break a girl's heart in a wink of one of his baby blues."

Tell me about it. Elaine feared she was halfway there already.

"You should go for him," Mirna Mae said, spraying a layer of hairspray across Mozelle's growing web of tangles and curls.

Mozelle shoved an elbow into Mirna Mae's side. "Iffn' she don't care for the boy anymore, don't go puttin' ideas into her head."

"Do that again, and I'll shave you bald!" Mirna Mae rubbed her side and glared at Mozelle.

"Even if I decided to go after him, Craig's way out of my league." The blond beautician finished applying conditioner to Elaine's hair.

Craig was out of Josie's league? Elaine couldn't stop herself. "Why?"

Josie plunked a fist on her hip, staring into the mirror at Elaine. "I'm a small-town girl. What could he possibly see in me when he has high-powered women fallin' all over themselves to catch his eye?"

Elaine looked around the shop and out through the window. What high-powered women? "Around here?"

Mozelle answered before Josie, "Yes." She seemed eager to change the subject. "Josie, you're young and date a lot. What do girls do nowadays to snag a man's attention?"

"Why, Mozelle?" Josie's eyebrows rose high on her forehead. "You thinkin' of going on the prowl?"

"Maybe I am, maybe I'm not, but that's neither here nor there." She motioned her head toward them and said, "Elaine's got a hankerin' for one of the local boys and hasn't had much practice in man-catchin'. Seein' as you've had plenty—practice, that is—you'd be the best coach to teach her."

"Oh really? Which boy?" Josie's hand paused en route to the wire brush caddy.

Elaine wished she could sink through the floor. How embarrassing to have your social limitations aired in front of complete strangers. And she couldn't tell Josie she had the hots for Craig, not after all the blonde had said of her dreams about the man. "I'd ... rather not say."

Josie began to comb Elaine's wet hair, parting the wet waves into sections, and then twisting the long strands and pinning them out of the way. She pulled the bottom layer of hair as straight as the curly tresses would allow, and lifted a strand, pulling it tight. "Since you won't fess up on who, I won't be able to give you specific pointers. But there are a few techniques sure to attract any red-blooded, heterosexual male." With a crisp, clean stroke, Josie snipped off three inches of hair.

When the curls fell to the floor, Elaine barely noticed. Having grown up too smart to fit in with kids her own age, she'd missed the much-needed education only peers could provide. She listened with interest to what the younger girl had to say.

"You got all the right equipment." Josie snipped her way across the bottom layer. Then she unclipped a section, letting it fall over the shorter strands. "You just need to package it properly and display it to your best advantage. I learned that in beauty school."

Great. That advice was real useful. Elaine still didn't have a clue. "How?"

Josie removed another clip and cut her way through more curls. "We're doin' it right now. A new 'do will go a long way toward instillin' confidence and sex appeal."

"Yeah, but surely looking good isn't enough to sustain a relationship."

"No, but you can hardly get one started if he doesn't even see you. And if you don't have some kind of sex appeal, you're not going to hold his attention for long. Maybe only long enough for a quickie in the sack."

Damn. Elaine blushed again. Why couldn't she control the chemical reactions in her body?

Josie had a way of zapping to the core. Her words struck entirely too close to home for Elaine. Was she only a two-night stand with the Cajun sex god? Her heart dropped like a lead weight into her stomach. She glanced down at the shapeless smock she wore over khaki slacks and a plain white shirt. "I don't think I have what it takes."

"Horse-hockey!" Mozelle shouted from beneath Mirna Mae's attack with the back comb. "Listen to what Josie's got to say. She knows what she's talkin' about."

Mozelle's adamancy was infectious. Elaine could sit there and list all her faults or she could come up with a way to compensate. What did she have to lose? She glanced up apologetically and smiled. "You're the expert, what should I do?"

"You need a little makeup, a sexy outfit, and a great hairdo, of course. Then you need a few pointers on how to act to get and keep a man's attention. Let's start with knowing Your Man. Here's where you gotta do a little homework."

"Homework?"

"Yeah, you need to know a little about your man. What's his favorite sport and food? What does he do for a living? Occupation tells a lot about a man, his dreams and aspirations."

Elaine nodded, soaking it all in. So far, everything Josie said was common sense.

"Take Craig, for instance. I know a lot about him already on account he useta hang out at the house during the summers. If I wanted to go after him, which I'm still thinkin' about, I already know the basics. He's a lawyer, his favorite food is shrimp gumbo, he likes football, and the N'Awlins Saints are his favorite team."

One word jumped out of Josie's description, clunking against everything Elaine thought she knew about Craig. "He's a what?"

"Lawyer." Josie frowned and stared at Elaine in the mirror. "Didn't you know that?"

"I thought he worked for his uncle at the marina." Her head spun with this new bit of information.

"That's just him helpin' out. He useta spend his summer vacations with his Uncle Joe. Larry says he came to Bayou Miste to meet with Mr. Jason Littington on business."

Craig wasn't a small-town guy? Elaine's singed brain grappled with the revelation. "So you're saying he's only in town on business?"

"Yeah."

"Where does he normally live?"

"N'Awlins."

Elaine's heart turned flip-flops in her chest. Craig lived in the same city as she did. Their relationship didn't have to end when they left Bayou Miste. The flip-flops stilled. Craig considered her only a passing distraction. Hmmm . . .

"I'm surprised you didn't know all this. You two have been out on the swamp for the past few nights. What did you find to talk about?"

"Nothing much." What talking they'd done hadn't included a word about Craig's professional life. He'd led her to believe he was nothing more than a helper at his uncle's marina. The louse! Like the little silver ball in a pinball machine, Elaine's mind bounced between the joy of knowing Craig lived in New Orleans to the stunning knowledge he'd lied to her all along! *Ping. Ping. Ping.* Elaine massaged the bridge of her nose to still her ricocheting thoughts.

"Anyway. Back to lessons on love—Packaging 101." Josie dropped another section of hair and continued cutting. "You appear to have all the right equipment. You just need to package it in such a way as to knock a man on his butt. Honey, the khaki slacks have gotta go."

Elaine's hand dropped to her lap and she stared up at Josie. "They do?"

"Definitely. You could wear a brown paper bag with more appeal than those. What you need is something that's form-fitting and shows every curve to its advantage. I've got just the dress for you."

"Dress? But I work in a lab. Dresses aren't practical in a lab."

"Maybe not in a lab, but definitely at the Raccoon Saloon."

"Huh?" The confused frown between Elaine's brows seemed permanently etched in her skin. Josie's energy and thought processes left Elaine's head spinning. "You lost me."

"Tonight's ladies' night at the Raccoon Saloon. You're coming with me." Josie cocked an eyebrow at Mozelle. "You too, if you have enough gumption to crawl out of the bayou."

Mozelle stared over at Elaine, her eyes wide and considering. "I'll go if you go," she challenged. "Been needin' to get out for a long time." She stared up at the ceiling. "Been since 1991 that I last set foot in that place. I'm way past due for a night of foot-stompin' fun."

"What exactly is the Raccoon Saloon?" Elaine asked.

"Honey, it's only the most happenin' place in the basin on a Tuesday night. It's just outside of Bayou Miste, so it's close to home. All the guys come out on ladies night cause that's when the women put on their finest and strut their stuff."

"Strut?" Knots formed in Elaine's stomach. "I don't know how to strut."

"Girl, by the time I'm through, you'll have every man in the parish panting after you."

Elaine gasped. "I don't want every man's attention!"

"Honey chile, every single, able-bodied man will be there. Your man, whoever that might be, most likely will be there too. Which brings me to the next love lesson—Making Your Man Jealous."

"This is getting way too complicated."

"No, this is the easy part. All you gotta do is pay attention to someone else while your guy is watching."

"Isn't that duplicitous?" Elaine asked.

"I don't know about duplicitous but it gets a guy's blood boilin' if he's interested." Josie snipped one last time and stepped back to look at her handiwork. "Oh, my."

With the beautician standing between her and the mirror, Elaine couldn't tell what she meant. Her heart pounded in her ears as she expected the worst. "Is that a good 'oh, my' or a bad 'oh, my'?"

"Sometimes I amaze myself. Take a look, honey." Josie stepped out of the way.

In the mirror, a stranger stared back at her. Gone was the bush of hair spread in a V from the tip of her head to below her shoulders. In its place were soft, layered curls brushing the tip of her shoulders and providing a frame around her face. Elaine lifted a hand and actually ran her fingers through the tresses without getting hung up in snarls. "Wow."

"I don't think you need the highlights. Your own hair color is beautiful on its own. Wooo!" Josie fanned herself. "Look at me, talking a customer out of a paying job. I must have sniffed swamp gas."

"Probably all that hairspray I used on Ms. Mozelle." Mirna Mae stepped up and smiled. "Nice work, Josie.

Better watch out, Craig'll look twice at this one, and you'll have yourself a bit of competition, after all."

"Really, I'm not interested in Mr. Thibodeaux," Elaine insisted.

Josie shot a sly grin at Mirna Mae. "I think she doth protest too much."

"She's new in town; give her a break, Josie." Mozelle said.

"So are you with me or not?" Josie challenged, shooting a glance between Elaine and Mozelle.

"I'm in." Mozelle crossed the room to stand beside Elaine. "Well?"

"Oh, no." Elaine pulled the cape from her shoulders and stood. "I have too much to do."

"Come on." Josie turned her around and grabbed her hands. "You have to show off your hairdo. Lord knows I could use the advertisement. And you bein' new will be like a man magnet. All the guys will be clamberin' to meet you and maybe some of them will rub off on me."

"No, really, I can't." Elaine searched her brain for the perfect excuse. "I don't feel right borrowing a dress from you. You hardly know me."

"Fiddlesticks! I feel like we're old friends already." Josie pulled her toward the door. "Now get on home and take a long soak in the tub."

"But . . ."

"No buts. I'll be by at 8:30 with the dress. We'll have a great time. I guar-an-tee it."

Mozelle took over from Josie, taking Elaine's arm and pushing her out onto the sidewalk. The door closed and Elaine stood staring back through the glass window of the beauty salon.

Josie wiggled her fingers, smiled and then turned back

to Mirna Mae, pumping her arm with a sharp downward thrust. Even from outside, Elaine could hear Josie say, "Yes!"

Steamrolled. Elaine shook her head and tried to look at the bright side. Craig was a lawyer. Surely he wouldn't be caught dead in a rowdy establishment like the Raccoon Saloon. And maybe a night without Craig would prove to her she wasn't interested.

CHAPTER SIXTEEN

Throughout the day, as Craig slept beneath the bed, dreams plagued him. In them, his father repeatedly reminded him of his responsibility to carry on the family business. In the dream the words "it's your legacy" rang out over and over, until they were more of a chant intermingled with the beat of voodoo drums.

When Craig felt his brain would explode from the constant barrage, Elaine's voice could be heard as if in the distance, "We have to stop them. We have to do what's right."

Instantly the drums stilled and his father's voice faded. Craig relaxed and fell into a long, deep sleep.

When he awoke he lay facedown on a hardwood floor. Boards pressed against his back and dust bunnies tickled his nose.

Ah-choo! Ah-choo! Ah-choo! He banged his head against the solid object behind his head and swore.

"Craig, is that you back with the human race?" Uncle Joe called from another room.

Craig's eyes flew open and he glanced around. Where the hell . . . ? Oh yeah, he'd crawled under the bed to keep from being eaten or stepped on while he slept.

What had been a cavern of space to a frog was now a weight on his shoulders. Craig wriggled his way from beneath the bed, stood up and tried to brush the fuzzy stuff from his chest and other body hairs. He flexed his shoulders. The wound from the night before gave him a twinge, but seemed to be healing nicely.

"That scientist lady dropped by before dusk and said she wouldn't be goin' out on the swamp tonight." Uncle Joe stuck his head around the corner, got one glimpse of Craig's naked form and raised a single eyebrow. "You also got a couple friends out on the porch waiting for you. Might want to put on more than dust fuzzies before greetin' them." Uncle Joe chuckled and ducked back into the bait shop.

The pillow Craig lobbed through the air bounced off the door frame. "Funny, very funny." Craig grabbed a pair of jeans and a T-shirt from the antique dresser in the corner and slipped into them. Why had Elaine called off the night? He should be glad. Things were getting too hot and heavy for his liking. Elaine wouldn't understand when he went back to New Orleans and resumed his life as a scumbag attorney.

Whoa, where'd that thought come from? Scumbag attorney? The adjective was high-powered, not scumbag. Craig shook his head. The bayou was getting to him. Not a good sign.

So he didn't have to escort Elaine through the swamp. That left him with a night free to pursue other women in the hopes of finding a cure to his . . . er . . . problem. The whole voodoo thing still grated on his nerves. "This situation is impossible."

"Then do somethin' about it," Uncle Joe called out.

Craig walked barefoot through the bait shop and out onto the porch overlooking the dock. Night had settled in and flying insects danced around the light fixtures.

Mo lounged against the porch rail while Larry sat on a bench whittling a stick with the knife he kept strapped to his boot.

"Found you a female yet?" Larry asked without looking up.

"No." Craig leaned against a square pole.

"That's what we thought." Mo said, pushing away from the rail. "Put on your dancin' shoes. It's ladies' night at the Raccoon Saloon."

Even though he'd been thinking about going out to find a woman to break the spell, when it came right down to it, he really had no desire for a night on the town. "I don't feel much like dancin'."

Mo crossed his arms over his chest. "We're not takin' no for an answer. I don't much like havin' a frog for a friend."

"Like I enjoy being a frog?" Craig didn't like the way Mo assumed the same position he had a few days earlier when Madame LeBieu had issued her summons.

Larry sheathed his knife and stood. The two men each grabbed an elbow and marched him back through the bait shop.

"Come on guys. You don't have to rough me up again." He sighed. What choice did he have? "I'll go."

When they reached the back room, Mo and Larry dropped his arms and stood with their feet spread, determined looks on their faces.

"We wouldn't be doin' this if it wasn't for your own good," Larry said.

"Yeah. Just like the other night." Craig fished his deck shoes from beneath the bed and slipped into them.

"You'll need a nicer shirt, if you want to attract a nice-lookin' woman," Mo said. "Unless you prefer someone like DeeDee Dubois."

"And comb your hair," Larry added.

Great. Now he had Mo and Larry telling him how to dress.

Twenty minutes later, the four were on their way to the Raccoon Saloon to get the best table before the band cranked up at nine. Uncle Joe had volunteered to drive. By the amount of cologne his uncle wore, he'd planned on going with or without the trio. Craig elected to take his own car to provide a quick escape route if the evening turned out even half as depressing as he knew it would.

As they passed the little rental cottage, Craig could see the lights on inside. Elaine was home. He'd much rather be with her than out at a bar looking for another woman. Boy, he had it bad. If he didn't watch out, he'd find himself head over heels for the woman. Good thing he was a confirmed bachelor, although his confirmation had been slipping lately.

"I can't believe I let her talk me into this," Elaine muttered. The noise coming from the Raccoon Saloon was so loud, she could have shouted and no one would have heard her. She gave another tug at the miniscule dress and groaned.

"Don't you worry, sweetie, you look beautiful. You won't sit down once for all the dancin' you'll be doin'," Mozelle said on one side of her.

The ramshackle establishment appeared to be pieced together out of weathered boards, corrugated tin and aged advertisements. By the size and shape of it, the Raccoon Saloon had probably been an old barn at one time. Cars lined the parking lot and the music blared from beneath the eaves.

"Come on. I know one of the band members and if I hurry, I can get in a few requests." Josie rushed ahead, darting in the darkened doorway before Elaine could protest her desertion.

She should have known she was in big trouble when the beautician had come by earlier dressed in a hot pink micro-miniskirt and a pink and black polka-dotted Daisy Mae midriff shirt worn off the shoulder.

When she'd tossed an electric-blue swatch of stretchy fabric at her, Elaine caught it in one hand. "This looks like a sleeve; where's the rest of it?"

Josie's mouth quirked up on one side and she planted a fist on her hot-pink hip. "Honey, that's it. Now run along and pour yourself into it. The band starts at nine and I want to be there for the first dance."

Now she felt altogether too conspicuous in the barely-there blue piece of fabric. Half a dozen men had already whistled at her—and she hadn't even made it inside yet! She'd never been subjected to such lewd behavior before in her life.

Appalled at the familiarity, she felt a strange sense of power fill her gut and stiffen her spine. She flung back her newly cut hair and straightened her shoulders. This movement had the added benefit of pushing her chest out a little farther. She hoped the sleeve wouldn't slip down and expose the tight strapless bra Josie had seen fit to provide as well. It fit a little too tightly, pushing her boobs up higher to emphasize her already generous cleavage.

She could imagine the horror of her fellow professors

213

at Tulane if they could see her now. They'd have her fired on the spot.

But who knew her in Bayou Miste? Here, she could be anything she wanted to be and the thought was strangely exhilarating. That and the new 'do went a long way toward blocking one tall, dark-haired, blue-eyed Cajun from entering her mind.

When Mozelle and Elaine entered, the floor was already crowded with people dancing to a mix of Cajun and country-western tunes from the jukebox. Josie met them just inside the door and led them to the bar, where she grabbed them three stools with a good view.

Not two seconds after they sat, three dark-haired guys sauntered over and asked them to dance. Josie and Mozelle immediately slid off their stools and led their guys to the crowded dance floor.

Feeling suddenly shy, Elaine shook her head. "Not yet. I'd like to order a drink first." She smiled, hoping the big guy wouldn't push the issue.

Without a word, the man nodded and turned away.

Elaine swung around on the barstool and ordered white wine. "Make that two!" she said, on second thought. The little false bravado an alcohol buzz could provide was just what she needed.

The first glass of wine she swallowed in one long, steady chug. With the second glass in her hand, she turned back to the crowd. The song changed to a slow tune and half the couples left the floor. The other half swayed to the music. The band milled around on the stage, pushing equipment into position.

Elaine gazed at the couples locked in each other's arms as if they were the only ones on the dance floor. She found herself envious of them and wishing she had someone to hold her tight and make her feel that way. Little tingles reverberated from her insides to the outer layer of epidermis. The wine had the effect of giving a fuzzy halo effect to the bare bulbs hanging sporadically throughout the open room. She wasn't drunk, just mildly buzzed and a tad less inhibited.

The big guy from a few minutes earlier appeared in front of her. "You wanna dance now?" he asked.

Not nearly as concerned this time, Elaine nodded and slid from her stool. She remembered the slinky blue dress and tugged the hem down and the neckline up, to ensure the fabric covered all the right places. Then she threw back her shoulders and practiced one of the moves Josie had taught her earlier at the cottage. Swing your hips side to side. If she put one foot in front of the other, the swaying motion would be automatic.

Following the big brute, Elaine pasted a smile on her face and swayed. She caught a number of men looking her way, appreciative smiles on their faces.

Wow. Who knew Elaine Smith could attract so many admiring stares? *Brian, eat your heart out.*

Before Elaine had time to bask in the glory of her successful sauntering, the guy pulled her into his arms and snugly up to his barrel chest.

Elaine gasped and tried to pull away. "Please, I can't breathe."

"Oh, sorry." He loosened his hold only a little and snuggled his cheek against her hair. The man smelled of woods and tobacco and he held Elaine entirely too close for her comfort.

She was just trying to think up a good reason to excuse herself when the song ended. Thank goodness.

But the man showed no intention of letting go of her.

While the jukebox played, the band had completed setup. Most couples either split or drifted back to their seats, leaving Elaine and her bulky captor standing with only a few die-hard couples amid the sawdust. She tugged and tugged, but the guy wouldn't let go of her hand.

"The song is over," she said, since the idiot didn't quite grasp the obvious.

"Ah, come on. Just one more dance," he said, his grip tightening until Elaine felt her bones would crunch.

"There's no music," she insisted.

"Howdy y'all!" The lead singer shouted into the microphone, drowning out Elaine's protests. "Welcome to the Raccoon Saloon. We're the Ragin' Cajuns and the first song for the evening is "Devil with a Blue Dress," a request in honor of one of our guests tonight. Anyone care to give it a guess as to which one?"

Elaine groaned. Just what she needed, more attention and music when she couldn't get rid of the overgrown baboon clutching her hand.

"Really, my foot hurts." And it did from being stepped on several times. "I'm going to sit this one out." When he loosened his hold, Elaine quickly stepped away and glanced around, trying to get her bearings. This evening was turning out to be a huge mistake. How could she gracefully escape back to her safe little cottage?

Craig sat peeling the label off his longneck bottle, wondering for the hundredth time what the hell he was doing in the Raccoon Saloon. He hadn't made a single move to find a woman. Every time one came up to ask him to dance, he'd muttered something about not enough beer yet.

Mo, in a clumsy attempt at a two-step, danced by with a brassy redhead and stopped in front of Craig's table. "How 'bout dis one?" he asked.

Craig squelched a cringe and shook his head ever so slightly.

Larry waltzed by, completely out of step with the music and pumping his partner's arm up and down. The man really had no business on the dance floor. As he passed Craig, he shouted, "What about her?"

Craig ducked his head and continued peeling paper from the brown glass.

"Ain't gonna get any closer to findin' a cure for your spell by staring at yer beer, boy," Uncle Joe commented.

"Leave it, Uncle," Craig growled. His mind wandered back to his uncle's rental cottage. What was Elaine doing right now? Was she reviewing her notes from previous experiments? Or was she on the phone with her ex-fiancé? Craig tensed and almost left his seat to go find out.

He barely noticed when the song on the jukebox ended and didn't even look up when Jacque, the lead singer, called out for everyone's attention.

When the band started playing "Devil with a Blue Dress," Craig decided he'd had enough. He looked across the dance floor for an escape route. His gaze collided with an electric-blue dress and the desperate expression of the one woman who'd been on his mind all evening. Escape was no longer an option.

The strains of "Devil with a Blue Dress" registered in Craig's suddenly feeble brain. She was the devil for plaguing his every thought since he'd woken up. And she looked damned sexy in that dress.

Before he could engage logic, he was across the floor standing in front of her, eyeing her like an apparition that would easily disappear if he spoke. "Dance with me."

Elaine didn't protest or question his high-handedness; she just melted into his body.

He crushed her to his chest. God, she smelled good. Their bodies fit perfectly together on the dance floor just like they had in bed. Their moves were smooth and natural, a form of foreplay, igniting longing for a more intimate setting. "Why didn't you want to go out on the bayou tonight?" Craig whispered against her ear.

"Mmmmm . . . this is much better than swamp water and mosquitoes." She snuggled closer.

"Agreed." He shifted his knee between hers and pressed his thigh against her pelvis. "I like the dress. I barely recognized you."

"I'm glad you did."

"Me too," Craig replied. "And here I thought this evening was going to be an incredible bore."

"And now?"

"I'm completely enchanted."

"Big words for a dock hand," she said against his shirt. Her warm breath heated his chest.

"Us dock hands have hidden talents that would amaze the untrained skeptic."

Elaine lifted her head and stared up at him, her eyebrows rising into the short curling strands caressing her forehead and cheeks. "Or perhaps you dock hands aren't revealing the whole truth."

Craig frowned down at her. "What do you mean?" Did she know about his condition?

She stopped dancing and stood staring into his face. "I know your secret, Craig Thibodeaux."

His heart hammered in his chest. "But how?" If Elaine knew about the spell, she'd be out of the running to help cure him of Madame LeBieu's trickery. An empty, sick feeling spread through his chest and into his gut. Would he lose the chance to make Elaine love him? Did he want her to love him?

A sweaty, meaty hand clamped onto his shoulder, pulling him away from Elaine. "What the hell?" Craig spun to face his attacker.

A man as broad and solid as a hundred-year-old cypress frowned down at him. Craig didn't consider himself short at six foot two inches, yet this guy towered over him in height and circumference. As with all bullies of gargantuan proportions, Craig followed the rule: Never show fear. "Beat it Gator."

Gator frowned down at Craig and shot an accusing glance at Elaine. "She said her feet hurt. Otherwise, she'd be dancin' wit' me."

"Maybe her feet are feeling better now. I can be pretty hard to resist." Craig joked, hoping to soothe Gator's irritation.

Instead Gator's frown deepened. "Are you sayin' I'm easy to resist?"

Damn, he'd done it now. He'd stepped smack-dab in the middle of Gator's sore spot. "No, Gator, I was just implying that I didn't really give her the chance to say no."

"Are you sure you weren't makin' fun of me? It sure sounded like you were makin' fun."

"No, no, Gator. You're hard to resist too."

"I don't think I like you, Craig Thibodeaux. I think I'm going to smash your face."

Craig's heartbeat ratcheted up a notch. Surely the big oaf wouldn't take a swing? Not in a public place. Craig was wrong.

A gigantic, meaty fist came out of nowhere and clipped him on the chin, knocking him halfway across the dance floor and flat on his back.

Stars swam before Craig's eyes in bright white, red and gold, and that was while they were closed! When he opened them, Gator was headed his way.

Elaine yelled and leaped onto the big brute's back, pummeling him with her fists.

Gator's thunderous expression was enough to make a grown man cringe. Craig didn't think even Gator would kick a man while he was down, but obviously Elaine did.

She rode piggyback, with her dress crawling up her thighs and revealing way more than she'd want to know. Her screams intensified and she yelled every curse word in the dictionary and some he thought might be in Latin.

The picture was priceless. He could already see tomorrow's headline: SCIENTIST GONE MAD ON THE BACK OF GIANT APE. A chuckle rose up in his chest and escaped in a rush. One chuckle led to another and soon his sides were splitting and tears poured from the corners of his eyes.

Gator, with Elaine still on his back, stopped in front of Craig and stared down, confusion written into the frown between his eyes. "You laughing at me, Craig?"

With a quick swipe at his eyes, Craig stood and looked up at Gator. "No, not at all."

"I didn't mean to hit you so hard." Gator stared down at his hands. "Darn hands. Momma says I don't even know my own strength. Guess she's right."

Elaine stopped pummeling and slid from Gator's back, her skirt riding up even farther to reveal lacy white bikini underwear. She rushed to his side. "Are you okay, Craig?"

Craig's laughter ceased as a red-hot surge shot through his veins to his groin. "I was until I saw those sexy-as-hell undies you're wearing."

Elaine's face suffused with color all the way out to her ears. She stood and tugged frantically at the hem of her dress, cursing in a most unladylike fashion. "That's what I get for worrying about you, Craig Thibodeaux. I'm leaving." Elaine spun on her spiked heels and took off across the dance floor, pushing against anyone standing in the way of her and the door.

Craig shot to his feet and lit out after her. No way in hell was he going to let her get away without exploring those white lacy panties a bit further.

CHAPTER SEVENTEEN

The jerk! Here she'd been upset by Gator's punch and all Craig could do was point out her exposure in front of God and everybody else at the Raccoon Saloon. Elaine could do without his type. She shoved past the same men who'd admired her earlier and shot quelling looks at them when they dared to make crude comments about her underwear.

Just as Elaine reached the door, Josie caught up with her. The blonde hugged her and smiled. "Congratulations, Elaine. You graduate with honors!"

Elaine frowned. "What?" Then she looked back.

Craig was threading his way through the crowd, gaining ground. If she didn't hurry, he'd catch her before she could make her escape.

"Hold up, Elaine," Craig called out.

Panic seized her and she ducked out the door into the night air. Once outside, she realized her mistake. She hadn't brought her car and she didn't have a ride home.

Her heels teetered on the gravel in the parking lot and she winced. *Great! I've succeeded in cutting off my nose to spite my face.*

She'd turned to go back in and round up Mozelle and Josie, when Craig burst through the door.

"Thank God I caught you," he said, reaching for her hands.

Elaine pulled away. "You didn't catch me. I don't have a car here. I was on my way back in to get Josie."

"If you want to go home, I can take you," he offered.

"I don't trust you to get me there." Why did he have to look so damn delicious all in black?

His smile curved the corners of his mouth and his eyes sparkled in the few lights shining over the parking lot. "If you can trust me to take you out on the water, you can trust me to get you home."

"I believe I'd be in way over my head if I trusted you again."

Dark brows drew downward over ice-blue eyes. "What's that supposed to mean?"

"I know your secret."

His body stiffened. "What the hell are you talking about?"

She flung her hand in the air. "You're not a dock hand. You're an attorney!"

Craig inhaled deeply and let the breath out, his body relaxing. "Is that all?"

"You mean there's more?"

"No, of course not," he replied, a little too quickly.

Elaine's eyes narrowed. "I don't know what to believe."

"I'm an attorney." He shrugged. "So, what's my occupation got to do with us?"

"Trust! Don't you get it? I can't trust you to tell me the truth, and I can't trust myself when I'm with you." Elaine clapped her hand over her mouth, her eyes growing rounder with her slip of the tongue.

Craig's gaze softened, and he closed the gap between them.

All the fight leached out of Elaine's body. She didn't put up an iota of resistance when Craig pulled her into his arms. "Problem is, I can't trust myself when I'm with you either. For some strange reason, I can't keep my hands off you." He leaned closer, his mouth hovering over hers. "Nor my lips."

When he still hovered, Elaine reached up behind his neck. "Then kiss me, damn it." She pulled his mouth to hers and fell deeper and deeper into an abyss of mindless sensuality.

Her hands roamed over his shoulders and into the front of his shirt, ripping through buttons with a frantic urgency driven by her raging hormones, her body's natural reaction to a sexy man. That's all it was. Hormones.

Yeah, right!

Craig captured her hands and pulled them away from his skin. "Let's get out of here."

Elaine's glazed eyes cleared and she stared around the parking lot. Every nerve ending screamed for more. If she didn't get him naked in the next five minutes, she'd explode. "Do you have a car?"

"Yes. Thank goodness I insisted on driving separately." He fished around in his pocket and pulled out his keys. With a quick kiss, he pulled her to him and steered her toward a midnight-black sports car. Once inside, he started the engine and shifted into reverse. "Where to?"

Feeling a little racy and altogether more uninhibited than she'd felt in her entire life, she answered, "Where did you go to make out as a teenager?"

"Huh?" Craig stared at her as if she'd lost her mind.

"I've never made out in a car before."

"Never?"

"No."

"Well then, sweetheart, you're in for a real treat. I promise this night will be unforgettable."

"I'm counting on it." She was more than determined to show him she could be every bit as aggressive and sexy as he was. My, what a new 'do and a sexy dress could do for a woman . . . or was it the Cajun sitting next to her stirring her blood to boiling? *I am woman, hear me roar!*

Craig parked on the edge of a moonlit lagoon. The moon kissed the water with diamonds, a perfect setting to initiate Elaine in the art of car bouncing.

When he shut off the engine, the silence in the interior of the car was broken only by the sound of their breathing—rapid breathing, at that. Craig stared around at the cramped interior of the sports car and almost cursed his idiotic choice of vehicles. Whatever happened to backseats? A seventies-model Cadillac with a roomy backseat would be handy about now.

His gaze shifted to Elaine.

Her hand reached down to unclip the seat belt.

Oh boy. The simple motion caused Craig's heart to rev into overdrive. He fumbled for the side levers and adjusted the seat all the way back, providing a pretty decent amount of space between him and the steering wheel. But would it be enough?

Out of her seat belt, Elaine smiled at him and shifted in her seat until the hem of her dress rode up, exposing the white lacy panties he'd glimpsed earlier.

He reached across the console to touch her thigh.

Her hand stilled his before he could caress up her leg to the center of that tempting triangle of material.

"Not yet. I'm experimenting." Her hand moved inside her white panties and preceded to stroke the very place Craig longed to be.

Suddenly, his jeans were entirely too tight, with the strain of his arousal pulsing a tattoo against his zipper. He groaned and looked away, unable to bear another moment of her teasing. "You're killing me, woman."

"Then my experiment is a success."

Craig glanced over at her.

She slid the white panties down her legs and kicked them off her ankles. With a wicked smile, she climbed over the console and planted a knee on either side of his thighs, facing him. She leaned forward and levered the seat into a full reclining position before she turned her attention to his zipper.

Was this the shy scientist he'd met only a few short days ago? The one who stumbled over her words as well as her feet? Craig could hardly believe it. How could one man get so lucky?

Perhaps it was the wine, perhaps swamp gases. If Elaine were honest with herself, she'd admit she'd sprung free of her inhibitions and was riding hell-bent for the finish line. Damn the microscope and full speed ahead!

With her hands on the metal button holding the waistband of Craig's trousers together, Elaine paused.

"Honey, don't stop now," he begged.

"I wouldn't dream of it." She slipped the button through the hole and paused again. "You're sure this road is deserted?"

"Absolutely."

"Good." She unzipped his pants until his erection sprung forward against his black briefs, creating a tent. "My, aren't we excited?"

"More than you could ever imagine."

Elaine's blood burned through her veins. She felt capable of conquering any problem or, more difficult, her deepest fears—rejection, not fitting in and her fear of water. Tonight, Elaine was on top of the world, and on top of the sexiest Cajun this side of the Mississippi. Now, to show him she had what it took to keep a man's attention.

Excitement swirled in her belly, spreading fingers of desire ever downward to pool at her core hovering over his thighs. With her dress hiked up to her hips, Elaine gave Craig a moonlit view of what she had to offer, and the thought made her even hotter than before.

She leaned back and rubbed her sweet spot against the rough fabric of his black-denim-clad thighs. Flames of pleasure leapt through her and she gasped.

Craig grasped her buttocks and kneaded the flesh, driving the hem of her dress up around her waist. "I want to be inside you," he said through clenched teeth.

"And so you will," she promised. She leaned forward and ran her hands up the inside of his shirt, threading through the hairs on his chest, tweaking the hard little nipples. With eager fingers, she pulled his shirt from the waistband of his jeans and unbuttoned the last of the remaining buttons. Pushing the garment over his shoulders, she paused. "Does it still hurt?" She eased forward and pressed her lips to the jagged line where the bullet had skinned his shoulder.

"No." A strong hand circled her hip to the front to cup the juncture of her thighs, a finger sliding easily into her warmth. "God, you're so wet." His other hand traveled up her side to fit over a rounded breast. Looping a finger into the stretch fabric, he pulled it down until the strapless bra was the only thing between her and the night air.

Even the bra was too much. She wanted to be naked with him inside her. Now. Elaine reached behind her back and unclasped the bra, her breasts springing free from the tight confines.

"Glorious," Craig breathed, wrapping his fingers around a glowing orb. He massaged first one, then the other, pinching the nipples into hardened peaks.

Elaine leaned forward and rubbed her breasts against the mat of hair on his chest, reveling in the coarseness against her tender skin. He was a big strong man, she was a soft-skinned woman. Such was the way of nature, and nature had outdone itself in Craig.

His erection pressed against her belly, an insistent reminder of his growing need and her burgeoning desire. With smooth precision, she eased her way down his chest to his narrow waist. Trailing kisses and tongue flicks all the way to the elastic waistband of his briefs, she reveled in every touch and taste along the way. With a nudge, she parted his legs and slid between his thighs until her knees touched the floorboard. Only then did she unwrap the package. First she ran her hands up from his balls over the hard shaft beneath the cotton. Heat warmed her fingers. Then she grasped the elastic and eased the briefs downward over him until his member was completely exposed.

"Ah geez, Elaine." His fingers dug into her shoulders. "Come up here."

"No," she said, her gaze completely focused on his magnificent manhood. "I've only just begun."

Craig moaned and lay back, his hands grasping the seat on either side of him. "I think I've died and gone to heaven."

"You bet your BVDs." Her voice was low and husky, her own desire spinning out of control. "You'll be singing with the angels before I'm done."

"God help me." Craig said to the ceiling of the car and gasped when her hands wrapped around him.

With sure strokes, Elaine massaged his length, up and down. She moved forward and pressed her breasts around him. His hips rose and fell as he slid his shaft between her cleavage.

Elaine hovered over the velvety tip and slid her tongue around the curved edge.

He tensed, his shaft quivering and incredibly hard. "I need to be inside you now, Elaine. I can't take any more of this."

"What about protection?"

"In my wallet, in my back pocket."

Elaine and Craig both fumbled for the wallet, rifling through until they found the little foil packet. When Craig went to open it, she held her hand out. "Let me."

Still on her knees, she tore the foil while she licked his arousal. Then she rolled the condom down over him until it fit snugly against the base.

As soon as it was in place, Craig grabbed her shoulders and pulled her up onto his chest. He nudged her thighs apart and brought her knees up on either side of him.

With her dress nothing more than a belt around her middle, Elaine had never felt more attractive or sexy. The humid night air kissed her breasts and the man beneath her followed suit.

She eased down over his shaft, her moist opening accepting him without hesitation.

He slid farther inside until her buttocks rested against his thighs. He stopped. "Are you all right?"

"Oh, yesss," she breathed, the flood of sensations pulling her closer to the edge.

"Then let's shake this buggy!" He lifted her hips, setting her in motion.

When she pushed upward, he withdrew. When she dropped back onto him, he met her with force enough to shimmy the little car. She rode him hard, meeting him thrust for thrust.

Craig clutched her thigh with one hand while the other tangled in her pubic hairs to find her most sensitive zone.

Already aroused to the point of mindlessness, Elaine toppled over the edge with one flick of Craig's finger. Her body tensed and burst into a kaleidoscope of sensation, rocking her to the very core.

Craig thrust one last time and joined her orgasm with one of his own. He held her fully sheathing his member, his expression one of utter concentration. Inside her, he pulsed his release.

As one, they relaxed. Elaine dragged in a deep breath and collapsed across Craig's chest, reluctant to sever their connection. "Is it always this good in the front seat of a car?" She buried her face in the crook of his neck and licked his earlobe.

His chest rose and fell in labored breaths, but Craig didn't answer.

Elaine leaned up on one elbow, peering into his shadowed face. "Did I do something wrong?" Her heart beat against her ribs.

Craig stared at her, his brows drawn toward the bridge of his nose. "Don't you have a clue what you do to me?"

She shrugged. "Not really." With a glance down his torso to where they connected, she smiled. "Beyond the obvious physical reaction, I figure you're used to this." She didn't delude herself into thinking she'd touched him on an emotional level.

With gentle hands, he reached up and turned her face toward his. "Don't play this down. What we just shared not only shook the car, it shook me too."

She touched a finger to his lips. "Don't."

He frowned his confusion, kissing the end of her finger.

"Don't say something you don't mean," she continued. "Our time together is limited, let's not muddy it with false sentiment." If he said something he didn't mean, she'd leave Bayou Miste with a broken heart.

Craig's frown deepened. "You know, for a smart lady, you've got a lot to learn about relationships."

"And you're the expert?" She leaned away from him, allowing his flaccid length to slide free. When she glanced up, headlights hit her full in the face. "There's a car coming!" She rolled over the console, banging her knee on the shift. "Ouch! I thought you said this road was deserted?"

"It usually is." Craig struggled to get his jeans up, buttoned and zipped. He levered his seat into an upright position.

Red, blue and gold lights strobed behind the car.

"Damn!"

"Cops?" Elaine squealed and fought to shimmy her twisted dress up over her breasts and down over her hips. She'd just covered the important stuff when a flashlight beam pierced the interior of the car.

"Craig, is that you?"

Craig pulled the edges of his shirt together and glanced over at Elaine. Apparently satisfied she was decent, he rolled the window down. "Hey Billy Ray, whatcha doing way out here on a Tuesday night?"

A man dressed in a dark uniform and sporting a polished gold badge peered through the window, shining his light into Elaine's eyes and down over her breasts. "Usually find some kids working on increasing the population of the parish. Could happen any night of the week, but especially on ladies' night at the Raccoon Saloon."

His light panned the interior of the car until it shone on the rearview mirror where Elaine's strapless bra dangled.

If Elaine could have sunk through the floorboard, she would have. Of all the stupid, adolescent stunts to pull . . .

Her embarrassment faded, pushed out by the elation of having done something she'd missed out on in high school. She'd necked in a car with a boy, *and* she'd been caught doing something naughty by the police! What an achievement. She only wished she had a girlfriend to share it with over a cup of hot cocoa.

"You okay there, miss?" Billy Ray asked, practically poking his head into the narrow window. "Craig ain't pullin' a fast one on you, is he? I could haul him in, if you want." The officer grinned. "Can't think of anything I'd like better. I'm sure I owe him one or two for all the pranks he pulled on me back when we were kids."

Craig frowned. "She's fine, Billy Ray. Now, could you scram?"

"I didn't hear her say she's fine." Billy Ray planted his feet wide and crossed his arms over his shoulders. "Well, are you, miss?"

Elaine struggled to keep a straight face and answered him with all the gravity befitting an officer of the law. "Yes, sir, I'm fine."

The deputy's arms dropped to his sides and he shrugged. "Rats. I could have used a little excitement. You two shouldn't be hangin' out on this old road. Sets a bad example for the teenagers. Now, get on outta here."

"Will do." Craig rolled up the window, revved the engine and spun the car in a circle to head back up the road.

Before they cleared the headlights of the police cruiser, Elaine exploded, laughing so hard she clutched her sides.

"What's so damn funny?" Craig asked, his voice a little on the cranky side.

Elaine gasped for air. "I've never . . . you should have . . . I can't believe . . ." Giggles interrupted every sentence she attempted until she gave up and doubled over.

When she could finally sit up and breathe, she glanced over at Craig.

His lips quivered and jerked upward on the corners. "You're some kind of nutcase."

Elaine wiped moisture from her eyes. "Why?"

"I'd have thought you'd be mortified beyond belief. Instead, you're bustin' a gut." He reached over and chucked her under the chin, then paused to stroke the side of her cheek.

Elaine leaned into his palm. "It was an experience I've never had." She pressed a kiss to his palm. "I'm glad I got to share it with you."

For a second, Elaine thought she'd destroyed the moment by her words.

Then in a quiet voice, Craig answered, "Me too."

For the rest of the short ride to the cottage, Craig held Elaine's hand. Neither spoke, nor did Elaine feel they needed to.

When Craig finally pulled into the gravel driveway of Elaine's temporary home, he sat for a few minutes staring straight ahead. "Elaine?"

"Ummmhuh?" she murmured, unwilling to end the evening.

"Did you leave the door open when you left?"

"Huh?"

CHAPTER EIGHTEEN

Elaine flew out of the BMW before Craig could stop her.

"Damn." Before she could put her foot on the porch, he caught up with her. "Wait."

"Why? All my equipment is in there."

"Yeah, and whoever broke in might be too." Craig crossed in front of her, keeping a tight hold on her hand, forcing her behind him. "Go back to the car."

"No. This is my stuff."

"Then stay behind me."

"Okay, but don't do anything macho."

Craig eased forward. "What? You mean you care?" he asked flippantly, his eyes focused fully on the house before him, yet his mind divided between the possible bad guy and her answer.

"No more so than you," she shot back.

Boy that was a non-answer if ever Craig heard one. "Hey, if anyone's in there, I've got a gun the size of a bazooka and I'm not afraid to use it."

Elaine whacked him on the arm. "You don't have a gun."

"I know that and you know that, but if there's someone in there, he won't know that. Well, he will now that we've discussed it loud enough for the entire parish to hear."

"I think whoever was here is gone now."

"It pays to be cautious." Craig crept up to the side of the open door and peeked his head around. The interior was dark and still. What little light shone in from the fractional moon revealed upset furniture and the clutter of items strewn across the floor. "Geez."

"Geez what?" Elaine jerked her hand loose and stepped around him to flip the light switch. "Geez."

The light illuminated the devastation. Craig listened for sounds of movement, but none came from inside the little cottage.

"Oh no!" Elaine clapped a hand to her mouth. Her eyes widened to round saucers and then filled with tears.

Craig stared at a spray-painted message on the wall. *Go home or die!* For the first time since he'd come face to face with a hungry alligator at the tender age of twelve, Craig knew real, gut-wrenching fear. The threat was written in red paint across the wall of the little living room and it was aimed at this scientist he'd come to admire. A person who wanted to help the swamps become a better place. The woman who'd managed to touch him as no other.

Craig wrapped an arm around her shoulders and pulled her to his side. "Don't worry, sweetheart. We can repaint the walls, and I won't let anything happen to you," he promised, wondering how in hell he could keep that promise when he turned back into a frog.

"I don't care about the paint." Her voice caught on a sob, and with a shaking hand, she pointed to a metal object lying amid the strewn papers and books. "My microscope," she whispered.

Leaving her side, Craig gathered the cold metal from the floor. He looked inside the lens and twisted the viewfinder until the image cleared. "The lens is intact."

"Oh, thank God." She took the tool from him and stared through the lens. Then she clutched it to her chest, tears slipping down her cheeks. "My parents gave me this microscope before they died."

"I didn't know your parents weren't alive." Craig frowned. He didn't know a lot about Elaine, and he found he wanted very much to learn more.

"I was in the last year of my master's program when they were killed in a car wreck."

"How old were you?"

"Twenty."

"Twenty?" Craig did a double-take. "You were twenty finishing your master's?"

"Yes." Elaine's back stiffened and her chin raised a notch higher.

"Damn, were you some kind of brainiac?"

Elaine winced. More tears welled in her eyes and spilled over.

Craig immediately felt like a clod. He reached out to take Elaine into his arms.

Like an animal avoiding the trap, Elaine jerked his hands loose and backed away. "I guess leopard frogs can't change their spots."

Craig's arms fell to his sides. "What are you talking about?" he asked.

"Oh what's the use?" Elaine hugged the microscope to her chest and stared down at the floor. "Even with the sexy dress and haircut, I still don't fit in any more than I did growing up."

"What do you mean, fit in?"

She turned and walked a few steps away. "I finished my undergraduate degree when most kids were graduating high school. I never knew what it was like to be a teenager because I was never around kids my own age."

The pain in Elaine's voice drew Craig forward. "So that's why you've never been necking." He slipped his arms her and her microscope and pulled her back against him. He leaned forward and nuzzled her neck. "I could never have guessed. You were fantastic."

Slowly, her body relaxed into his. With a deep sigh, she tipped her head back onto his shoulder, giving his lips full range of her neck. "Do you really think of me as a brainiac?"

The hope in her voice was almost his undoing. Craig turned her in his arms and tipped her chin up, forcing her to look into his eyes. "I'm very much attracted by your intelligence and passion for knowledge. And your bravery to face your deepest fears humbles me. And babe, in that blue dress, *mon Dieu*, you're incredibly hot. But even in khaki slacks at the bottom of a boat, I can't keep my hands off you." He proved it by sliding his hands down her back and over her rounded buttocks.

His movements had the desired effect when any remaining tension in Elaine's body eased and she snuggled against him. "You're not just saying this to get me in bed, are you?"

"Will it help?" He grinned.

She backed away enough to look at him.

Immediately, he wiped the stupid look from his face. "No really, I'm telling you the truth." He stared down at her creamy breasts pushing up out of the strapless top of her knock-'em-dead dress and leaned down to press his lips to the cleavage before he looked back up into her eyes. "And if you look like the sexiest devil with that blue dress, that's just icing on the cake."

"It's not even my dress." Her hands slipped around his waist and dropped down to slide into his rear pockets.

Craig found it difficult to concentrate with Elaine's hands in his back pockets. Every movement was an incredible turn-on without even having skin-to-skin contact.

"What about the threat?" she asked against his neck.

"It's just paint." He kissed a path from her jawline down to her collarbone.

"Shouldn't we call the police?" Her tongue did wicked things to his earlobe.

"Tomorrow." Craig's lips hovered over hers. "I've had enough of the police for one night."

Leaning back, Elaine frowned up into his face. "But won't your uncle be upset about his house?"

"Uncle who?" His hands tangled in her hair and he pulled her head back for better access to her soft lips. "Are you going to worry all night?"

"Yes," she breathed, her eyelids drooping over near-black irises.

"Then let me help you forget." He touched his mouth to hers, barely brushing the skin in a feathery stroke and coming back up to stare into her face.

"My memory's clouding," she whispered huskily.

He kissed her again.

"What's my name?" Her hands circled his head and brought him back to her.

"It's Elaine," he answered and claimed her lips, skimming his tongue past her teeth.

The fire in Craig's chest scorched his veins, making a beeline to his groin. His hands circled her waist and he pressed his bulging zipper against her tummy. "I find you far too sexy for my own good."

"Me too," she whispered.

"And even though tonight wasn't my first time necking . . ." Craig could feel her stiffening, ". . . it was the best time I've ever had in a bucket seat. You were so incredibly . . ." his lips hovered over hers, ". . . hot."

Elaine rose up on her toes to meet his kiss. Her tongue tangled and teased while her hands tugged his shirt from his trousers. Then soft fingers ran up his back and down into the waistline of his jeans. She ground her hips into his, pressing the thin fabric of her dress against the hardened ridge of his desire.

Without pulling away, he said into her mouth, "Woman, you're killing me."

Elaine backed up in his arms and did an amazing thing, for her. She batted her eyes and smiled teasingly. "I'm sorry, should I stop?"

Craig had never seen her do this before. "Are you flirting with me?"

Her smile faded, and she blushed a devilish shade of pink. "I've been taking lessons."

"Lessons in flirting?" Craig shook his head. The woman who knew more about science than he'd ever known or wanted to know had to learn how to flirt. "You really did miss out on the finer things in life, didn't you?"

"Yes." Again, her chin rose and a little frown wrinkled the skin between her eyes. "But I'm a quick learner."

"And, pray tell, who would be teaching you how to flirt?"

"My new friends, Josie and Mozelle." She braced her hands on his arms to push him away.

"What else did they teach you?" Craig's hold tightened. "Although, I'm afraid to ask."

"Let me go, and I'll show you." Her voice dropped to a husky whisper.

Like a shot, he dropped her arms and practically salivated for her next demonstration. He wasn't disappointed.

Elaine stepped away, turned around, and walked toward the tiny bedroom, her back to him, her hips swaying with every step. When she reached the threshold, she took a deep breath, and squared her shoulders. Then she planted a hand on one hip, and, swinging a shoulder back so he could view the profile of one breast, shot a sexy smile in his direction. "Follow me, Cajun."

The blue dress, the come-hither look and those incredibly already-been-kissed lips reached out imaginary fingers, grabbed his manhood and jerked him forward. "Remind me to thank those ladies."

He swept in behind her and pressed his hips to her buttocks. With a slow not-so-steady hand, he ran his fingers up the curve of her waist to cup that tantalizing breast. "I never knew school could be so exhilarating."

"You ain't seen nothin' yet."

Craig glanced over Elaine's naked shoulder at the clock and stifled a groan. With his body spooning her backside, he wanted nothing more than to lie in bed and make love to Elaine into the light of the early morning. In fact, making love to Elaine could easily become a twenty-four-seven occupation, and he'd be perfectly happy.

Who needed a successful law practice, especially when it didn't provide nearly as much satisfaction as lying here with Elaine?

He sighed. Dawn would come and he'd be a frog in a few short minutes. He needed to get to his uncle before he transformed.

With one last, gentle squeeze of her warm hip, he slipped out of the bed and into his clothes.

Elaine rolled onto her back, one arm flung over the pillow next to hers. A small frown wrinkled her brow, but she didn't wake.

Craig leaned close, drinking in how her naturally dark eyelashes fanned out over her cheekbones and her tangled hair stood out darkly against the white sheets. He pressed a kiss to her lips, then turned and left before he couldn't.

He picked his way through the living room, avoiding broken glass and crinkly paper. The angry red writing on the wall sent a chill through his soul, strengthening his resolve to take this person apart, limb by limb.

A quick glance at the lightening sky forced Craig into a jog to his uncle's house. He needed to warn Uncle Joe to keep an eye on Elaine during the day and to not let her out on the swamp under any circumstances.

He leaped the last few steps up to the front porch of Uncle Joe's house and pounded on the door. The white clapboard house could have been identical to the one Elaine slept in a few doors down. Another glance at the sky and Craig banged even louder.

From inside the house sounds of furniture crashing to the floor were followed by loud cursing.

"Come on Uncle Joe—" Craig shouted.

The sun popped up over the horizon. Craig's skin and bones tightened, shrinking and contracting. *Damn!*

The front-porch light glared to life, temporarily blinding Craig.

"Who the hell's knockin' on my door at this time of the mornin'?" When Uncle Joe, wearing only black boxer shorts decorated with bright red and pink hearts, opened the front door, the morphing was halfway over.

Craig hunkered in a squatting position, his features half man, half frog. "Uncle Joe," Craig croaked. His words were barely understandable.

"That you, Craig?" Uncle Joe rubbed his eyes and

peered closer. "You look a little green around the gills, boy." He chuckled.

Alternating between words and croaking, Craig fought to get his message across before the transformation was complete. "Elaine . . . trouble . . . don't—"

Three words. Three lousy words. The transformation complete, he sat with his belly on the floor, kicking himself for not getting there earlier.

"What's that, Craig?" Uncle Joe squatted down. "I didn't understand a single word you said." With a wry smile, he shook his head. "You really need to find you a woman."

Like I don't know that?

"Joe, honey, is there someone at the door?" called a familiar female voice Craig couldn't quite put a name to.

Uncle Joe turned to yell, "No, sweet *thang*, musta been the wind."

Uncle Joe has a female friend sleeping with him? Interesting. Craig peered around his uncle's leg, but couldn't see anything in the darkened house.

"You gonna make it back to the bait shop all right?"

Craig nodded his froggy head.

"Snookems, you comin' back to bed?" called the voice from inside the darkened house.

His uncle's face turned beet red in the porch light. "Gotta go."

As the door closed, Craig turned to hop off the porch. He needed to get back to Elaine. Even if he couldn't do anything to protect her, he could at least keep an eye on her.

The sun streaked through the window and shone across the bed before Elaine budged from sleep. Without opening her eyes, she indulged in a long stretch in the warmth of the late-morning sun. Wouldn't it be nice to make love all day long? Maybe she'd look for Craig today and suggest it.

Her eyes popped open, and she sat up in bed. Was she actually considering propositioning a man in broad daylight? Her? Elaine Smith? Social cripple and egghead extraordinaire?

Recalling last night's performance, and her major role in initiating it, Elaine's lips curled upward and she sank back against the pillows. She'd really done it. She'd seduced a very sexy man. Not once, but twice! And in the bucket seat of a sports car! Wahoo!

She really was becoming a wild woman, wasn't she? By allowing her sexuality full reign, she'd discovered a sense of power and confidence lacking in her life up until now. She could conquer the world.

With a flick of her wrist, she tossed the sheets aside and leapt out of bed. She had work to do and time was wasting. After a quick shower, she bravely stepped into the small living room.

I can handle this. I can handle this. She stood staring around the room, assessing the damage. Nothing a broom, a can of paint and a little elbow grease wouldn't cure. *Remember, I am the new improved Elaine. The Elaine who isn't afraid to go after what she wants.*

Before she touched a thing, she called the police.

Half the morning flew by as Elaine filed a report, and answered the same questions asked separately by each of the three Bayou Miste deputies who'd shown up on her doorstep. When they'd taken all the pictures they wanted, including one of her white lacy undies lying on the floor of her bedroom, the deputies filed out the door, promising to get right on it.

Finally Elaine could get on with the task of cleaning up the mess. Shoving the sleeves of her white oxford-cloth shirt up her arms, she dug in. She had a lot of work to do, to put the place to rights. And maybe afterward, she'd go shopping to replace every pair of khaki slacks in her wardrobe.

Two hours later, she stood back and examined the results of her cleaning spree and inventory. Aside from the paint on the wall, the cottage appeared almost normal. Some of the furniture was a little dented and scarred, and one chair needed a leg glued back on, but nothing major.

What worried her most was that every bit of her research from notes to specimens was gone. Even her dissecting tray with the frog she'd kept in the refrigerator, and the frozen fish in the freezer had been taken. The anonymous sample she'd received at the university, the catalyst that had set this entire effort into motion, was nothing more than a broken jar on the wooden floor of the living room.

If she wanted to pursue this investigation, she'd have to start over. Did she have the stamina and courage to do that?

Damn right!

But first, she wanted to do a little background investigation. She needed to find out what industries were nearby that could be dumping that much pollution into the swamp. The best place she knew of to get information was from a local who liked to talk a lot. Now, who did she know who fit that description?

"Elaine? You up for visitors?" Mozelle Reneau stood outside the screen door carrying a basket covered with a dish towel. "I got pipin' hot beignets."

"Please, come in." Elaine hurried to open the door. The sweet smell of hot pastries filled her nostrils, reminding her she hadn't stopped to have breakfast. A glance at the clock made her realize she'd even missed lunch. Her stomach growled.

Dawg sprawled on the porch in front of the door. Elaine had to forcibly push him with the door to get it open enough for Mozelle to enter.

"That's got to be the laziest hound dog this side of the Mississippi." Once inside, Mozelle exclaimed, "Good Lord!" She stood just inside the living room, staring at the red paint on the wall. "What happened?"

"Someone paid me a visit while I was out last night at the Raccoon Saloon."

With a shake of her head, Mozelle carried the basket to the kitchen. "I don't know what gets into people to act so rude."

"You and me both."

"Well, don't you worry none. Nothin' a little paint won't cure." She stood with her hands fisted on her hips. "There's just no excuse for threatenin' a woman like that."

"Agreed."

"I'll speak to Joe about it today." She smiled a Mona Lisa smile.

"Thank you, Mozelle." The strange smile wasn't lost on Elaine. She wondered what the older woman was up to.

"I noticed you didn't stay long at the Raccoon Saloon," Mozelle said, arranging plates on the table while Elaine measured coffee into the coffeemaker.

Not sure how to respond, Elaine asked, "Was that a question or a statement?"

"Just an observation." Mozelle set forks next to the plates, and then turned to face Elaine. "So did the lessons work?"

Heat crawled up Elaine's neck as she recalled how well the lessons had worked. She couldn't restrain the smile that tugged at her lips. "Yes."

"Well, bless my soul, that makes two." Mozelle grinned and turned back to unnecessarily polish a fork.

Elaine leaned her back against the counter and crossed her arms over her chest. "Mozelle Reneau, what do you mean by two?"

"Oh, nothing." She waved her hand in the air and remained uncharacteristically evasive for Bayou Miste's biggest gossip.

"You know you can't throw out a comment like that without filling in the details." Elaine crossed the room and circled Mozelle to get face to face. "From what I've learned about you in the past few days, you have got to be bursting to tell me, so spill it."

Twin flags of color rode high on Mozelle's pale cheeks. She sank onto the bright red vinyl-covered chair and smiled up at Elaine. "I asked a man to dance last night."

Having hurdled that barrier herself, Elaine nodded, suspecting that wasn't all Mozelle had done. "Is that all, just one dance?"

Mozelle darted a glance toward the far corner ceiling. "Well, no. We danced several dances." Her face flushed brighter.

"And?"

Mozelle stopped staring at the ceiling and looked directly into Elaine's eyes. "We danced all night. There, I said it." She heaved a huge sigh, and her hand fluttered to her throat.

"Does the Raccoon Saloon stay open that late?"

The older woman's forehead wrinkled and she stared at Elaine as if she were dense. "Nooo. If I must spell it out, we danced in the sheets."

Elaine sat in the seat across the Formica table from Mozelle, her eyes widening. "Oh." What did you say to top that? The older woman had scored.

Mozelle popped out of her chair and pulled mugs from the cabinet. Over her shoulder she commented, "I haven't had sex that good since Mr. Reneau passed away over ten years ago. For that matter, I hadn't had sex. I was almost afraid I'd forgotten how."

Elaine cringed and prayed she didn't go into the gory details. She liked Mozelle, but there was such a thing as too much information. "I'm really happy for you."

With two cups of hot coffee, Mozelle returned to the table. "I never thought I'd get Joe to notice me. He's been avoiding me for years."

"Joe? As in Joe Thibodeaux? Craig's uncle?"

"The one and only." Mozelle tipped her head to the side. "I think the alcohol had something to do with it, but I'm sure in the light of day, he'll realize we were meant to be together."

Elaine clapped a hand to her forehead. "Did you get him drunk and take advantage of him?"

Mozelle stared at her. "Of course I did. How else was I gonna get him to dance? The old coot's been pinin' away for Craig's mamma for the past forty years. It was about time he got over it."

"Whoa! Wait a minute. Joe was in love with Craig's mother?" Elaine sat back in her chair. This was an interesting tidbit. "And she didn't love him?"

"I have my suspicions she might have, but Joe didn't get around to askin' afore his brother did."

"Wow. And she said yes. How sad." Elaine wondered if Craig knew anything about this. "That had to hurt Joe."

"Yessum." Mozelle smacked her palms on the table. "That's been quite a while back and, like I said, it was about time he got over it. I just gave him a little push. Don't know why I hadn't done it sooner. Must be the new 'do. Makes a woman feel like she could conquer the world."

Elaine almost groaned. Here she'd been thinking along

the same lines just that morning. Hearing Mozelle say it didn't make her feel all warm and fuzzy like she had earlier. The same words that had empowered her now only made her feel like a fraud.

Had she coerced Craig into bed last night? Had she taken unfair advantage of him? She closed her eyes and thought through their activities. No. He'd been just as eager as she had. Whew!

Still. Maybe she shouldn't get so carried away and overinflate her opinion of her sexual prowess.

Time to change the subject. Elaine opened her eyes. "Mozelle, what are the local industries in this area?"

"Huh?" The change in topic had Mozelle wrinkling her brow.

"I'm studying the impact of pollutants on the swamps around Bayou Miste. I figure since you've lived here for a good portion of your life, you might know what industries are nearby."

Mozelle waved her hand. "That's easy. There's only one between here and Morgan City. Littington Enterprises."

"Littington?" Elaine mentally scratched her head. Where had she heard that name before? Then it hit her. "Does Jason Littington have anything to do with Littington Enterprises?"

"Yessum, he owns it. That place employs most of the people in the three surrounding towns. Without it, none of us could afford to stay. My husband worked there for thirty years before he retired. You don't suppose that's where the pollutants are comin' from, do you?"

Elaine sure hoped not. "I plan to find out."

Mozelle sipped from her mug. "Be a shame if it causes trouble for the refinery, bein' as how most people depend on it for their livelihood." She stared over at the angry red letters on the wall. "You thinkin' someone from the refinery's doin' this to you?"

"It's a possibility. All my specimens and research are missing. Whoever did it is trying to keep me from proving the swamp is being polluted."

"And is it?" Mozelle asked.

"Yes."

The older woman shook her head. "It'll be a shame if they close down that refinery."

"It'll be a bigger shame if everything in the swamp dies due to negligence." And a shame if she had to stand up in court against attorney, Craig Thibodeaux, who just happens to represent Jason Littington.

"Yes, yes, you're quite right." Mozelle stared across at her. "So whatcha gonna do about it?"

"I don't know." Elaine pinched the corner off the powdery end of a beignet, popped it into her mouth and chewed on the sweet and her thoughts. The lump in her chest that used to be her heart, hurt with every beat. She couldn't believe Craig hadn't bothered to tell her. Had he only helped her collect specimens to keep an eye on the enemy? If so, he was a slimeball that didn't deserve her heartache. "I need to get back out on the swamp and collect more evidence."

Mozelle reached across the table and grasped Elaine's hands. "It could be dangerous."

"I know." All her life Elaine had lived safely within her parent's home, safely within the walls of the lab, and safely behind her microscope. But some efforts demanded that one conquer her fears and leave her safety net behind. Elaine stared at the writing on the wall, a chill slipping down her spine. "This is something I have to do."

CHAPTER NINETEEN

Exhausted from his late-night activities, Craig had hunkered down next to Dawg on Elaine's front porch and slept like the dead. He didn't wake until Old Lady Reneau showed up carrying a basket of heaven.

As Ms. Reneau had stood on the porch talking to Elaine, the voice clicked in Craig's memory. This was the voice he'd heard earlier that morning at his uncle's cottage. Craig stared up at her as if seeing her for the first time. Uncle Joe was sleeping with Old Lady Reneau?

He'd rolled the revelation over and over in his mind. For a woman in her sixties, he guessed she was okay to look at. Although she'd chased the local teenagers out of her peach trees, she'd shared beignets with them on occasion, and darn good ones at that. She'd been alone for the past ten years, and Uncle Joe had never married. Why not?

When Elaine had pushed the door open, Craig leapt out of the way to keep from being stepped on by Ms. Reneau or crushed by Dawg. He hadn't hopped fast enough to get inside, but figured it was just as well. Ms. Reneau could talk the ear off a frog when she had a mind to.

Once the door closed, Dawg had rolled back over and blocked it again. Craig could only stare up at the door, but after a few minutes, he'd thought he might want to hear what was going in there after all.

He'd hopped down off the porch and around the house, trying to get close enough to overhear some of Elaine and Ms. Reneau's conversation. After the success of last night's love lessons, he was anxious to see if the older woman had more advice for Elaine. He was also interested to see if Ms. Reneau planned to talk about her visit to Uncle Joe's last night. Craig had a lot to discuss with his father's brother.

No matter where he'd stood, he couldn't hear the conversation inside the cottage. He would have loved to have been a fly on the wall. Speaking of flies . . . He shook himself. Save the hunger pangs for nighttime. No more flies for this guy!

What felt like two hours later, Ms. Reneau emerged with an empty basket dangling from her fingertips and a promise to drop by the next day.

"Thanks for the beignets. They were wonderful," Elaine called out.

The sound of her voice bathed him in the same afterglow as their previous night's foray into foreplay and hot steamy sex. He wanted nothing more than to take her into his arms and hold her throughout the day. But he couldn't as long as he remained a frog.

"Oh, hi, Todd. I didn't see you out here earlier." Elaine squatted next to him in her khaki slacks and white blouse. She had her satchel and bucket in one hand, and a little powdered sugar on her chin. "Is Dawg taking good care of you?"

Craig stared up at the powdered sugar. If he stretched

far enough, his tongue could reach out and wipe that sugar right off her. But what would that buy him? She'd freak out at being licked by a frog and he'd still be a frog.

Mon Dieu! What the hell had he done to deserve this?

Elaine stood, walked down the steps and across the street toward the marina.

When Craig could pull himself together and quit thinking about that little speck of powdered sugar, he hopped after her. Where in the heck did she think she was going at this time of day? The sun wouldn't go down for another hour.

Craig hopped faster.

He'd just reached the marina parking lot when Elaine eased out onto the dock. Uncle Joe was pumping gas into the outboard tank of a small skiff.

"Mr. Thibodeaux?" she called out.

"Oh, hello, Miss Smith. Didn't expect to see you here so early."

So far, even from a distance, Craig could hear everything. He prayed she wasn't there to go out on the swamp yet.

"I had a break-in at the cottage last night while I was at the Raccoon Saloon. I thought you ought to know about it."

Good. She was telling Uncle Joe about the trouble at the house.

"Really?" His uncle hung the gas pump back up and scratched his head. "Never had anything like that happen around here. Any of your equipment missing?"

"No, but all my specimens and research are gone."

"Sorry to hear that."

"Actually, that's why I'm here." Elaine looked around the dock and back up at the bait shop. "Is your nephew around?"

Uncle Joe rubbed his chin and nodded. "Likely."

Craig hopped down onto the wooden planks and closer to the pair.

"Do you suppose he could take me out earlier this evening?" Elaine asked.

"Depends on how much earlier."

Craig would have smiled if he could. His uncle had a way of dancing around the issue when he wanted to. Must have been all the practice he'd gotten as a lawyer more than thirty years ago.

Elaine shrugged. "I was hoping to go out now. Do you suppose he could take me?"

With a slow shake of his head, Uncle Joe answered, "Not hardly."

"Maybe I could ask him myself. Is he here?" Elaine stared back up at the bait shop.

"Maybe he's here, maybe he's not."

Way to be evasive, Uncle Joe! Craig inched closer.

The fine lines of Elaine's eyebrows drew together behind her glasses. How long before she got tired of Uncle Joe's riddles and decided to go home?

Soon, Craig hoped.

"Could you take me out on the swamp?" Elaine stared at Uncle Joe with those big brown eyes. "Out to your friend Bernie's old fishin' hole?"

Craig might have fallen for those eyes, but not Uncle Joe. "Now, I don't know about that. My eyesight ain't what it used to be at night."

"I really need to get those samples as soon as possible. If we go now, we could be back before dark."

Rubbing his chin, Uncle Joe dipped his head to the side. "You sure you can't wait until Craig can take you?"

"After what happened last night and the other nights

we were out on the swamp, I don't feel comfortable going out after dark. Besides, to stop the polluting I need to get solid evidence to show the EPA."

Joe rubbed his chin again, and stared up at the sky.

Don't do it Uncle Joe! Craig hopped up and down to get his uncle's attention. *Don't let her coerce you into something dangerous.*

"Well, if you think we can make it back by dark, I guess I could take you."

Oh, Uncle Joe, you caved. Craig croaked his disappointment.

"Thank you, Mr. Thibodeaux." Elaine kissed the old man's cheek.

If Craig could have, he would have groaned. Uncle Joe was a goner. The kiss just sealed the deal.

"Could we leave right now?" Elaine asked.

"Sure. Let me lock up the bait shop. Business has been kinda slow, anyway."

Elaine moved to the side to allow him passage on the boardwalk.

While Joe climbed the steps to the bait shop, Elaine eased over to the skiff and tossed in her bucket and satchel. With careful precision, she placed one foot at a time into the little boat while clinging to the wooden planks on the dock. Finally she sat on the metal bench and breathed a huge sigh.

Craig admired her spunk, even if he didn't agree with her decision to go out on the bayou. She'd gotten into the boat all by herself this time.

"I left a note for Craig telling him we'll be at Bernie's old fishin' hole, in case we're late getting back," Uncle Joe called out from behind Craig before he stepped into the boat.

Craig took a flying leap and landed on a pair of rubber

hip-waders piled in the front of the little boat. No way he'd let Elaine and Uncle Joe go out in the swamp without him. Too many crazy things had happened in the bayou lately.

He glanced up at the sky. The sun was low, but not quite low enough for Craig to change back into a man. If they ran into trouble out on the water, he couldn't help them, but he'd at least be there to know what was going on.

Craig had an ominous feeling about their little trek. He felt it all the way to his diminutive frog bones. Maybe the sensations had a little to do with the voodoo curse he was caught up in. But he was absolutely certain something was about to happen, and he wasn't going to like it.

In deference to her fear of the water, Craig had driven the boat slow and smooth, easing around twists and turns.

Not Mr. Thibodeaux. He drove like a madman.

Elaine clamped her teeth on her tongue and kept her eyes glued shut most of the way. When they slowed, she looked around to see the overhanging Spanish moss guarding the entrance to what she'd begun to think of as hers and Craig's lagoon—a polluted lagoon, but theirs nonetheless.

How strange to be out on the bayou without him. She missed his teasing and his understanding of her fears. Much as she liked Joe, he wasn't Craig and she didn't have the same comfort level. "Could you take me close to that little island?"

Joe aimed for the small outcropping of land. Then he shut off the motor and allowed the craft to drift to a stop with a gentle thump against the bank.

Elaine stared around, but she didn't see a single frog jumping into the water. "Where are all the frogs? And I don't see any dead fish," she mused aloud. "There were at least a half-dozen the last time we were here."

"Maybe someone came in and cleaned up the evidence." Joe dipped a paddle into the water and maneuvered the skiff to another position farther along the island.

At the very least, she could take some water to test. Carefully bending over the boat's side, she collected a sample in a tube, labeled it, and slipped it into her satchel.

When they reached the end of the lagoon, Joe dug his paddle deeper into the water to turn the boat around.

Thunk!

Elaine's gaze met Joe's.

As one, they peered over the side and into the water. In the shadows cast by the late-afternoon sun, they could just make out the curved edge of a barrel below the surface.

"Holy Moses," Joe said.

"No kidding," Elaine responded. "We've found the source of the pollutants."

Joe glanced up at the sound of an engine. "I think we'd better get the heck out of Dodge, or we'll be sittin' ducks in this pond."

"Let's go." Elaine sat up straight, trying to see through the dense foliage and lengthening gloom.

Turning in his seat, Joe pulled the crank rope, and the motor leapt to life.

Thank you, God. Elaine sent a silent prayer to the heavens. Now would not be a good time for the motor to be stubborn. As far as she was concerned, Joe could drive any way he pleased as long as it was fast and furious.

They'd just cleared the low-hanging tree at the entrance to the lagoon, when the same deck boat she'd seen before stormed around a bend in the bayou and headed straight for them.

Joe spun the skiff around and gave it all the gas the little motor could take.

The wind whipped her hair out of its neat ponytail, and the strands lashed at her neck. She alternated between watching out for low-hanging branches and glancing over her shoulder. The closer the other boat came, the more she looked back.

"Hang on, I'm gonna turn," Joe yelled.

Already clinging with a death grip, Elaine leaned into the sharp turn. Just as they completed the ninety-degree angle, Elaine looked back. The other boat bore down on them, aiming for the back end of the skiff where Joe sat.

"Look out, Joe!" Elaine yelled.

The force of the collision lifted the smaller boat sideways, launching Elaine from her seat. Joe catapulted into the water several feet away.

Although petrified of the tea-colored water filling her nostrils, Elaine forced herself to be calm. Last time she'd fallen into the bayou, she'd only been in water about chest deep. If she just waited to get her feet under her, everything would be all right. Her lungs burned for a breath of air when her knees finally touched the soft silt at the bottom.

Quickly, she scrambled to get her feet beneath her and pushed to a standing position. Oh, no. Even erect, her head didn't quite clear the surface. Panic surged through her veins, pooling in her gut, threatening to overwhelm her senses. She pushed hard against the slimy bottom, bouncing up to the surface where she gasped for breath before submerging again.

When her head was above the water, she could see dusk

had settled over the bayou. Below, fragments of dirt and decomposed vegetation swirled around her, and a bullfrog swam by. She had to get to Joe. He may be hurt.

Craig didn't see the other boat coming. He'd only seen the terror on Elaine's face seconds before the skiff flipped over. He tried to leap aside, but the heavy rubber of the hip-waders dragged him below the surface. For a few panicky seconds he thought he'd be forever trapped and ultimately drowned beneath the rubber.

Just when he thought he was one dead frog, the rubber waders stopped their downward drift and buoyed upward. Craig kicked his webbed feet and swam free. As he reached the surface, the sun plummeted below the horizon, melding shadows together into full darkness.

Before he could locate Elaine and Uncle Joe, the change hit him with the force of a Mack truck. With the strain of bones and skin stretching and growing, the pain dragged him beneath the surface.

With only enough breath in his lungs for a frog to survive, his fully formed human lungs burned with the need for oxygen. His vision blurred and he fought against the fuzzy haze preceding the black abyss of unconsciousness.

Elaine was in the water somewhere nearby, possibly drowning, trapped in her worst nightmare. And who knew how Uncle Joe fared in the collision? The old man meant a lot to Craig. He'd been the balance in Craig's upbringing, the roots to which he'd clung in his youth. Craig couldn't give up; he had to stay awake and find them.

He pushed through the haze and the darkness, propelling his fully transformed body through the brackish water to the surface. "Elaine! Uncle Joe!"

His gaze strained against the gloom, and he listened for the slightest sound of splashing.

"Joe!" A gurgling feminine cry rent the air a few yards to Craig's left. He launched himself in that direction. In the meager light eking its way through the dense canopy overhead, Craig could see ripples disturbing the water's surface. He dove into the middle of the circles, his hand connecting with hair. Winding his fingers into the floating tresses, he dragged her up until he could hook his arms beneath hers and lift her to the surface.

Expecting her to kick and scream hysterically, Craig was surprised when Elaine hung limply in his arms. His heart alternated between racing and standing still. Was she alive?

Then her body jerked and she coughed up water. "Joe," she gasped.

"It's me, Craig," he said, swimming her toward a small island, praying the alligators would give them a break this one night.

"Craig? How'd you get here?" she asked. "Where's Joe?"

Craig concentrated on keeping her head above water until his bare feet touched the bottom. He sat Elaine on a large root, grabbed a low-hanging branch, and shoved it into her hands. "Can you hold on until I find him?"

She nodded, tears slipping down her cheeks. "Yes, go."

Craig threw himself back into the murky water and swam out to the overturned boat. With a deep breath, he dove beneath it and resurfaced on the other side. No uncle.

He swam in wider circles, bumping along the bottom of the bayou in case his uncle had submerged. In the shadow of a giant bald cypress tree, he found a still form draped over a knobby cypress knee. Uncle Joe.

His face was out of the water but the man wasn't moving. "Uncle Joe?" No response. Fear swirling through his stomach, Craig searched for a pulse. For a moment, he couldn't feel the reassuring beat of the older man's heart. Pain shot through Craig's chest, threatening to shut off his breathing. *Not Uncle Joe. Please, God, not Uncle Joe.*

"Craig? Is that you, boy?" Uncle Joe breathed in a raspy voice.

"Yes, sir. It's me."

"Thought I saw you hop in the boat." Uncle Joe coughed, grimaced and grabbed for his ribs. "Thank God for cypress knees. Kept me from drowning, but I think I busted a rib."

"Don't you worry, I'll have you outta here in no time." Craig glanced around for the boat.

"Where's Elaine?" Joe asked.

"I'm here," she called out from the darkness. "Are you all right?"

"Nothing a little alcohol won't cure," Joe yelled back. He coughed for his trouble. When he got his breath again, he asked, "What about the other boat?"

"Gone," Craig said.

"Good." Uncle Joe inhaled carefully. "Not up to a fight right now."

"No, you're not." Craig didn't remind his uncle they weren't out of trouble yet. With the alligator population up and the fish population down . . . well now, that made for a bad combination for humans swimming in an alligator habitat.

Uncle Joe pushed against the cypress knee, winced and looked around. "What about our boat?"

"I don't know," Craig said. "Hang tight while I check it out."

Craig swam out to the upside-down craft and quickly ran the tips of his fingers along the hull. One corner was dented in six inches, and a gash stretched from the dent up to the rim. He couldn't feel any other holes. Whatever the damage, the skiff was their only option. He had to get Elaine and Uncle Joe out of the water.

Swimming hard, he pulled the boat to the shallows and struggled to flip it onto its belly. The skiff floated, but the motor was waterlogged and completely unserviceable. If they were lucky, they'd make it back to the marina before morning using good old-fashioned elbow grease and a paddle. He just hoped Uncle Joe's injuries weren't life threatening.

With one hand wrapped around the tie-off rope, Craig swam the boat over to Elaine. He shoved her over the side onto the cool metal bench.

Her teeth chattered and she clung to him even when she was seated. "I'm glad you found us." For the moment, Elaine pushed aside her anger and misgivings about Craig's part in the Littington organization. He'd been there when she needed him. What more could she ask?

"Me too." He kissed her hard on the lips and peeled her arms from around his neck. "I've got to get Uncle Joe. We're going to be all right." He swam the skiff to where Uncle Joe slouched over the cypress knees. "Need a hand?"

"Yeah, 'fraid I do." Uncle Joe never asked for help. The fact that he would meant he was in some amount of pain.

"Not a problem." Craig slid his arms under the other man and eased him over the side of the boat.

The older man grunted, but didn't cry out.

With both of the people Craig had grown to love in the boat, he realized he couldn't join them without a whole lot of questions.

He'd been swimming in the nude. As a frog, he didn't have a need for clothing. As a man, he'd have a tough time explaining his lack of covering. Just as he pondered the dilemma, the rubber hip-waders floated to the surface in front of him.

Craig sent a silent thank you to the heavens. The three of them just might make it through the night intact, both physically and mentally. His jaw tightened. And when he got back to dry land, he planned to catch whoever had done this to his family.

CHAPTER TWENTY

Elaine thought they'd never get back to the marina. Damp and in a state of semi-shock, her teeth clattered so hard against each other, surely they'd chip.

Without the engine and with only the one paddle Craig wielded, progress was slow.

Cupping her stiff fingers, Elaine bailed water out of the bottom of the boat. She wished she could do more to help them along.

Uncle Joe had lapsed into silence. Elaine couldn't see his expression, since he sat facing Craig in the middle of the boat.

Elaine worried he wasn't doing well. She hoped he hadn't punctured a lung with the broken rib. He could also have a concussion, which meant he should stay awake.

"Mr. Thibodeaux?" she called out. "Joe?"

A few seconds went by before he grunted.

"Are you okay?" she asked.

"Yeah."

He didn't sound okay. Elaine tried to think of something to say that would keep him talking. "How long have you had the marina?"

"Since I quit law."

Not quite the answer she expected. "I didn't know you were in law. Was everyone in Bayou Miste an attorney and I didn't know it?"

"No, just the Thibodeauxs," Craig said.

"Why did you quit practicing, Joe?" Elaine asked.

"Had my reasons." His words were clipped, not inviting more digging. The night grew silent with only the sound of the paddle dipping in the water.

Elaine couldn't help herself, she had to ask. "Was it a woman? You don't have to answer. I was just curious." She rubbed her hands together to get the blood flowing in her cold fingers.

For a long time, Joe was quiet. Then out of the darkness he said, "Yeah."

Just then, Elaine recalled Mozelle's comment about Joe loving Craig's mother, and the pieces fell into place. Damn! She should have kept her big mouth shut. And she would for the rest of the journey back to the marina.

But Joe had more to say. "It was a long time ago. And I still think about her every day of my life. Kinda hard not to."

Elaine pried only because Joe seemed to want to talk about it. "Why, if it was such a long time ago?"

Joe nodded his head in the direction of Craig. "This big doofus keeps coming back to remind me."

Uh-oh! Looked like Uncle Joe had kept a secret from his nephew and Elaine had busted it wide open. She wished she could crawl under a rock or slip over the side of the boat. She shrank back on the metal bench hoping she hadn't started a family feud.

"Me?" Craig frowned.

In the light from the half-moon shining through the gaps in the leaves, Uncle Joe stared across at Craig. "Yeah, you."

"What do I have to do with your love life?"

What can of worms had she opened with her line of questioning? Elaine had only meant to keep Joe talking until they could get him back to land and a doctor.

"I fell for the wrong girl back when I was about your age."

"Why was she wrong?" Elaine thought about her predicament with Craig. She was a scientist; he was an attorney, representing a client possibly responsible for polluting the ecosystem of the bayou. How much more wrong could they be for each other?

"She was in love with another man."

Okay, so Joe had a stronger reason for her being the wrong one for him.

"Did you tell her how you felt?" Elaine asked.

"Yeah."

"And what happened?"

"She married my brother anyway."

Craig's gaze bored into his uncle's. "Why didn't you tell me?"

Uncle Joe attempted a shrug, and winced for his effort. "What did it matter? She married your father, I moved to Bayou Miste, and the rest is history."

Craig leaned forward, the paddle dragging in the water. "Why did you run away?"

"I left. Your father wouldn't have wanted me hangin' around like a dadgum fifth wheel."

"You're brothers." Craig dipped the paddle into the water. "Couldn't you have worked things out?"

Uncle Joe shook his head. "For years I couldn't be around her knowing she wasn't mine. And I couldn't forgive myself for betraying my brother."

"For loving my mother?" Craig couldn't see his mother, queen of the social scene, with Uncle Joe.

A half smile tilted the corner of his uncle's mouth. "No. For telling her on their wedding day."

"Oh." Craig sat back, the wind knocked out of his sails.

"Yeah, the timin' . . . how do you say . . . sucked."

"No kidding," Craig muttered.

"I've kicked myself all my life, wondering if it would have made a difference if I'd told her sooner. When you were old enough to come visit, I pretended you were our son. I probably even wished it. Then you grew up and haven't been here in so long, I thought I'd lost you as well."

Craig ran a hand through his hair. "I didn't know."

"No, you weren't supposed to." Joe shifted on his seat. "When you went on to join the family business, just as your father wanted, I thought you were well on your way to making the same mistakes I did. Not taking any risks, living the life your family expects rather than the one you choose isn't the way to find happiness."

"I like my life," Craig insisted.

"Do you?" Uncle Joe stared up at him.

"You like representing men like Jason Littington, who very well could be killing Bayou Miste?" Elaine, who'd been sitting quietly in the front of the boat, chose that moment to speak up. "I heard you were only in town on business and that business was with Littington of Littington Enterprises, the only refinery or major industrial anything between here and Morgan City."

"That's right." Craig felt like he was on the wrong end of a judge, jury and hangman's noose.

"I'll bet if we pull that dumped barrel we saw out of the swamp, we'll discover Littington at the bottom of it." Elaine tipped her head to the side. "And you're proud of representing people like that?"

"I don't judge until I hear both sides of the argument."

"And you tell no more of the truth than absolutely necessary, either." Elaine's voice broke at the end of her words. "Is that one of the first lessons you learned in Law 101?"

"I didn't lie to you, Elaine."

"You didn't tell me the truth, either." Elaine wrapped her arms around herself as though she could ward off his words.

"But I didn't lie," he insisted.

"What else haven't you told me, Craig?" She sniffed, and Craig wished he could see her face more clearly. Was she crying? That was the last thing he wanted.

"I've told you everything I can. For anything else, you'll have to trust me."

She shook her head. "How can I trust you, when you don't tell me all the truth? Like how did you get out in the swamp and find us? And why are you wearing those . . . those . . . rubbery things . . . instead of clothes?"

If he told her he was a frog by day, she'd never believe him. And she would never trust him again if he didn't tell her. Damned if he did, and damned if he didn't. If she witnessed his transformation to an amphibian she'd know the truth, but she would also learn of the spell, and make herself ineligible to be the woman who loved him and broke the curse. Craig couldn't risk that happening. At this point she was his best chance for getting his human form back permanently. "I can't answer your questions now."

"Can't or won't?" Her shoulders rose and fell. "There's no trust."

Craig stared from Elaine to his uncle and back to Elaine. His heart squeezed tight in his chest. Elaine was slipping away from him and he couldn't do anything to get her back. "I guess that's it then."

"I guess so." Elaine stared down at her feet.

"What are you going to do with the information about the swamp?" Craig asked.

"I'll go to the EPA," she said, her voice low and her head still down.

"Then there's nothing more to say." Craig dug the paddle into the water. The quicker he got back to the marina, the sooner he could get away from her.

"Bull feathers!" Uncle Joe shouted, followed immediately by several tentative coughs.

"Stay out of it, Uncle Joe," Craig warned.

"Didn't you hear anything I said to you just now?" Joe whispered in deference to his sore rib.

"Yes, but this is different." He dug the paddle in again, propelling the boat forward and a little to the left. He compensated by dipping in on the opposite side.

"Bull feathers!" Uncle Joe repeated. "You're crazy about this girl. Don't screw it up like I did."

"Uncle," Craig said, his voice low and dangerous. If ever there was a time for the Coast Guard to show up, now would be good.

The sound of a motor hummed softly in the night.

"Do you think they came back for us?" Elaine asked.

"Shhhh." Craig tilted his head in the direction of the noise. "Sounds like a trolling motor."

"Larry, you gotta turn de motor off if you wanna gig dose frogs." Mo's voice could be heard before Craig actually saw him.

"But we be gettin' there much faster with it than without," Larry argued.

"Don't do no good for frog giggin' if you scare de frogs all away."

"Why we be giggin', anyway?" Larry asked. "Ain'tcha 'fraid we might catch our good buddy?"

"He ain't a frog at night, bonehead. An' I got a hankern' for some fried frog legs."

Craig turned and stood in the boat, waving his paddle high over his head. "Mo, Larry, over here!"

A jon boat similar to the one they were in trolled into view.

"Craig, whatcha doin' out here on de bayou? Shouldn't you be findin' you a woman or something?" Mo called out.

"Had us a little accident, guys. Think you could give us a lift back to the marina? Uncle Joe could use some medical attention."

"You all right, Mr. Thibodeaux?" Mo pulled the boat alongside the damaged skiff.

"Okay," Joe wheezed. "For an old man with a broken rib, I guess."

"Woooweee! What happened here?" Larry stared at the skiff's damaged corner.

"Had a run-in with a deck boat." Craig tossed them the towrope.

Mo whacked Larry in the gut. "I tol' you, der be some powerful bad magic on dis bayou tonight."

Larry rubbed his belly, frowning. "You didn't tell me dat."

"Well I felt it. I shoulda tol' you."

"You see what I have to put up with?" Larry said to Craig. He grabbed the rope and tied it to a metal loop at the back of their boat. "Ready?"

"Thanks guys," Craig said. As usual, his buddies came through for him. Mo waved aside his gratitude. "Dat's what friends are for."

Question was, would Craig come through for them? He had a mess to clean up and it stunk just as bad as the polluted barrel at the bottom of the bayou. He had to get to Jason Littington and find out what the hell was going on before he could convince Elaine he was not working for the bad guys. Although why her opinion of him meant so much, he couldn't imagine. But it did. A lot.

About fifteen minutes later, they reached the marina. The bait shop had been closed since Uncle Joe had left earlier, but in the parking lot stood a shiny red Mercedes sports coupe.

Uh oh. Craig's mess had just exploded to gargantuan proportions.

Once Mo and Larry had tied the skiff to the dock, Elaine hurriedly accepted Mo's beefy hand to pull her to the wooden planks. "Thank you, Mo," she offered, then turned to march up to the bait shop and as far away from Craig as she could get.

Not until she'd reached the parking lot did Elaine realize she wasn't alone. A woman stepped out of a bright red Mercedes, a female like no other Elaine had ever encountered.

She was everything Elaine was not. From sleek, tailored suit to perfectly straight blond hair hanging to an ideal length, not too long, not too short, she was classically beautiful in every way.

With her clothes dripping dry on her body, Elaine felt certain she looked like a reject from the Salvation Army with a Little Orphan Annie hairstyle.

The woman looked down her nose at Elaine and immediately turned her attention to the men coming up behind her. "Craig!" she called out and rushed to him, flinging her arms around his neck and pressing her perfectly tailored suit to his hip-waders. "I've missed you so much."

"Cassandra, what are you doing here?" Craig's voice was clipped and didn't sound too happy.

"I came because you asked me to, silly."

All of Elaine's righteous indignation about the Littington fiasco paled in comparison to the way her heart hit rock bottom. Apparently, there were other things Craig had failed to tell her, proving he hadn't meant for their relationship to last. He already had a girlfriend, one who could blend in with his circles in New Orleans much better than a dweeb scientist who was afraid of the water.

While loverboy was hugging his Cassandra, Elaine slipped away to shower the smell of bayou water from her hair. If only she could wash the heartache away with the smell. Exhausted beyond belief, she trudged her way to her rented cottage, locking the door behind her.

Tonight would be her first night alone since she and Craig had started their steamy romps in the sack. She could only stand to be in the bedroom long enough to gather fresh clothing on her way to the bathroom. She'd sleep on the couch and pack her stuff tomorrow. Her stay in Bayou Miste was over. Time to face reality and get back to the university. *So you can resume hiding behind your microscope?* No way. She'd overcome that phase in her life. Damned if she'd let herself backslide.

* * *

Two hours at the hospital, with Cassandra yammering in one ear while his uncle read him the riot act in the other, gave Craig a splitting headache. Finally convinced his uncle had no more lasting damage than a broken rib, Craig dropped him off at his house with a bottle of painkillers and a lecture on taking it easy.

Cassandra was another story entirely. Trying to get rid of her was like a fly trying to shake sticky flypaper. Until she saw his sleeping quarters in the back of . . . as she put it . . . the worm-infested bait shop, she thought she was going to sleep with him. Craig put his foot down and sent her back to Morgan City and the closest Holiday Inn with room service.

Finally alone, he grabbed a phone and dialed Jason Littington. He had some business to conduct with the man. Never mind that the clock read three A.M. Craig's life was crashing around him and he didn't have time for pleasantries.

"Mr. Littington? This is Craig Thibodeaux."

"Craig, why the heck are you calling me at this hour?"

"You got trouble, sir. If you don't want to go to jail, meet me at my uncle's bait shop, ASAP."

"What—"

"Just do it." Craig said, his voice firm. "And come alone."

CHAPTER TWENTY-ONE

Elaine blinked at the sun streaking through the cottage window to her makeshift bed on the couch. Once again, she'd slept the day away when she should have been working. Didn't she have some frogs to dissect or specimens to investigate beneath her microscope?

She'd tossed and turned on the couch cushions until dawn before she'd drifted off. Her sleep hadn't been any more restful. With voodoo drums beating and ominous chanting filling her dreams, she felt like she'd been offered up as a sacrifice in some pagan ritual only to be rejected. Even in her dreams she didn't fit in.

What was it she was supposed to do today? Something big. She sat up and pushed the mass of tangled curls from her face and waited for her fuzzy head to clear. When it did, her empty stomach grumbled. Or was that her empty heart? Oh yeah. The beautiful Cassandra had come for Craig and Elaine was supposed to be packing to leave Bayou Miste.

If Cassandra was the type of woman he wanted, no way Elaine Smith could measure up. Nor did she want to. If she'd learned one thing, she'd learned she couldn't be who she wasn't. She could improve on herself, but she couldn't and wouldn't change deep down. Hers was a case of "love me as I am, or don't love me at all."

Unfortunately, Craig would choose the latter, if he hadn't already. Besides, he wasn't the man she'd thought he was. Why hadn't he told her he was involved with Littington Enterprises and trusted her to either understand or give him the chance to explain? He hadn't done that. He'd strung her along to further his own interests, just like Brian.

Well, who needed him, anyway?

You do. The little voice in her head sounded very much like the chanting she'd heard in her dreams.

A knock sounded at the door. Who could that be? Elaine looked down at her Tweety-Bird T-shirt and flannel boxer shorts and shrugged. With her new "what you see is what you get" attitude, she opened the door.

Mozelle stood there with her requisite basket full of sweet-smelling pastries and a smile bright enough to light the Chrysler building. "Howdy, neighbor. Thought you could use a little midday snack."

"Oh, hi, Mozelle." Elaine opened the door for the woman. With all the enthusiasm of one marching to the guillotine, she turned and padded barefooted into the kitchen to start some go-juice in the coffeemaker.

"What's wrong dear? Are you not feeling well?" Mozelle set the basket on the table and touched her hand to Elaine's forehead. "No fever."

"I'm fine." *If you don't count a broken heart.*

"I heard y'all had some trouble out on the swamp."

Elaine shook her head. "Good news travels fast around here."

"I was by to see Joe earlier." Mozelle blushed. "Needless to say, I was shocked to find him injured. And you, my dear, were you injured as well?"

"No, I wasn't injured." *Just my heart.*

"Joe told me that Cassandra woman showed up lookin' for Craig last night." Mozelle peered closer at Elaine. "Is that what's got your panties in a wad?"

Good news really did travel fast. Elaine forced her tone to be light. "Why should it?"

"I know I'd be upset if I saw the man I was head over heels for huggin' some other woman."

Turning her back to Mozelle, Elaine said, "I'm not head over heels for him. Who said I was?"

"Honey, your words say one thing, your face says another."

Elaine raised a hand to her cheek and sank to the shiny red vinyl chair. "Oh this is awful. I can't be in love with Craig."

Mozelle stood next to Elaine and wrapped an arm around her shoulder. "Sweet pea, there's nothing awful about lovin' someone. It's a gift."

"A gift if the feeling is returned, a curse if it isn't." Elaine laid her head on the table. "He wouldn't want my love, even if I offered it up with a free sports car."

"How do you know if you don't ask?"

"Ask? Mozelle, if you'd seen that woman . . . I couldn't compete with her. She's perfect, and I'm . . ." she glanced down at her faded Tweety, lifted a tangled curl and shook her head, ". . . I'm just me."

"Maybe that's what Craig wants. He's lived in New Orleans all his life surrounded by everything money has to offer. You have something he can't buy."

"I do?" Elaine looked up hopelessly. "Like what?"

"You have genuine compassion and a heart worth

takin' a risk for." Mozelle grabbed her hands and stared into Elaine's eyes. "Honey, you're real. From what Joe told me, Cassandra wouldn't know love if it hit her smack-dab in her chemically and surgically enhanced face."

"It's no use, Mozelle. I don't belong here. I need to go back where I do."

"You gonna tuck your tail between your legs and run?" The older woman folded her arms across her chest. "I thought you had more gumption than that. What did I tell you about fighting for your man?"

"He's not my man!" Elaine wailed. "I don't even know who he is. He knew I wanted to stop the pollution, yet he represents the man who's causing it. We have nothing in common, nothing." Elaine turned her back to Mozelle, fighting a losing battle to keep the tears from falling. First one slid down her cheek, followed by another and before too long, a steady stream dripped off her chin.

"Have you given him a chance to explain?" Mozelle asked.

With a shake of her head, Elaine stared down at her hands.

An arm draped over Elaine's shoulder, and the older woman pulled her close. "You got the most important thing in common, sweetie. You got love. Everything else can be worked out."

Steeling herself from the warmth and comfort Mozelle offered, Elaine stiffened and pulled away. "No, we don't, and no, it can't."

"That boy loves you. I saw how he looked at you at the Raccoon Saloon the other night."

"That wasn't love." Elaine smacked her palm against the table. "What you saw was an ordinary case of lust."

"Not the way he stuck up for you. I really, truly believe he cares. He just doesn't always know how to show it. Besides, it's just like a man to be stubborn and bullheaded about sharin' his feelin's. You can't expect the impossible. Why, look at me. I've waited the past ten years for Joe to notice I exist. Ten years too long. Sometimes you gotta take matters into yer own hands."

Elaine scrubbed the back of her hand over her eyes. "I can't, Mozelle. I just can't."

The older woman planted her fists on her hips and tapped a toe against the wooden floor. "So that's it? Yer just gonna hightail it out of here without a goodbye, by yer leave, or kiss my grits?"

"Yes." Elaine grabbed a tissue and blew. "The sooner the better."

"What about the pollution? Who'll make sure they stop?"

"I'll call the EPA and give them the information I know over the phone. Joe can show them where we found the barrel. They'll investigate and prosecute as necessary."

Ms. Reneau wrapped her arms around her middle and shuffled to the window, her shoulders hunched, appearing older than she had since Elaine had known her. "What about the friends you made here? Don'tcha think we'll miss you?"

"Oh, Mozelle." Elaine crossed the floor and pulled the other woman into a tight hug. "I'm going to miss you." She fought against the tears choking her vocal chords. "You can come see me in New Orleans."

"Don't have much call for goin' to the Big Easy. They drive too fast for my likin'."

"You could get Josie to bring you."

"Don't know that I like how fast she drives either," Mozelle said.

"But you'll do it?" Elaine held her at arm's length. The woman's answer meant more to her than she thought possible, considering the few short days they'd known each other. "Won't you?"

"Sure, honey. I'll come see you. But I still think you ought to reconsider and give Craig a chance to explain."

Elaine's gaze settled on a far corner of the room. "I can't. I have to go home."

Mozelle hugged her close, patting her back like a child. Then she set Elaine away and lifted her apron to wipe the tears from her eyes. "Well then, I guess there's not much else I can do to talk you out of it."

"No, there's not," Elaine said, mist fogging her eyes. "In fact, if I'm to get on the road before dark, I'd better start packing."

Mozelle squeezed her tight once more. "I'm gonna miss you, Elaine Smith. You've been a little ray of sunshine in Bayou Miste. I hate to see you leave."

"Thanks," Elaine said over Mozelle's shoulder, ". . . for being my friend."

Mozelle broke free, scrubbed a hand across her face and looked around. "Is there anything I can do to help?"

"I think I'd rather be alone to pack." If Mozelle didn't leave soon, Elaine would be blubbering all over again. Who'd have thought in the little bitty town of Bayou Miste, she'd have found such a good friend in a woman old enough to be her mother?

"If you're sure, I'll just go check on Joe." Mozelle's mouth lifted at the corners. "I think that ornery ol' poot likes playin' sick."

Elaine forced a smile for Mozelle's happiness. "Go on, he needs you." She only wished Craig needed her.

After Mozelle left, Elaine dragged boxes out into the living room and tossed in books, papers and pencils. When she got to her microscope, she hesitated, recalling the night Craig had held her after the house had been ransacked. At the time, she'd felt cared for. Craig had made love to her all night, his touch gentle and his passion equal to her own.

Had it all been an act? Elaine set the microscope on the table and looked around for newspaper to wrap it.

"Leaving?" a feminine voice asked from behind her.

Elaine spun to face the infamous and infinitely beautiful Cassandra. She wore a finely woven silk skirt suit with dyed-to-match strap sandals. Every one of her straight blond hairs was pulled back and secured in a neat French chignon. Not a stray tendril dared escape to destroy the perfect symmetry.

Elaine closed her eyes to keep from heaving air from her hollow belly. Tweety Bird still hung like an old rag from her shoulders over her flannel boxers whose hem had given up threads to the washing-machine monster years ago. What she wanted to do was crawl under the nearest paper bag and ignore the world.

Unfortunately, hiding was not an option. Elaine opened her eyes and plastered a smile on her face as if Cassandra's visit was no big deal. "Hi, should I know you?"

Cassandra's gaze ran the length from Elaine's disastrous hair to her bare feet. "I don't know. I had to come meet the woman everyone's been talking about."

"Me?" Elaine squeaked.

"Since ten this morning, I've had no less than four visitors and at least two threatening phone calls, warning me to stay away from Craig and someone called Elaine."

"You have?" Elaine's vocabulary escaped her. What was going on?

"Some man named Mo even threatened to turn his pet alligator loose in my hotel room."

Mo? Elaine barely knew Mo. Why would he be warning Cassandra off Craig? "I don't understand." Elaine pushed her hair away from her face.

"I don't either, especially since Craig called me last Saturday, begging me to come all the way from New Orleans to this godforsaken swamp." Cassandra glanced around the interior of the cottage and back to Elaine. "Craig mentioned he had something important to ask me and he needed me down here as soon as possible." She held out a hand and studied her coral-tipped fingernails.

"And it took you three days to get here?" Elaine could have pulled her tongue out and stomped all over it. Why should she care how long it took Cassandra to come to Bayou Miste after Craig's call?

Had Craig phoned Elaine with the promise of asking an important question, she sure as hell wouldn't have waited three days to mosey her way down to the bayou. She'd have broken speed limits in every parish from New Orleans to the center of the Atchafalaya Basin.

Is this woman kidding? Apparently looks weren't everything. She left a lot to be desired in mental faculties. Yet Craig had begged her to come to Bayou Miste with the promise of an important question.

Elaine's heart sank at what that important question had to be.

"Although Craig came here under the pretext of business, I figured he was here to contemplate the next step in our relationship and maybe to . . ." Cassandra's gaze flicked to Elaine, ". . . sow a few wild oats."

Elaine gasped at the blatant slam. Try as she might, she couldn't halt the flood of heat to her cheeks as she recalled the wild oats they'd sown together. Irritation quickly followed embarrassment and she forced a hand to her hip. "Are you finished inspecting the oat fields? If so, I have work to do."

As she studied Elaine, the luscious blonde's eyes narrowed, a considering gleam sparkling in their depths. "You're a bit more intelligent than his usual flings. He has a hit-and-run reputation, but make no mistake, he always comes back to me."

Elaine flinched. Craig had said he wasn't the commitment type. Was Cassandra the reason?

A carefully plucked eyebrow rose over clear gray eyes. "You didn't think he'd stay with you, did you?"

Cassandra's words hit like a punch to the gut. "Look, if you've come to gloat, save your breath. Craig means nothing to me." Elaine swallowed the lump rising in her throat. "Now if you don't mind, I really have work to do."

"You're making the right decision to leave. Craig and I have an understanding, and once we're married, I'm sure his little indiscretions will end." Cassandra drew in a deep breath and blew it out. Then, with a cardboard smile, she stuck out her hand. "Ellen, it's been . . . interesting. I'll show myself out."

Staring at the proffered hand, Elaine kept hers at her side. She had no intention of shaking the woman's hand or following her to the door.

Cassandra's smile slipped, and she dropped her hand and swung her purse over her shoulder. Her bag caught the microscope perched on the edge of the table and sent it flying to the floor. The device landed with a crash and the distinct sound of breaking glass.

The woman responsible for smashing Elaine's heart turned and stared down her nose at the microscope. "Did I do that?" She shrugged. "Just send the bill to Craig. He won't mind; we'll have joint accounts soon enough."

Numb and hurting at the same time, Elaine moved around the cottage gathering her belongings, yet stepping around the broken microscope. She'd save that for last.

Packing took her longer than she'd thought. Just before the sun dropped below the tree line, she shoved the final box into the backseat of her sedan and retuned to the house for one last look and to collect her treasured microscope.

The place looked the same as the first day she'd set foot inside the front door, except for the angry red words on the wall.

The quaint cottage with vintage furniture stood ready for the next renter. Elaine walked over to the dinette with its speckled tabletop and bright-red vinyl seat cushions. She smiled, running her finger across the surface. Who'd have thought they still had tables like these? She switched the light off in the kitchen and turned toward the bedroom.

She'd left this room for last. The old white iron bed conjured memories best left behind. Craig lying there in nothing but a smile, stroking the hair from her face, trailing kisses down her neck.

Given Craig's concern for his uncle and his love for the swamp, representing Littington and his polluting factory didn't make sense. Why would he jeopardize a place he'd loved as a child?

Elaine could picture a smaller version of Craig running through Mozelle's peach orchard. Whether the boy was a younger version of Craig from the past or the possible child he'd bring to Bayou Miste someday, Elaine couldn't tell.

A sob caught in her throat. Why torture herself? They weren't meant to be. Hadn't he said he wasn't one to commit?

Elaine touched the light switch, leaving the room and

that chapter of her life in the dark. Now all she had to do was get her microscope and go.

In these few short days, she'd connected with Bayou Miste more than the years alone in her house in New Orleans. She stared down at the old microscope lying on its side on the hardwood floor, its gray metal full of memories of her parents, and now Craig.

But the microscope was a thing, not a warm, living, breathing person. If she had a choice between keeping the 'scope or having a single shot at getting her parents back, she'd toss the 'scope in a New Orleans minute and fight with all her heart for her parents.

So why wasn't she willing to fight for Craig? He wasn't married to Cassandra yet. From the little Elaine had gleaned from their earlier conversation, they weren't even engaged. She didn't have a legal hold on the man. Problem was, Elaine didn't know anything about Craig's feelings for her or for Cassandra.

And did she, Elaine Smith, the woman afraid of water and relationships, love Craig enough to go after him? Was that what she was considering?

A woman used to analyzing scientific phenomena and developing a hypothesis, she hadn't done her work here. She'd observed a change in herself. That change she'd describe as a feeling of completeness when she was with Craig and a corresponding emptiness when she wasn't. The only logical hypothesis she could come up with was love. How was she to know if it was the real thing if she didn't hang around and experiment?

What if he doesn't want me?

Was the possibility of rejection so abhorrent she'd refuse to expose her heart? Even if she only had a one-in-a-bazillion probability of Craig returning her love, wasn't it worth the risk?

Hell, yes! The voice in her head sounded loud and clear.

Assuming the phenomena was love, how would she feel if he discarded it? Horrible. But at least she would have tried. She'd know for certain one way or the other, and she'd have no regrets for missed opportunities.

What about his dealings with Littington? Could she form a relationship with a man who didn't trust her enough to tell her the truth? Elaine stared down at the microscope. The answer came into focus. As Mozelle had so plainly put it, she needed to fight for her man. If that meant giving him a chance to explain and going toe-to-toe with the intimidating Cassandra, so be it!

Elaine set the microscope on the table and marched out to her car. When she bent in to grab a box, a voice sounded behind her.

"Going somewhere?"

"No." Elaine answered before she realized the question had not been a friendly one. A chill raced down her spine, and she spun to face the intruder.

With his hip leaning against her car and his face partially concealed in the shadows, Randall Pratt's eyes glowed with strange intensity.

"What are you doing here?" she demanded.

He pushed away from the car and walked closer, like a snake sidling up to his next meal. "Now is that any way to greet a friend?"

"You're not my friend." Elaine knew what friends were, now that she'd met Mozelle and Josie.

"Tsk, tsk." He lifted a strand of her hair. "I came to make sure you left town for good."

"I'm not leaving." Elaine planted her feet slightly apart, refusing to back away from his threatening closeness.

"Oh, but I think you will." Randall lifted his hand,

pointing a gun at her midsection. "You're coming with me. You've caused more than enough trouble."

Her heart pounding in her chest, Elaine inched backward until her shoulder blades bumped against the cool metal of her car door. "What have I done to you?"

"Don't play stupid. You and the fancy-schmanzy lawyer been nosing around where you don't belong."

Pieces fell into place and lodged in the pit of Elaine's stomach. "You're the one dumping the barrels in the bayou."

"Give the lady a prize." Randall jerked the gun toward the door. "Let's go."

"Don't be ridiculous." She infused as much confidence into her voice as she could with a gun pointed at her vital organs. "You might get away with dumping pollutants in the bayou, but you'll never get away with murder."

A swaggering smile slid up one side of his mouth. "I could bury a Mack truck in the bayou and no one would find it."

Elaine inhaled a long slow breath and glanced toward Mozelle's empty house.

Randall's gaze followed hers. "Don't even think about screaming. A nine-millimeter bullet may be small, but it leaves a big hole in a person's gut. Makes for a big mess."

Cold metal pressed against her sternum. All the breath left Elaine's lungs in a whoosh.

"That's more like it." Randall said. "Now, get in the car."

CHAPTER TWENTY-TWO

The meeting with Jason Littington had concluded better than Craig had hoped and they had a good idea who was responsible for the illegal dumping. As the first gray reminders of sunrise lightened the sky, they had a plan in place.

Craig had hurriedly shoved the refinery owner out the bait shop door, locking it behind him. Wouldn't sit well with Littington if he had stepped back into the shop and found Craig in the throes of frog metamorphosis.

Unfortunately, Littington's departure had left Craig no time to leave the shop before the change occurred. After shrinking to his bullfrog form, Craig had hopped to a quiet corner and slept. The business of staying up all night and changing forms twice a day had exhausted him.

His sleep had been intermingled with disturbing dreams of voodoo ceremonies and an effervescent, full orange moon. When he woke in the late afternoon, an urgent sense of impending doom settled in his gut. What did the night hold in store for this man-frog serving a penance he probably deserved?

Uncle Joe hadn't made it to the shop today, no doubt convalescing with his new nurse and lady love, Mozelle Reneau. The marina had remained locked throughout the day.

With the CLOSED sign still displayed in the front door, customers came, peered in through the windows and left without bait or tackle. Trapped inside by his size, Craig impatiently awaited sunset and his transformation back to human form. He worried about Elaine, alone in her cottage, a target to whatever maniacs had been terrorizing them in the swamp. With Uncle Joe out of commission and Craig locked in the shop, she didn't have anyone to protect her.

The hands on the wall clock crawled through each hour until Craig knew he'd explode with the need for action. Finally, the sun dropped below the horizon. Craig welcomed the pain of his stretching, growing, and lengthening bones and tissues.

As soon as he could focus, he slipped into jeans and a shirt. Then he reached for the phone and dialed home. "Hey Mom, this is Craig. Let me talk to Dad. Tell him it's urgent."

"Hello, Craig." His father's brisk voice cut across the line. "What's the problem?"

"Dad, I need you to call the EPA and get them down here right away."

"What's this all about?" Craig's father demanded. "Did you seal the deal with Littington?"

Trust his father to be more worried about the Littington deal. "Not exactly."

"You've been down there a week. You should have all the paperwork signed and delivered back to New Orleans by now."

Craig breathed deeply to squelch his rising impatience. "I know, but more important things have come up."

"What could be more important than bringing in new business to the family firm?"

People's lives, the environment, loving someone. "Lots, Dad," Craig answered.

"I sent Cassandra down there to bring you back. She should be there by now."

"She's here." So Cassandra hadn't come because he'd called. She'd come because the boss had ordered her to. "I sent her up to Morgan City. I won't be coming back with her."

"She's an aggressive attorney, son. And a fine woman. You could do worse." His father cleared his throat, a prelude to his usual advice to his son. "It's time you started thinking about your future. Maybe even settle down and raise a few kids."

Craig pinched the bridge of his nose, a headache building behind his eyes. "I'm working on it, Dad. Only not with Cassandra."

"Don't tell me you're foolin' around with one of those Cajun swamp gals?"

Craig bit down on his tongue and breathed through his nose several times before answered. "Dad, I'll choose who I want to spend my life with. If she happens to be a Cajun swamp rat or an Alaskan Eskimo, I'll be the one to make that choice, not you."

"Don't take that tone with me. I still control who works for Thibodeaux and Associates."

With a sigh, Craig realized the time had come. "No, Dad, you don't. I quit."

"What do you mean, you quit?" His father paused. "What's got into you, boy? Did you drink too much swamp water? Has my brother been filling you with crazy ideas?"

"No, Dad." How could he explain to his bottom-line-driven father? "I want to do more with my skills and degree. I want to make a difference."

"You make a difference to your clients back here."

"Yeah, a difference on how much money they get from their fifth divorce in as many years. Or who gets to keep the family pet that cost as much as some people make in a year." This conversation wasn't getting him anywhere. "Dad, I don't have time to discuss this. I appreciate everything you've taught me. Now it's time for me to get out on my own."

Richard Thibodeaux paused as if grasping for something to say to change his son's mind. "You're making a big mistake."

"Maybe so, Dad, maybe so. But sometimes you have to go after what you believe in." Like Elaine. "Will you call the EPA?"

His father hesitated, and then breathed an audible sigh over the line. "I'll call. But don't think we're done with this discussion. When are you coming back to New Orleans?"

"I don't know." Craig ran a hand through his hair.

"Your mother will be upset."

Cheap shot, Dad. "I'm pretty sure Mom will understand." Craig sucked in a deep breath. No matter how he felt about the family firm, he loved his father. "Dad, this may be hard for you to comprehend, but I know this is the right decision for me."

"You should think about it more," his father said. "Take a vacation. Sleep on it."

"I have, Dad." Craig looked out at the dark sky. "I have to go. Tell Mom I love her."

"Son—"

With a steady hand, Craig set the phone on the hook. Wow, he'd actually quit. All his life, he'd been geared toward following in his father's footsteps, becoming a part of the family business. Now he didn't have a job. But he had something he hadn't had in a long time, a purpose. He slipped into shoes and headed for the door.

Adrenaline pumped through his veins as he headed across the street and straight for his uncle's rental cottage. Before he launched his mission for the night, he had to be sure Elaine fared well from the previous night's disastrous outcome.

The dark, silent cottage appeared asleep among the row of houses. Elaine's car wasn't in the driveway and the front door stood ajar.

Craig's heart skipped a beat. Then, leaping to the porch, he slammed through the doorway and into the living room. "Elaine?" His voice echoed through the empty house. None of her papers or notebooks lay scattered across the couch and every other available surface. The little table she'd set up against the wall was gone. He ran into the bedroom and pulled the drawers out of the dresser. Empty. The bathroom was clean of any toiletries.

Elaine was gone. She'd packed up and left without a goodbye or anything.

Craig wandered back out into the living room and stared around in a numb stupor; the only thought in his head reverberated in incessant repetition. *She's gone. She's gone. She's gone.*

Except for the ugly writing on the living room wall, the house looked as if Elaine Smith had never been there. Every item of furniture had been moved back to its original location, the room swept and the dishes cleaned and shelved. Had Elaine been nothing more than a figment of his imagination, another trick played on him courtesy of Madame LeBieu?

Out of the corner of his eye, Craig saw the microscope standing on the kitchen table. No, she hadn't been only in his imagination. Elaine had been here and left her mark on the town, the swamp and most of all, him.

A lump lodged in his throat. When he lifted the instrument, a sickening rattle indicated the tool had suffered damage. Elaine loved this microscope. Could she have been mad enough about his betrayal she'd leave behind the last evidence of her parents' love?

Craig stared down at the gray hunk of metal as if the cold steel would answer his unspoken question. Had Elaine left it as a message to him that their relationship was over? Craig's hand tightened around the grip.

The clock on the wall bonged. A glance confirmed that the time had come to catch the polluting perpetrators. As much as he wanted to follow Elaine and bring her back, he knew any hope he had with her hinged on tonight's activities. His love life would go on hold until he dealt once and for all with the people who dared to dump in what he considered his own backyard.

A quick duck into his uncle's house for the new camcorder Craig'd gotten him for Christmas last year, and Craig was off to Littington Enterprises.

He backed his car in between a stand of oleanders and Magnolias just past the only open entrance to the plant. With the windows rolled down on his black BMW, he inhaled the moist warmth of the Louisiana night air. The fragrant scent of flowers reminded him of Elaine and of the perfume Madame LeBieu had sprayed in his face.

Craig frowned. Hadn't the voodoo priestess spoken of a woman who'd come into his life? One who'd love him warts and all? Had that woman been Elaine? And he'd thrown her love away through a silly lack of communication.

With his head tipped to the roof of his car, Craig prayed to God and the voodoo queens of the swamp he wasn't too late to woo Elaine back into his life. He'd never met anyone who brought out the best in him. She'd helped him discover the emptiness in his career and the need for more meaningful work. She'd shown him how important it was to commit to a worthwhile goal and throw your heart into it, no matter how scared or distracted you might become.

He smiled. Elaine was one hell of a woman and he'd let her walk away. With or without the curse, he'd be a fool to let her get away. But if he wanted to live the rest of his days with her, and he was beginning to think he did, then he needed to break the curse. With the full moon just days away, he didn't have time to waste. If Elaine was the woman of Madame LeBieu's spell, Craig had some serious back-paddling to do in his canoe to make her see him as worthy of her love. He prayed some day he'd be able to tell her about the curse. Maybe her scientific mind wouldn't let her believe his tale, but as long as he had her in his arms he wouldn't care. She could laugh and think him fanciful all she wanted. As long as they could spend all their days and nights together he'd be happy.

A dingy gray truck lumbered up to the gate, stopped, then passed through. Craig could barely make out the faded letters on the side panel: PRATT CHEMICAL DISPOSAL.

Bingo. Let the games begin.

Craig switched his engine on and waited for the truck to come back out with its load of barrels, supposedly headed to a safe disposal site. All Craig needed was evidence of Pratt and his partner dumping the barrels into the swamp and he'd go straight to the cops, the Coast Guard and the EPA with the video.

Littington had agreed to foot the bill for the cleanup. Disturbed by the damage to the environment and the negative publicity the press would give, he'd embraced the opportunity for the company itself to find the culprits and make amends for the damage done. He just wanted the bad guys to be caught and put away for a long, long time. He'd insisted he wasn't even aware of what was going on until the previous day. Pratt Chemical Disposal had been the low bidder and all his disposal licenses had been up to date. With no one else collecting the chemicals for disposal, Pratt or someone in his organization had to be the culprit.

Craig had secretly jumped for joy. He, of all people, knew how long and expensive litigation would be if the refinery refused to provide the necessary reparations.

But Jason Littington proved to be open, honest and concerned, much to his credit and unlike many of Craig's previous clients from New Orleans. Littington still had kids growing up in the parish and he hated the thought of pollution poisoning his home.

The truck reappeared, slowing to clear the gate. Craig's heart pounded in his chest. He'd never played the role of private detective. He didn't know what to expect from the thugs who'd already shot at him and tried to kill Elaine and Uncle Joe by capsizing their boat. Perhaps he should have gotten a gun from Uncle Joe's collection, but there wasn't time now.

Lights off, he maintained a discreet distance from the lumbering truck, following it to a nearby boat launch.

Craig parked behind bushes, left the car running and snuck out with the video camera. Ten barrels stood in the back of the truck. He recognized Randall Pratt and Gator Brouchard as the men rolling the barrels to a boat tied to the pier. Craig was amazed at their gall. They hadn't even attempted to take any of the barrels to the appropriate disposal sites. They'd gone straight from the refinery to the swamp.

With video recorder in hand, Craig caught them on film rolling the barrels one by one into the boat. Neither man spoke as they worked to move the toxins.

When five of the ten barrels were on board, they returned to the truck. This time when they went in the back, they came out carrying something long and skinny, wrapped in an old blanket. They hauled it on the boat and laid it down on the deck.

Craig frowned. He could guess what was in the barrels but what did Randall and Gator have in the blanket? By the shape of it, it could have been a body. Thank goodness Elaine was on her way back to New Orleans. Craig would rather she was mad at him and safe than the target for these two thugs on yet another attempt to harm her.

"I didn't sign up for no killing." Gator's voice carried loud enough for the video camera to pick up.

So the lump was a body. Craig's imagination hadn't been working overtime, creating threats where none existed. A trickle of sweat ran down his back. Maybe he was in for more than he'd bargained for. If he was smart, he'd get his butt back into his car and go find the police.

"You're getting paid, aren't you?" Randall tossed a strap to Gator. "Tie those barrels down."

"I didn't sign up for no killing." Gator leaned over and wrapped the strap around a barrel and the deck railing. "You said we were just going to scare people away."

"Look, dumb shit, if the cops get wind of our little disposal operation, not only will the money stop flowing, we'll go to straight to jail. We won't pass go, we won't collect two hundred dollars." Pratt stepped closer, face to face with Gator. "You ever been to jail?"

"No." Gator stepped backward, his legs up against one of the seats.

"Neither have I." Randall poked a finger into Gator's chest. "And I don't plan to. Littington still thinks we're a legitimate disposal company, and as long as he thinks we are, the money he pays our company goes right in our pockets. I'm gonna keep that cash coming in. Don't forget this has been the best money you or me ever made. Do you like that big truck you bought?"

"Yeah."

Randall poked Gator's chest again. "And that fancy house you got down in Gulf Shores?"

"Yeah, but—"

Another poke to Gator's chest. "No buts. We keep our mouths shut and take care of the problem." Randal tipped his head in the direction of the body on the deck.

Gator grabbed the finger still pushing against his chest. "I'll do it, but don't poke me again."

Randall's eyes narrowed. But when Gator dropped his finger, he nodded and stepped off the boat. "Time's wastin'."

Craig hoped his camcorder was picking up the scene. As dark as it was, he doubted it. At the least, the voices should be discernable.

Once the boat had been loaded with as many of the heavy barrels as it could hold and remain afloat, Gator stashed the truck in the trees and hurried back to climb aboard. Randall started the engine and pulled slowly away from the ramp.

Damn! How the heck could Craig follow without a boat? Familiar with the swamp in this area, Craig knew this tributary emptied out where several converged into a large lake area close to his uncle's marina.

If he hurried, he might catch them before they disappeared in the maze of channels. Craig sprinted for his car, and sped along the country road back to Thibodeaux Marina, breaking every speed limit on the country roads. At the parking lot, he leapt from the car, and raced across the dock to a skiff tied to the second pier.

One, two, three yanks on the motor's pull start and he was on his way across the swamp. Thank goodness the channels merged close to the marina or he didn't stand a snowball's chance in the bayou of finding the thugs.

As he approached the central lake, he spied the boat headed toward Bayou Black. Craig followed, praying they wouldn't hear or see him and start shooting.

Several miles out, the larger boat slowed and turned sharply into what Craig could only guess was a dense outcropping of overhanging trees and brush.

Instinctively, Craig killed the engine on his skiff and grabbed a paddle. As he drifted toward the spot where the boat had disappeared, he heard the other engine shut down.

Craig dipped the oar into the water, silently propelling the small craft forward. A murmur of voices grew louder as he approached. When he drifted within a couple yards of the outcropping, he could see the entrance to a lagoon. He pushed the boat against the muddy banks of an island and stepped out onto land. The foliage was too dense to forge a path through without alerting Randall and Gator.

With an uneasy search for alligators, Craig slipped into the inky water, hefted the camcorder onto his shoulder and swam around the trees into the lagoon, hugging the shoreline to hide in deep shadows.

"Hey, watch where you're going. You almost rolled that thing on my toe," Randall complained.

"If you'd get your toes out of the way, I wouldn't roll across them," Gator responded, his voice terse. He grunted and shifted a barrel across the flat deck to the edge and shoved it over. The barrel landed with a huge splash and sank straight to the bottom.

Craig stood on the silt bottom hidden by a tree branch not five yards from the boat, completely undetected. He hefted the camcorder to his shoulder and aimed the lens at the two men maneuvering another fifty-five gallon barrel to the boat's edge. With a quick flick of his finger, Craig pressed the record button.

"Gator, you idiot! You're tipping it too far my direction. If you're not careful it'll—"

Wonk! The barrel slammed sideways on the deck and rolled toward Randall, knocking him to his butt mere inches from the boat's edge.

"Sorry, Randy, my hands slipped. This one's a little oily."

"I swear, if I didn't need your help, I'd dump you over the side along with Littington's barrels."

Craig smiled grimly. He had video proof of the two dumping barrels into the bayou and the audio was sure to give the police positive identification of the culprits. Along with the samples he was sure Elaine planned to give the EPA, Craig knew the authorities would have good reason to start a full-scale investigation. After the fifth barrel plopped into the water, they turned to the blanketed lump.

Gator nudged the blanket with his toe. "What do you want to do with her?"

Craig's ears perked. Her? Gator had said "her"? Craig's heart pounded in his chest as the pair unwrapped the lump. When he saw the wild bush of frizzy hair lying against the deck, his heart stopped, lodging in his throat.

Elaine.

All this time he'd thought she was safely on her way to

New Orleans. He should have known. The microscope was as clear a message as he could have gotten. She'd never leave without it.

Craig tossed the camcorder onto the shore and swam for the boat, circling around the back to the ladder.

Please don't be dead. Please.

With blood pounding in his ears, he pulled himself up the ladder, risking a peek over the edge. A loud ripping sound pierced the night. The still form jerked and gasped as duct tape was torn from her mouth.

"Get up girly!" Randall reached down and hauled Elaine to her feet. "Cut it, Gator."

Craig braced to leap forward when Gator pulled a long hunting knife from his boot and slipped it between Elaine's wrists. With a quick upward thrust, he cut through the thick gray tape.

Elaine staggered but remained on her feet, peeling the tape from her skin.

"So, what'er we gonna do with her?" Gator asked.

"Shoot 'er and leave 'er as alligator bait." Randall said.

Elaine gasped.

Gator and Randall stood sideways to Craig. He feared if he made a lunge for Gator, the big guy would fire the weapon and hit Elaine. With every ounce of concentration, he willed Elaine to look his way. Craig hadn't believed in magic up until Madame LeBieu had put the hex on him. Now he rallied every possible force in the mysterious swamp, praying for a little voodoo whoodoo. *Look at me, Elaine.*

Elaine glanced up and stared right at Craig. Her eyes widened, her mouth dropping open.

Craig pressed a finger to his lips.

With an almost imperceptible nod, Elaine turned her attention back to Randall and Gator.

"Whatcha waitin' for? Shoot 'er," Randall ordered Gator.

Gator swung toward Randall, gun and all. "Why me? You're always makin' me do the dirty work."

"That's what you're getting paid for. Now, shut up and shoot."

"Don't do it, Gator." Elaine backed away from Gator, Randall and Craig.

The two bad guys turned toward her, their backs now fully to Craig.

Craig smiled grimly. Smart girl. Exactly the reason he loved her.

"You can't give me orders," Gator said. "I'm the one with the gun, not you."

"Yes, you're the one with the gun." Elaine nodded and spoke in a slow, calming voice. "But so far, you've only dumped chemicals in the bayou. Do you really want to go to jail for murder?"

"Don't listen to her, Gator. She don't know what she's talkin' about. Besides, who'll ever find her body after the alligators eat it?"

Elaine tipped her head in Randall's direction. "Don't you see? He wants you to shoot me so you'll be the one committing the murder, not him. You'll be the one charged with it—you'll be the one facing the death penalty."

Craig eased out of the water, thankful Elaine had Gator and Randall's full attention.

"Here, give me the gun. I'll shoot her."

When Randall grabbed for the pistol, Craig lunged.

"What the—" Randall yelled.

Hunkered down like a football player about to sack the quarterback, Craig hit Gator at full throttle, knocking him off his feet.

"Craig, look out!" Elaine yelled.

A loud crack split the air. Sharp, fiery pain ripped into Craig's shoulder, knocking him backward. Over the edge of the deck boat he flew, hitting the bayou's surface with a huge splash. Water covered his face and he sank into the black abyss.

CHAPTER TWENTY-THREE

Elaine screamed. Blind rage and fear for Craig flushed blood over her eyes. Acting on pure instinct, she crouched low, balled up her body and steamrolled into Randall's midsection, knocking him sideways. A seat caught the back of his legs and he flipped upside down on the deck floor. The gun flew from his hand, landing a couple feet from Elaine.

Should she go for the gun or . . . She spied a paddle next to her feet. If she went for the gun, she'd probably shoot herself, or Randall would get there first and use it to kill her.

As Randall struggled to his feet, Elaine reached down, lifted the paddle and whacked the man in the stomach.

"Oomph!" He bent double and Elaine whacked him on the back of the head as hard as she could.

Randall fell to the floor and lay still.

Elaine glanced from one unconscious man to the other to ensure they weren't going anywhere, then she scooped the gun off the deck and slung it as far as she could out into the swamp.

She peered over the boat's edge, squelching the panic before it could rise up and incapacitate her. "Craig?"

No sign of the man could be seen in the light from the moon. Only a couple of bubbles popped to the surface. The panic she'd held in check burst like a leaky dam. Without giving herself time to think, she threw her body overboard at the spot where she'd seen the bubbles.

Craig couldn't die. So what if he'd lied, so what if he represented Jason Littington, so what if she couldn't swim . . . Elaine wasn't going to let the man die!

False bravado lasted as long as it took for Elaine's head to sink below the surface, then real terror set in.

Just as her fear threatened to overwhelm her, she bumped into something solid with her foot. Craig!

Reaching down, she grabbed a handful of hair and yanked him up to the surface. The push to get him up sent her down. Her feet touched the silt on the bottom, but her head stayed well underwater.

Her lungs burned for air. What good was she to Craig if she drowned trying to save him? She pushed hard against the floor of the swamp and sprang to the surface, gulped air and glanced around for the boat. Then she sank again, propelling Craig up at the same time she went down.

Her knee bumped hard metal. By the shape of it, she'd found one of the barrels Randall and Gator had worked so hard to dump into the swamp. Desperate, she grasped the edge and pulled herself to stand on the barrel, rising above the surface to gasp for breath. Then she grabbed for Craig, tugging him toward her. With one arm around his neck to keep his head above water, she used her other arm to feel for a pulse. She found it, but he wasn't breathing. How could she push the water out of his lungs when he was still in the water? Her only solution was to wrap her arms around his middle from behind and hug with a sharp upward thrust to his diaphragm.

Craig coughed up water and spluttered. When he didn't start breathing, Elaine hugged again.

This time, Craig coughed and then inhaled as if he would suck the trees into his lungs, followed by a round of gut-wrenching coughs.

Thank God, he was breathing on his own again. Elaine held him tight to keep him from going under again.

"Elaine?"

"I'm here," she said softly into his ear, squeezing tighter with her cheek against his back.

"I love it when you hug me," he wheezed, "but could you loosen up a bit?"

Immediately, she let go and Craig sank into the water. She grabbed him before he gulped another gallon of the swamp into his lungs.

"I'm sleepy." Craig's head dropped forward.

She had to get him on the boat and back to civilization and a doctor. "Craig." She forced her voice to be strong.

Craig's head lolled and then came up. "Huh?"

Elaine scooted around the barrel to face him. "Craig, I need to get to the boat."

"Can't swim," he mumbled.

"You don't need to; you just need to stand here."

"Too deep," he said.

"Put your feet down." Elaine quelled the urge to laugh hysterically at her words, an echo of Craig's advice to her not too long ago. She braced herself and helped him find his feet on the barrel. When he stood, weak but steady, she kissed him. "I'm going for the boat."

"No, I'll go." He shook his head as if to clear the haze.

"Don't be silly. You can barely stand in the water."

"You can't swim."

"I'll manage." She gripped his arms and kissed him full on the lips. "Keep your head above the water." Then she gulped a deep breath and stepped off the barrel in the direction of the boat.

Praying for calm, she sank to the bottom, pushed off the silt and bounced in what she hoped was the right direction. Up, she surfaced to find the boat only two more bounces from her. Down and up again put her within reasonable dog-paddle distance.

Minus the dignity of a dog, she paddled and kicked until she reached the ladder and clung until she had sufficient breath to climb aboard.

A quick glance behind her proved Craig still stood with his head high above the water, but how long could he last before he passed out?

Once on board, she stepped over Randall, who stirred and made as if to rise.

Elaine grabbed the paddle from the floor. "Get up and I'll hit you again. Don't piss me off!" Her voice rose, the pitch shrill and past any reasoning.

Randall slumped back to the floor and moaned. "I should have killed you while I had a chance."

Several attempts at starting the boat finally met with success. She eased the lever forward, setting the boat in motion, and executed a wide turn in the tiny lagoon. She aimed for Craig and at the last minute swerved to miss him, cutting the motor as he had done when they'd gone specimen hunting.

Unfortunately, she cut it too late and the boat propelled forward faster than she would have liked. They were sure to drift by too fast for Craig to grab on.

Elaine leaned over the edge, extending the paddle. "Grab hold!" she yelled.

Craig caught the paddle's edge and hung on until the boat slowed to a stop.

With the paddle firmly in hand and her arms screaming from the strain, she walked it and Craig around the side of the boat to the ladder.

Craig tried to haul himself on board one-armed, favoring his injured shoulder, but he fell backward into the water.

Elaine leaned over, grabbed his shirt and pulled while he pushed his way up onto the boat, and then collapsed on a seat.

When Elaine switched on a lamp, she got her first look at his wound. Blood soaked through and around the bullet hole in his shirt. So much blood. "Oh geez, Craig." She swayed, the boat's light blurring around the edges.

"Don't faint on me now," Craig said through clenched teeth.

"I'm not." So it was a half-truth. She shook her head to clear her vision.

"Good,'cause I think I am . . ." his voice faded and he slid sideways, almost falling off the seat before Elaine could catch him. Blood seeped from the wound onto her hand at an alarming rate. His face glowed a pale sickly green in the light from the moon.

Without a thought for modesty, Elaine stripped her shirt from her back, ripped off a piece, wadded it and pressed it against Craig's shoulder. "Don't you die on me, Craig," she said, her voice low and tears streaming from her eyes.

He blinked and muttered, "Didn't know you cared."

"I do, damn it! I love you, you big stupid idiot, so dying is not an option!"

Craig's head fell back against the seat, a brief smile lifting the corners of his lips.

"Don't pass out, now. I don't know my way out of this

bayou." She tied the wad of fabric around his shoulder with the rest of her shirt. Gator stirred and moaned. Without backup, she couldn't risk leaving the criminals untied. A quick search of the boat produced a roll of fishing line and Gator's knife. Working quickly, she tied the two men's hands and feet. Convinced they wouldn't cause any more trouble, she started the engine and steered through the lagoon's entrance.

Elaine slowed the boat, leaned over and shook Craig. "Craig, honey, wake up."

"Am I dead?" His head lolled to the side and he opened one eye.

"No, not a chance."

"But I see an angel."

"You're worse than I thought." She smoothed the hair off his brow and pressed a kiss there. "You're hallucinating."

"No, really, you're my very own angel, sent by the voodoo queen."

Elaine frowned. He really was losing it. "Craig, stay with me long enough to get us back to the marina."

"I'm with you, honey. Wild bullfrogs couldn't drag me away." He lifted his head, squinted in the moonlight and pointed with his good arm. "That way."

After what seemed to be an eternity, the boat glided up to the dock at Thibodeaux Marina. Craig had drifted in and out of consciousness, with Elaine waking him at every fork in the bayou to beg the next round of directions. She'd remained patient with him when he couldn't think straight. Actually, she was looking very tempting in her lacy white bra. Too bad he didn't have the energy to reach out and touch her, pull her close and kiss the rest of her clothes off.

Yup, she was his very own guardian angel. He just hoped he could hold on to her and keep her from leaving him again. He didn't even want to consider her walking away from Bayou Miste without him.

Was it part of his hallucinations, or had she really said she loved him? If she was just trying to make him feel good, it worked. He wished she'd say it again, just to be sure. His heart beat faster when she leaned close enough for him to feel her breath on his ear. Would she tell him the three words he longed to hear? She lifted his hand and wrapped his fingers around the boat paddle. "Hit them if they give you any problems."

A quick kiss and she jumped out of the boat, like a confident sailor. How unlike the frightened waif of the first night he'd taken her out on the bayou.

Too weak to get out of the boat, he waited and watched her run across the dock in her jeans and lacy white bra. Wow! Even in his weakened condition Craig couldn't help but admire his brave and sexy angel.

He couldn't quite see up to the bait shop. But he heard a loud crash, the distinctive sound of shattered glass. She hadn't just broken a window in the bait shop, had she? Mild-mannered microscope junkie Elaine Smith?

Craig glanced down at the paddle in his hand and the two men bound in fishing line, glad he was on her side.

He must have passed out again. When he opened his eyes, the dark wasn't quite as dark and bright lights flashed in the distance up by the bait shop. Someone was talking to him.

"Craig, they're here to take you to the hospital."

He looked up into Elaine's liquid green eyes. She wore a white T-shirt sporting a largemouth bass and the words "I'd rather be fishing" across her breasts.

"Will you be there?" he asked.

She smiled. "Wild bullfrogs couldn't keep me away." She squeezed his hand and then backed away.

Two men in Emergency Medical Service uniforms helped him out of the boat and onto a stretcher. His legs were no longer useful. He hated being so weak when he needed to be strong for Elaine.

She followed close behind until they reached the parking lot where the ambulance stood, lights flashing, and the entire town out in force.

When they moved him to the wheeled gurney and pushed him toward the open doors of the ambulance, Craig stirred enough to say, "Wait." He stared around at the familiar faces.

Mo was closest to him. "I heard all de commotion. Thought maybe T-Rex was causin' trouble. Glad to see it wasn't." He nodded toward a sheriff's car where a deputy was handcuffing Randall and Gator. "Dem's bad ones, dey are. I should have been dere with you, man."

Craig looked up at Elaine. "I had backup."

Larry stepped up beside Mo. "She's a keeper, all right."

Craig's gaze never left Elaine's. "I know."

"So, whatcha gonna do about it?" Ms. Reneau moved closer, towing Uncle Joe by the hand.

"What do you mean?" He knew what Ms. Reneau alluded to, but he didn't want to declare himself in front of everyone. He wanted to tell Elaine he loved her. But he wanted to present her with all the bells and whistles of a romantic evening, planned and choreographed to elicit the desired response. Or was he just scared? He'd lived so long at arm's length from real relationships; could he break old habits?

Uncle Joe stepped up beside him. His white hair stuck straight out and his T-shirt was on backwards. "She broke the window."

"I'll buy you a new one," Craig said.

"I'm not worried about the window." Uncle Joe leaned closer and whispered, "If she'd do that for your rotten carcass, you stand a good chance of breaking that spell."

"I know that, Uncle Joe. I also know I don't deserve her." What the hell. "Elaine? Elaine?" He looked out in the sea of faces and almost panicked when he couldn't find the one he sought.

"I'm here." She slid between him and his circle of friends, and scooped up his hand.

"Did you mean what you said out there on the bayou?"

In the grayish light he could tell the colors in her face deepened and she looked away. "Mean what?"

He understood her hesitation. "I worked out a deal with Littington to clean up the contamination." That wasn't exactly a declaration of love, but he was warming up.

"I know. Littington's here somewhere. He told me."

"I quit my job with the family firm."

She leaned over and kissed his lips. "Uh huh."

He was getting a lot warmer. He inhaled deeply and blurted, "I love you, Elaine Smith. Marry me."

She turned his face to hers. "Are you sure? I thought you were allergic to commitment."

"I was." He reached up and hooked his good arm around her neck and pulled her down to him. "Until I met a scientist with just the right chemistry for me. I love you because you're smart, passionate and completely committed to your work. I want to spend the rest of my life with you. Did I mention passionate?"

She smiled and nodded.

"Look, I know I don't have a job and I don't really deserve you, but do you think you could love me anyway?"

Uncle Joe stared out at the bayou. "Guess you'll find out right about . . . now."

Mo and Larry's gazes followed Uncle Joe's. While they'd been talking, morning had come to the bayou. Bright orange sunlight streamed through the base of the trees, spreading a fiery trail across the black waters.

But Craig focused all his attention on the one woman with all the answers he needed.

She leaned close and whispered against his ear. "I love you more than all the frogs in the bayou, Craig. I would like nothing more than to spend the rest of my life with you." Then she kissed his very human lips in the red and pink light of dawn.

Since the night he'd fallen victim to the bizarre hex, he never thought he'd be saying it, but he sent a silent prayer to the voodoo gods in the bayou. "Thank you, Madame LeBieu."

Spellbound
KATHLEEN NANCE

As the Minstrel of Kaf, Zayne keeps the land of the djinn in harmony. Yet lately, he needs a woman to restore balance to his life, a woman with whom he can blend his voice and his body. And according to his destiny, this soul mate can only be found in the strange land of Earth.

Madeline knows to expect a guest while house-sitting, but she didn't expect the man would be so sexy, so potent, so fascinated by the doorbell. With one soul-stirring kiss, she sees colorful sparks dancing on the air. But Madeline wants to make sure her handsome djinni won't pull a disappearing act before she can become utterly spellbound.

- -